THE SONG

OF AN

INNOCENT

BYSTANDER

iAN BOnE

DUTTON BOOKS / New York

Copyright © 2002 by Ian Bone

CIP Data is available.

Published in the United States 2004 by Dutton Books,
a member of Penguin Group (USA) Inc.
345 Hudson Street, New York, New York 10014
www.penguin.com

First published in 2002 by Penguin Books Australia,
250 Camberwell Road, Camberwell, Victoria 3124, Australia

Typography by Heather Wood

Printed in USA • First American Edition

10   9   8   7   6   5   4   3   2   1

ISBN 0-525-47282-7

To you, Liz.
You teach me more than gladness.

A variety of innocent bystanders have helped shape this book in one way or another. Thanks to Simon Higgins and Patrick Bellamy for their useful information. And to Victoria Wilkins: that seemingly unrelated conversation at Black Point actually brought about this madness. Thanks to Anne Bartlett for reading with such grace and generosity. To Laura Harris at Penguin for believing so strongly, and to my mum and family for being such brilliant fans, especially my sisters, Stephanie and Helen.

THE SONG

OF AN

INNOCENT

BYSTANDER

JOHN WAYNE

O'GRADY

One bitterly cold afternoon, a handful of customers lingered inside the Family Value hamburger restaurant on Grange Street, their meals finished, their welcome scattered in scraps on the discarded food trays. There was just a smattering of people, caught in the lull that followed the Sunday lunch rush, when the "Noonburger" would soon become the "Dinnerburger" (complete with your choice of coleslaw or fresh garden salad), when the price of coffee would inexplicably rise by ten cents, when the plastic surfaces would gleam anew, coaxed into a sparkle by cheerfully named cleaning products. These people were just irregular color and shape among the plastic decor of this all-new, pride-of-the-company underground restaurant.

At precisely 2:45 P.M., a man stood on one of the small tables near the service counter. He had a black sports bag clutched to his chest. Nobody noticed him until he spoke in his unremarkable voice, until his words echoed across the near-empty expanse of fake wood below him.

"It's time to pay your dues, Family Value," he said. "You've been sucking the lifeblood of the masses for too long, peddling your lies, your poisons."

Most of the customers turned their heads to look up at the loony on the tabletop, expecting a bit of entertainment. John Wayne O'Grady stared back at them, fumbling with the zipper on his bag.

"I've locked the doors," he said, "so everybody stay where you are."

Then he removed a semiautomatic Barrett shotgun from the bag and aimed it at the bustling, fat restaurant manager who was making his way over, dripping with conciliation and calm.

"Open your mouth and I'll shoot you dead," said O'Grady matter-of-factly.

The watching occupants of the all-new, underground Family Value restaurant were chilled by these words—snap frozen into an instant silence.

O'Grady reached into his pants pocket with his non-trigger hand and removed a white handkerchief (with the words *Family Value—we value you* embroidered around the edge) and wiped his sweating brow. The instant the handkerchief passed across his skin, more beads of perspiration burst free but were ignored. With the Barrett weighing heavily in his hand, O'Grady tried unsuccessfully to return the handkerchief to his pocket, missing with each attempt, until he eventually let it drop onto the shining red tabletop at his feet.

Twenty-three seconds had passed since he'd threatened to shoot the manager dead.

John Wayne O'Grady was caught in the moment, paused between intention and action, between words and the biting pressure on his trigger finger.

Into the pause came a question: Who took charge now? The manager, who felt responsible for the customers in his restaurant? The careworn man against the wall who'd fought in a war and knew what effect guns had on the human body? The hamburger cook hiding behind the freezer door, certain that the madman hadn't seen him yet? The mother who clutched her son to her stomach, thinking *Please don't harm my boy?*

O'Grady himself with his angry heart?

The barrel of O'Grady's Barrett stared at the manager's chest—cold, accurate, unshakable, and waiting. A twitch developed under the gunman's right eye. His finger tightened slightly on the trigger. A millimeter of extra pressure.

Fifty-three seconds had passed since the first threat of death when a voice spoke from the counter. A young girl's nine-year-old voice. A child who had been distracted on the stairs, who had not seen the gunman enter behind her, had not heard his angry words below. Who had marched up to the counter with a purpose, oblivious to the terror behind her.

"Can I please see the manager, please?" she asked in her most assertive tone. "You promised me a Wild West sticker with my Noonburger, but I didn't get one."

FREDA OPPERMAN

I don't think you can ever be too polite, do you? I was always brought up to believe that a simple "please" or "thank you," repeated often, will smooth the most troubled of waters. They are the little acts of kindness that help in any difficult situation. Be polite, be patient, and smile when you ask for something. But even with all that training, I never sent any thank-you cards after my rescue. I wonder if it would have put a smile on the emergency workers' faces?

Choosing the right thank-you card is an art in itself for the young survivor. She should give thought to color and decoration, for instance. No doubt it'd be a welcome touch to send a fireman a red card. Tactical response officers from the police force, on the other hand, would probably appreciate blue. And bomb squad heroes would be delighted if you took the time to create your lettering to resemble green, red, and black electric wire intertwined.

There are days when each tiny detail, from a chair scrape to a smell, will bring back the memory of my comrades. Will vividly recall their fear, their sweat, their whimpers. Then there are days when it is all an empty blank. Strange, isn't it? Have you ever noticed that memory is everything?

Right now I can't see what the policeman looked like who carried me from that restaurant. I can see his hands, though—calloused, hard, and strong—that gripped me so tight, as if I might squirm free and run back down those stairs.

Into that most dangerous of places. Into hell.

Not that you'd normally think of restaurants as dangerous. They're in the same league as supermarkets and shopping malls—kingdoms of politeness—where "Have a nice day" rules supreme, because you are the most important thing in the world. Not your wallet or your purse or your credit card. *You.*

It's as if you are loved.

There's something that disturbs me in this supermarket aisle. Right here where I stand. I've tried to ignore it, tried turning my back on it and pretending that it isn't there, but it *is* there. It's a gap. I can see it right now in one of the shelves. A gap is a statement, a lack of something, a clear message that there is a void. In this case it's a few cans of fruit that are missing, and I step forward, reaching to the back of the shelf to pull new cans to the front. A chubby boy in a white shirt and a red tie comes over, checking to see that I haven't messed up the secret code of cans. Satisfied with my arrangement, he gives me a warning look before going back to his job. Arranging cans is a job that should only be attempted by trained professionals, kids. DO NOT attempt this at home.

I stare at the line of cans, imagining hundreds and hundreds of similar rows behind them, stretching out to infinity like one of those bouncing mirror tricks. *There is plenty.* Isn't that what these shelves are here to tell us? This place? Isn't that why the neon lights stretch out across the tiled ceiling above me, creating a canopy of greenish white light that seems to settle like falling mist?

Once, when I was younger, I went into a grocery store with my mother to buy an ice cream. Sliding open the freezer, I saw a perfectly formed crystal of ice stuck to the frozen wall. Like a teardrop from God, snap frozen in all its perfection. Glistening and brilliant. I didn't move because I was afraid that something as insignificant as the heat from my hand would change its shape and make the angels weep. Then a snotty boy with close-cropped hair pushed past me, grabbed an ice cream, and knocked the iced teardrop into the deepest, darkest part of the freezer.

My mother is a very practical woman, like that boy. Ordinary things are expected to perform to normal standards. That way she can maintain a sense of control. There are no manuals that cover the spiritual life of freezers. The world she sees consists of problems to be unraveled until a solution is found. Look at the way she deals with this busy supermarket. She surveys the lines that have already formed at the checkouts, sizes up the piles of groceries in each waiting cart, assesses the speed and accuracy of each checkout operator. Should she go with the shortest line and suffer the trainee operator who is clearly having trouble with the code for cashew nuts? Should she go with the longer line and risk the possibility of the old lady at the head being a purse fumbler?

Finally, she decides, shooting her cart toward the end of the middle line with her single-minded determination that often frightens me. But there's competition—another steely-eyed woman, hell-bent on reaching the end of that line before my mother. They both arrive with a minor collision, their carts wedged into a ridiculous V.

"Excuse me," says the rival cart-lady.

"All right, I will," says my mother, and she rams her cart a little harder, pushing her rival's cart sideways.

"No! I didn't mean . . ." says the other cart-lady, wedging her cart back into the V. "I didn't mean that! I was here first."

"That's not how it would appear to me," says my mother with a smile. Then she sets about acting "normal," staring vaguely at her surroundings as if the other woman were not even there. The cart-lady should not take this as a sign that my mother is demented or has lost touch with reality. She should not be fooled by this. My mother is a woman with a powerful sense of justice. She has tackled governments, bureaucrats, bullies, and criminals. Everything she does is tactical.

"Freda," she calls, and I make my way over. "You seem very quiet today, even for yourself." Says Nancy Opperman, N.O., my mother. She wasn't born an N.O., the Opperman name was provided by my father. After he floated out of her life all those years back, Nancy decided to keep the O. Perhaps because it was associated with "that Freda Opperman girl," or perhaps the initials N.O. were too good to relinquish.

I nod in answer to her question but say nothing, aware that I've just reinforced her opinion of me—silent and weird—but what the heck? We've come to expect so much of each other. She expects me to be cold, distant, a strangeling with deep-set eyes and a dark inner secret. And I expect her to have the manners to politely ignore it.

The cart-lady beside us launches another attack, and I step back. This is my mother's event, not mine. I hear the cart-lady suggest that N.O. look for another line. What she doesn't understand is that Nancy Opperman is not the sort of person who looks, who seeks. There's not enough certainty in seeking. Nancy Opperman does not take risks. She works tirelessly to fill our lives with winners.

Ever since John Wayne O'Grady came along, I've learned that something bad is always waiting for you just around the corner. That a smile or a friendly gesture can rapidly change into the most sinister moment of evil, right before your eyes. And I suppose if bad things are waiting to jump up and bite you, then maybe good things are waiting, too.

I don't count myself among those who believe that, however. I cannot. You see, that would be allowing myself to hope. How could I take such a risk? Hope belongs to women with overflowing shopping carts who still think they'll get to the head of the line. Hope belongs to those who haven't seen what's around the corner.

My mother has finished her argument with the cart-lady for now, and an uneasy standoff exists between the two. Nancy gives me a pleasant smile. "I had a phone call this morning," she says. "It was a newspaper reporter." Then she looks at me, waiting for my response.

I snap out of my reverie and struggle with this news, wrestle it to the ground and sit on it, but it bucks me off and deals me a sly kick to the chest. Flattened, I let out an involuntary "Oh." I'm not given to long sentences with N.O.

"Will you move your cart now?" says the cart-lady beside us, still trying to remain polite through clenched teeth. She'll get it eventually.

Nancy pushes her cart farther toward the line, then carries on with her train of thought. Her enemy, she-of-the-other-cart, explodes into a tirade, but it falls on deaf ears.

"This reporter wants to write an article about you," says my mother, raising her voice above the background noise of outrage.

I open my mouth, but all I release is a short burst of air. It's been ten years now! Who would be interested? I don't want to have another article written about me. I refuse to cooperate with the "girl who got lucky" show and once again be a symbol of hope. My voiceless protest dissipates into a vague cloud that wafts around my mother's head.

Someone else speaks instead. "I'm waiting," says the cart-lady.

Not waiting for me, I hope? You should never wait for me.

Nancy doesn't wait. She lists off the contents of my wardrobe, making suggestions about what I should wear for the interview. She knows how important it is for me to plan ahead, but I'm not paying attention. Next to us, the cart-lady is slowly building up a head of steam, coming nicely to the boil, and Nancy is not paying attention to her. As a family we've taken the art of not paying attention to new and dizzy heights.

But really it's only the cart-lady who is getting dizzy. "I'll call the manager!" she shrieks.

This is what I hear: The sound of someone sobbing. A young boy whispering to his mother, "Is he going to hurt us?" Breathing, so loud and heavy that it might be my own. The dull, metallic click of the Barrett as he swapped it from hand to hand. The manager speaking.

"What a very good idea," says my mother. She launches her cart forward sharply. A bottle falls from the rival woman's groceries. It lands with a crash, and a sticky puddle of cordial spreads slowly toward cart-lady and her expensive shoes. She has no choice but to move back, allowing N.O. to march on into the line unimpeded.

"You'd better call that manager now," says my mother in a friendly tone, "get that mess cleaned up."

"It's not my mess," says the shocked woman, but it's all too little, too late.

It never is your mess in the end.

N.O. spends a good deal of time at the checkout watching every item go through the scanner. The pantomime of the sticky cordial is played out behind us, starring the chubby boy from "the gap," but Nancy ignores the show, her eyes on the register, intent on making sure the price that flashes up on the digital readout matches her own expectations. She is a woman of high expectations, my mother, mostly leaning toward the positive end of the spectrum—success, victory—that sort of thing. She knows that every item has its price, its own secret code to be read by the hard, sharp glow of certainty.

So, I'm to be interviewed by a newspaper journalist after ten long years. I was a bigger story back then. I was a darling girl, caught up in a dreadful siege in a family restaurant. Of course, I wasn't the only one in the restaurant. Many others walked up those stairs unscathed, but it was my face that was blown up on the front pages of the newspapers; it was my story that was examined in detail.

Having satisfied herself that the checkout girl hasn't short-changed us, N.O. pushes the burdened cart out of the supermarket. I follow, taller and stronger than the days of my previous glory. My height comes from my father's side. He was born into a family of quiet boys, beanpoles, who hunched their shoulders. A trait I seem to have inherited. The Opperman boys were so modest about their physical presence in the world that their mother used to say they had big feet, but left little footprints.

Nancy Opperman is different, of course, having inherited the Opperman name only. She is small, my mother, what people would call "wiry" or "birdlike," but that doesn't stop her from moving mountains. Her parents were "busy" people who kept the devil at bay by never indulging in an idle second. Nancy's mother was a tireless woman who decorated their entire garden in mosaics—starting with the outdoor furniture, moving on to the paving, and finishing with walls, borders, and plaques, which she hung from the trees. It became a lifelong obsession, and Nancy and her sister learned from an early age to manage the household chores, or starve waiting as their mother scratched through piles of broken plates and crockery, searching for the right color. Their father was an absent man, important in some bureaucratic department that kept him traveling for months on end. Nancy soon emerged as the organizer and boss of the household, even though she was the younger of the sisters.

I look at her now, pushing the cart, her tight little calf muscles showing through her stockings, a surprising amount of strength in her skinny little arms. Nothing stands in the way of N.O. I've seen her make mincemeat of corporate lawyers who have dared to stand between her and a just cause. But far greater than that, I've seen her part the waves of daily burden for me so that I can walk through life unscathed.

"I would have thought you'd be excited about this interview," says Nancy as she negotiates the cart over a speed bump in the parking lot.

It's a poor choice of words, coming from her. I've really had all the excitement a girl can take. A bitterly cold gust of wind tries its best to remove our clothing, to expose our frailties. We resist the wind, mother and I, stowing our groceries in the car. The former because the wind is no match for her determination, the latter because I hide in her wake and allow the icy blasts to swirl past me.

As we return the cart to its bay, I lift my head against the wind and ask, "Which newspaper?" She doesn't hear. My words are carried away, sent tumbling and swirling down the street to play tag with the stray pieces of paper and the odd plastic bag.

My ordeal started with words, a polite request for some stickers. A simple conversation with the manager would have satisfied me. Instead, I was locked away in an underground restaurant for thirty-six hours with a madman and a shotgun and a dozen or so terrified people. In the end, many words were spoken during that siege—hateful words, bitter and angry—but the only words that were remembered were the widely reported dying words of Theo Constantine, restaurant manager and hero, to nine-year-old Freda. "Make something of all this mess. Lead a good life."

The young survivor should really be wary of famous last words. They carry so many requirements. They place her in a position where she has to "live up to . . . ," as opposed to her natural instinct to "live away from. . . ." They ask her to expect more from the world than she has the right to.

As we drive home, Nancy starts drumming on the steering wheel. She'll be whistling soon. I hate it when she whistles. She's happy because after so many years of wandering in the wilderness, Freda Opperman might become a sought-after subject again. The impending ten-year anniversary of the siege could propel me back into the spotlight.

I wonder who initiated this interview? Did the reporter ring up out of the blue, or did N.O. work behind the scenes to make it happen? God knows it will make for great publicity, especially if I tell the story that Nancy wants me to tell. How N.O. and her standard-bearer, that Opperman girl, have done so much for the victims of crime over the past ten years. How N.O. and the kid (you know, the one that was in that siege) have ensured that all corporations tremble at the mere sound of the word *lawsuit*.

I almost feel sorry for this journalist. No doubt he'll want me to tell him everything. They all do. If I close my eyes I can see his nicotine-stained fingers curled around the mini tape recorder, his cheap cartoon tie askew against his crumpled white shirt, his eager expression as he waits for me to tell him the truth.

John Wayne O'Grady said that people are lazy, and they believe in lies because they're too afraid of what the truth might do to them. He said that the bigger the lie, the more successful it is. John Wayne O'Grady tried to show us the truth, but he knew that nobody would listen to him unless he backed it up with reinforcement, the Barrett version of "pay attention." John Wayne O'Grady peddled and paraded words, demeaned their dignity until they joined the grime and muck on the restaurant floor where he made us sit as he preached his sermons.

"There is no value in Family Value!" (His favorite saying.) "This is not food they serve here, this is poison. It is the poison of mass production. It is the poison of multinational greed and lust. Pack-raping corporations that prey on the masses. Filthy parasites who exploit your gullibility. They are the enemy. They destroy the rain forests, all in the name of beef cattle and hamburger buns."

I remember the elderly lady hostage in my group, with her cardigan buttons done up crookedly, leaning forward and whispering to the young hamburger cook with the "Family Value—we value you" tie, "Is he talking about locust plagues?"

"No," the cook whispered back to her, patting her wrinkled hand. "He's referring to the management of this restaurant. I don't think he likes them."

And Theo Constantine, the manager with the famous last words, let out a low moan and began to sweat.

Our car cuts a swath through the cold, afternoon fade-out. I search through the rivers of water on my window for distraction, but all I can see is a wet suburban landscape gone wavery and distorted. I wind my window down to feel the cold bite of the air, but Nancy protests, saying she's just paid good money to have her hair done. As if she could pay anything *but* "good" money.

"I'm glad you have the chance to do this interview, Freda. Aren't you?" she says.

"Mm?" I reply. It's near enough to a yes for N.O.

"These past few months have been a worrying time . . . what with you finishing school. You've just seemed so . . . listless."

As opposed to my half-listless state when I was at school? I sigh loudly, and Nancy has the decency to ask me what's the matter. "Do I have to do this interview?" I ask. Sometimes the young survivor will attempt to have a say in the management of her survival.

"This is a crossroad time for you, Freda," says Nancy. "You're young, so you probably can't see it. This is a time where you're . . . poised."

I turn and glare at her, but she doesn't notice. Are we going to have a "growing-up" conversation? I certainly hope not. I squirm in my seat, now that we've skirted so close to that sticky, embarrassing topic. She's already lined up a job for me. In one of her organizations. Straight in through the front door. No interview, no process, I start in two weeks' time.

Nancy glances at me, then quickly changes the subject. I'm not really listening. She has steered the conversation away from the maturation of Freda Opperman. She has put aside any mention of independence and self-determination, knowing how much they make my heart race.

"Anyway," says Nancy, "it won't take up more than half an hour of your life." She's talking about the interview again. This is her peace offering to me, a minimization that is supposed to make me accept my fate.

We leave it at that, survivor and mother, with an agreement that the interview will only take up a neat package of minutes, thirty of them, which will then be placed in storage with all my other packages, nestled on the shelves of my history.

I don't have an easy relationship with this history of mine, filled as it is with horrible stories, with people who sat alongside me in that foul place stinking in their own sweat and fear. History demands questions such as: If I remember *this,* then why can't I remember *that?* It has too many scribbled notes on dusty shelves, *Missing. May return later.* They are hypnotic, these empty spaces; they make you stare and stare until the light begins to blind you.

My mother is whistling now, I knew it would come. She has the most irritating style, forcing air out through her clenched teeth, a dreadful spitting-wheezy noise that she can keep up for hours. It is curious that she hasn't told me which newspaper the reporter is with. It's not the sort of detail she would normally neglect. Inwardly I shudder at the truth behind this oversight. It must be bad. A low-life rag perhaps? A suburban fire starter with badly aligned color photographs on the front?

Why do they bother? There's nothing new to say, not from my lips, at least. I'll be polite, and I'll answer his questions with a minimum of fuss, but in the end my words will boil down to very little.

N.O. pulls the car into our driveway, a spotlessly clean "sweep" of concrete, and sighs. The wind has blown some leaves onto the pristine surface of the drive, which means she'll be out here later pushing nature back to where it belongs. It's not as if N.O. is a fastidious gardener, quite the opposite in fact. Our backyard is a jungle of deliriously rampant growth. This neat front yard is exactly that—a front—a phony facade that gives the "right" impression. Nancy keeps it spotless in case anyone should bother to drive by and see where that "Opperman girl" lives. We haven't had a sightseer in years, but it doesn't stop Nancy from sweeping.

We carry the shopping inside the house, our comfortable little redbrick home that I have lived in all my life. It hasn't changed much since I was a girl, except for the security grilles on each window, the security doors, the electronic alarm system, the dead bolts, and the conversion of the spare bedroom into an office, because nobody comes to stay at the Oppermans anymore. There's no time.

I am tense as I help Nancy unpack the groceries, placing each box and can into her neat cupboards. Instead of putting the can of peaches in the canned goods section, I put them where the desserts are kept. Nancy sighs and corrects my mistake. I don't have time for visuals, it's sound that I'm focused on. A bird sings and I jump. N.O.'s sensible shoes squeak on the vinyl, and I snap my attention toward the phone.

I feel so foolish and tell myself that I don't care. I don't care, I don't care. But the news of this interview has unsettled me. I've been caught off guard. Wasn't this all over and done with? Hadn't my life taken on a new direction? The maturation of Freda Opperman; the girl on the train who goes to work, comes home again, then puts her feet up after a long day? Isn't that what we had planned? Now I have to remember the rules again. What I can say, what I can't say, and what I can never reveal.

The phone rings, and I have a curious sensation, as if my chest is being crushed.

"That'll be him," says Nancy in a confidential voice.

I turn to my mother with a questioning expression.

"His name's William," she says.

William? Why isn't he "Bill" or "Will?" I don't like the sound of "William." Is he fastidious and particular? Will "Will" want every single detail about me and my life? William is a very pretentious name to have. I won't cooperate. I shall pick up the phone, say something rude, then hang up. I shall rip the thing from the wall.

By the time I arrive at the phone, however, all I can manage is a mean stare. It ignores me, ringing shrilly, demanding that I do something and do it fast. Nancy shouts from the kitchen, "For crying out loud, Freda!" I take a deep breath and pick it up.

"Hello?" says a young man's voice. "Is this Freda Opperman?"

Here it comes, William. You are going to cop the tongue-lashing of a lifetime. You are going to receive the full fury of Freda Opperman.

"Yes," I croak.

And he begins talking. He begins our conversation.

Yes, William, it is me. Yes, William, I am here, raw, visible. Yes, William, I'll listen. Just say whatever you need to say.

You see, I'm all ears, William. All ears.

JOHN **WAYNE**

O'GRADY

It took precisely fifteen seconds for John Wayne O'Grady to respond to the sound of the girl's voice. Fifteen seconds for the dispassionate weight of the shotgun in his hands to become leaden and dead. He saw the girl at the counter with her hands crossed in front of her and an imperious expression on her face. He saw the fat man turn instinctively toward the girl and speak, asking her to sit down. He saw the manager's shoulders tense up as he remembered that he was under the threat of death if he uttered a word. He saw the manager turn back apologetically, eyes locked on the lethal weapon. He saw the girl register fear as she realized for the first time that there was an armed man in the room.

Then the gun grew uncomfortable in his hands, and he shifted his grip slightly. A barely audible gasp escaped from the manager's lips, enough to spark O'Grady back to reality.

Fifteen seconds.

"Didn't like that, huh?" A lopsided smile creased O'Grady's features as he watched the manager wipe his brow. He shifted the shotgun slightly, subtle movements that just might be the precursor to a more dramatic action. He seemed to take pleasure in the way the manager's eyes were locked on the Barrett's trigger, the way his skin was sweaty, his eyelids puffy.

Then the girl at the counter spoke again, this time in a small voice. "What's going on?"

The terrified customers in the restaurant watched as O'Grady shifted his gaze from the manager to the girl. The gunman was tall, so he had to look down a long way from his tabletop perch to meet the girl's eyes. O'Grady frowned, then rested the gun momentarily, eased it from the burden of threatener, and ran his hand through his thinning hair. Flecks of dandruff flew onto his shoulder. The face of O'Grady was inscrutable, a stone wall of emptiness, yet the terrified hostages studied it intensely as they waited, fearful of what he might do next.

"You," said O'Grady, pointing to the sweating manager. "You've been trained in the ways of Family Value restaurants, right? Trained to cook with packaged bread buns and frozen meat. You've been trained to deal with a sanitized workplace that fits into neat, plastic molds."

Close to panic, the manager, Theo Constantine, couldn't concentrate on the words. He was nervous at the best of times, spending most of his working day as if every mishap was a catastrophe. Right now the mildly jittery, bumbling, aloof manager was caught in a frozen state of hysteria.

"What's the procedure?" asked O'Grady, staring the manager in the eye.

Constantine squeaked a tiny, "What?" out of his constricted throat.

"I know how your multinational masters think," said O'Grady. "I know you were trained to deal with difficult children during the endless hours of manager's school you attended. So what's the procedure? Or weren't you listening as well as all the other managers? Eh? Those boys in their pressed trousers and clean white shirts and their *Hi, I'm Nobody* badges pinned neatly to their chests. What's the procedure to get her out of the way?" O'Grady nodded toward the girl.

"Her?" asked Constantine. He was met with the steely gaze of O'Grady. "You want me to deal with the girl?"

O'Grady didn't move. He watched as the manager sighed and walked over to the girl at the counter, asking, "Where are your parents?"

"I don't know . . ."

"Did they go to the bathroom?"

"I don't know!"

"So far, so bad," said O'Grady as the manager took the girl by the arm and led her over to the woman with the small boy. Both mother and son backed themselves farther against the wall.

"Is this your daughter?"

"No."

"Would you mind keeping an eye on her . . ."

He didn't bother finishing his sentence. The woman shook her head so emphatically she was in danger of tearing a neck muscle. The manager looked around for another possible mother or father figure and received equally flat refusals from the other customers. The girl clutched his hand tightly, a tense, almost squinting expression on her face. She looked up at the manager, her only port in this maelstrom of madness, but he didn't want her, either. He steered her to a fenced-in play area at the back of the restaurant with an order to stay put. But as soon as the manager had turned away the girl stood up, tears flowing down her cheeks, and followed him back to the counter.

O'Grady laughed out loud. "Can you see it?" he shouted. "The first lesson in the reeducation of the people has been played out to perfection. This girl represents everything that is wrong with the so-called Family Value code of conduct. She won't be shoved into a standard-sized hole. She won't be forced to fit into their artificial environment. *She* is real, not Family Value. There *is* no family value in Family Value. There's only plastic and wastepaper and tasteless saturated fats. There's only useless fools like this manager here who follow the company line and peddle their lies but can't deal with anything human!"

The manager flushed a deep red. Turning here and there for some kind of outlet for his embarrassment, he saw the girl behind him and spoke in a harsh voice, "I thought I told you to stay put!" The girl burst into hysterical sobs and a murmur of outrage broke out among the customers.

O'Grady nodded sagely, then raised the Barrett up higher and aimed it at the manager's head. "Get the hell back here," he snapped.

"Oh, jeez," quivered the manager, his eyes locked on the Barrett. "What do you want to point that thing at me for?"

Since pointing a weapon was such an unambiguous and clear act, O'Grady did not answer. Instead, he turned toward the terrified customers, seeking out the irresponsible parents who had allowed their child to be subjected to the humiliation of the "Family Value Way."

"Whose kid is this?" asked O'Grady. "Yours? Yours?"

The customers shook their heads, looked down at their feet, or adopted blank expressions. None claimed the child. No mother stepped forward to soothe her sobs, to hold her close. No father emerged to pick his daughter up and console her.

"What the hell is going on here?" shouted O'Grady.

"It appears that she's here without . . ." began the manager, but O'Grady silenced him with a wave of the Barrett.

"Where the hell are her parents? Are they hiding? Where are they?"

He pointed the shotgun at every corner, swinging the barrel around wildly, sweeping it past the heads of frightened customers and terrified children.

"I don't know," shouted the manager desperately. "Please calm down . . ."

"What the hell is going on here? Are they trying to be heroes?"

"No. They . . ."

"Because I'll kill 'em if they are."

"No one is trying to be a hero . . ."

"Come out now! Come out or I'll start shooting for the hell of it!" He cocked his shooting elbow up high, eye to the sight, his cheek muscles twitching with tension.

The manager opened his mouth to shout "No!" He sucked a deep breath into his lungs, swelling his chest cavity, expanding the musculature and excess fat around his rib cage. But before he could force the air out, another voice shouted.

"They're not here, you horrible man. They're not here!"

O'Grady lowered the shotgun slowly and stood on the table panting, the sweat pouring from his forehead.

"What?" he said.

"They're not here," repeated the girl, tears pouring down her cheeks.

FREDA OPPERMAN

I'm dressing for this interview with the journalist named William. It is quite a process. My wide-open wardrobe stands before me, but nothing really grabs my eye. Sometimes I stand here for hours, trying to choose what to wear. At least when I went to school the decision was already made for me. I didn't have to worry about which color was lucky today.

I have the Opperman disdain for decorations. I try to keep my clothes simple, my hair out of my face, and give as little thought as possible to color. After all, I dream in monochrome without any regrets. In fact, I couldn't think of anything more horrible than to dream in color. To see the underground, the faces, the girl on the stairs in splashes of red and blue and green. I prefer to wake with my muted gray memories. They fade quicker into the night.

Nancy likes color. She goes for the European hues, softer and more sensible. They suit her no-nonsense attitude. And I think they also act as camouflage, shielding her powers from unsuspecting opponents who might assume that she is an easy mark. Never underestimate N.O. I have watched her emergence, ever since the first press conference after the siege. Up until that moment she had been a talented lawyer who probably would have continued on with her private practice. But something happened as we sat at the press-conference table, the police commissioner at Nancy's side, his face rigid with tension after the private shellacking she'd given him because the police took too long to end the siege. There we sat, squinting in the lights, three unhappy campers confronted by TV cameras and journalists.

"Freda, how does it feel to be back with your mom and dad?"

Why did they want to know that? How did they think it felt? My chair was pushed up against Nancy's, my hand squeezed in her fine-boned hand under the table, my eyes looking down so the reporters wouldn't be able to see me. It didn't feel real.

"Freda, how does it feel to be back with your mom and dad?"

I glanced quickly at my father, Hugh, standing at the back of the room. He offered encouragement with his eyes. But he hadn't been invited to sit at the table.

"Freda, how does . . . ?"

Were they trying to trick me, these reporters? I was unable to remember anything. Unable to breathe properly. Panic was rapidly taking hold of me. And then I felt her hand squeeze mine. Nancy's.

"She's relieved and just needs rest and quiet to recover from her ordeal." That voice. So assured and strong.

The journalists were only momentarily diverted. "Can you tell us what happened in those last hours, Freda?"

Me, small again, not looking at anyone. "Not really."

Really, because all I could see at the time was that gun exploding in such a bright flash of color.

Then Nancy again. Growing. Taking charge. It was the birth of my protector.

"She doesn't remember much. Just Mr. Constantine on the floor . . ."

"Did he say anything?" That question directed at her.

We exchanged a quick glance. Then Nancy spoke again. "He told her to make something of all the mess that had happened. To lead a good life."

I nodded, and suddenly the whole room erupted with shouting voices, questions fired at me like bullets. "Is Constantine a hero?" "What did you say back?" "Did you hold his hand?" Nancy put an end to the press conference then, and we never held another. Since that debacle I have always answered my questions in more intimate, quieter settings.

Was Theo Constantine a hero? I guess he was many things. A manager, a frightened hostage, even a dreamer. I have a memory of him. The both of us sitting in the storeroom, me watching him, when he told me he'd had a dream about a man standing on a table in his restaurant, singing opera. I can see his face telling me this. He looked embarrassed. Poor Theo, he rushed toward John Wayne O'Grady in those opening minutes of the siege expecting to hear an aria.

I am to meet with Mr. William Something-or-other today for a "chat." I like the fact that he has tried to camouflage this interview with such a quaint description. Even his hesitant question at the beginning of our phone conversation, his checking for certainty, struck a chord with me.

"Is this Freda Opperman?"

I did think to myself, "Who else would it be?" but instead I answered with a "Yes."

"This is William . . ." he said, adding his surname, but it came out as a mumbled, garbled mess of a word. I spent the next minute or so trying to rerun the surname in my head, so I missed the next part of our conversation.

"It's on Grange Street . . . is that all okay?" asked William.

"Is your name really William?" I asked. "Or is it Will? Or Bill?"

"William," he answered.

"What newspaper are you from?" I wanted more information.

"I told you that before." There was a pause as he digested the fact that I obviously had not listened, then he repeated his introduction. "I'm from a university magazine . . ." My heart sank. This was worse than I'd first imagined. ". . . It comes out every month and this story would make a fabulous feature article . . ."

I suppose there are many shades of shame in our lives. There is the shame of being caught stealing, the shame of letting a friend down, the shame of being knocked over by a VW Beetle, and the shame of having your life exposed in a university magazine. What will Mr. William, the university journalist, make of this little life of mine?

"So . . . are those arrangements okay, then?"

"What arrangements?"

"The Blue House coffee shop . . . in Grange Street . . ."

"Yes," I mumbled. "See you then." And I hung up.

No doubt he'll want to ask about Theo Constantine's famous last words. They all do. He'll want to know what they mean to me now, and I shall talk about how one can either *be* good or *do* good or go for both. I shall remind him of the moral and righteous crusade Nancy Opperman has fought for the oppressed and downtrodden—victims of crime, powerless litigants, social reformers—and what a good fight that has been. That is how it has always been. They *all* ask about those words.

As far as the canon of famous last words go, Theo's are hardly spectacular. They have not been etched onto his gravestone, or chiseled into the base of a statue. They haven't even been engraved onto a paper-towel dispenser in one of the many Family Value restaurants around the nation. Yet everyone remembers them. Since the disaster of the press conference, I have been asked a hundred times what I said to Constantine after he uttered the words, and each time I have answered that I don't recall. It is all a blank. Yet an answer comes to me now, a fitting response that I doubt would be printable. I might tell William that I leaned closer to Theo Constantine and whispered, "I liked you better when you were dreaming about opera."

So, what do you wear to impress a journalist? I know what they're like, even university hacks. They make instant decisions based on the cut of your pants, the hang of your T-shirt, the spring of your shoes. They read hidden codes into your attire as if it might offer insights into your soul.

Perhaps a simple pair of jeans and a plain T-shirt? Casual Freda who does not care a hoot about a silly interview with this university magazine? Then why am I turning up in the first place? A quirky outfit, then? Something that would play to the stereotype? He'd tell himself he had no preconceptions, but in the end he'd see my peculiar attire as confirmation that I was a strange, peculiar girl. There's no sense in giving him a head start.

I choose a shirt from the rack. Even though colors are of no concern to me, I know that they affect others. This shirt is a nondescript pale blue that was probably never fashionable, but would not be seen as a disaster, either. It might remind William of a summer sky, of lying on his back on the lawn watching the clouds roll by.

When I was four years old, Nancy and I went in a plane to visit Auntie Glenda. I remember looking out the window and seeing the sun poke through the clouds in a radiant burst of light. I remember asking Nancy if that was where the angels lived. She leaned over my shoulder and smiled but didn't answer.

I wonder if William dreams in color? I might even ask him, if the interview's going badly. Selecting a pair of dark cotton pants to go with the shirt, I try them on and stand before the mirror. They make me look tall and slender, and even though I am tall (and relatively slender), instinct tells me to accentuate that today. Finally I choose an apricot cardigan because it is the first thing that comes to hand. Now I can dress.

I suppose that William would see his choice of meeting place as canny. He's hoping that the very sight of Grange Street, where the Family Value underground restaurant once stood, will poke at my memory and cause a flood of recollections. What he hasn't banked on is that I visit the city on a regular basis and have walked down Grange Street a thousand times since that ordeal.

Going by William's theory I would have accosted countless people by now. Bailed them up at the corner, "I remember how cold it was that day." Stopped them by the Scandinavian ice cream parlor, "The gun seemed enormous to my small eyes." Tripped them up at the cosmetics shop to whisper in their ear, "I wondered if I'd ever see my parents again."

So many stories told over the years would surely see my brain spent, dried up, left only with tiny scrapings of the event. Memory, however, is a mysterious drink that spills at the most unlikely of times. There have been umpteen occasions where I've walked Grange Street and not recalled a single moment of that time. And there've been other times when a smell, or the sound of a child's game, will bring it all back.

That afternoon—Nancy, Hugh, and me—on our way down the steps. Together, because this was N.O.'s plan. Why should she let divorce deprive me of the opportunity to go on outings with both my parents? And I loved it. Loved holding my father's hand, even loved hearing Nancy talking about her latest case. Hugh, listening in that half-an-ear way of his, nodding intermittently, being polite.

I'd won a hard-fought battle to come to the Family Value restaurant—a long shoot-out with my mother, although it more resembled a court case. I had chipped away at her defenses on a daily basis, ever since the planned outing was mooted. I countered her opening remarks ("The food is so plastic in those restaurants." *I like it!*), I rebutted her expert witnesses ("They exploit the young people who work there." *They always smile at me!*), and I shattered her summing-up speech ("It's not a comfortable atmosphere there." *Dad likes it. He takes me there on my visits!*). Eventually, the judgment fell in my favor. It was a tough case, but one that I had to win, because Nancy had plans to take us to an Italian restaurant, and everyone knows you can't get Wild West stickers at an Italian restaurant.

Seated together near the play area, our plastic trays so full of promise, my little heart was beating at the prospect of opening my stickers, just as I'd seen the boy on TV do a hundred times before. But the stickers weren't there, and when I wanted to complain, N.O. ordered that I "stay put" and eat my meal. I begged to be allowed to go and get my stickers. I appealed to Hugh, I put on all my best faces, but my mother wasn't going to budge. She didn't want to be left alone with the quiet, dreamy presence of Hugh Opperman. Didn't want an opportunity to find his diffident air irritating, his faraway look an annoyance.

Even as we breezed out of that restaurant past the counter, so close to the Wild West stickers, so easily attained by polite request, I did not speak. It wasn't until we were out on the street again and N.O. had decided to look inside a bookshop that little Freda saw her opportunity. I put my case to my coconspirator and he relented.

"Go on, then," Hugh said. "But be quick about it." These were the words that sent me back down those steps into hell.

I stand at my dresser now. How did I get here? There is nothing remarkable before me, just drawers containing socks and other unmentionables. My underwear drawer is open. How did that happen? My mind is a bit dazed. It's memory that does that.

There is a discordant note in my head, as if the elements are singing out of tune. I want to cover my ears, but that would not help. It is a crazy melody, racing toward a climax that frightens me. Something is very wrong. I'm being compelled to think up stories when everyone knows I *do not* tell stories. I'm being urged to step out of my room and into the unknown, when it is common knowledge that I do not trust the unknown. I just don't do that. It's not part of the plan.

Focusing on the mundane features of my room, I try to calm myself. Usually I can come down from the pinnacle of panic within a few minutes, but this time it seems to be lasting. I see my bed. My curtains. My desk. My dresser. Why *is* my undies drawer open? I look inside, seeking clues, and my hand brushes an ornate carved box. I pause, feeling a tingle on my skin, an unpleasant electricity that makes me shiver. This is wrong. Wrong. I slam my drawer shut and it makes a harsh crack, a shot that rips through the fabric of my room, opening up holes to another world, to other places.

I feel hunted. A young man waits to write about me. I feel cornered. The sanctity of my room is unsettled by sharp sounds. I feel trapped. The long stretch of material that has protected me for so many years feels frayed and distressed.

I switch on every light in my room—overhead, bedside, desk, night-light—I give them life and energy so that they can have a conversation with the gloom behind me and keep it occupied. I scan every corner of my room to remind myself of how it should look, then I walk out, close the door, and lock the three locks. My room is sealed now, forbidden to misbehave. It waits quietly for my return. Now I have the way ahead to deal with, and it bothers me. How do I make it behave? How do I train the light to shine in every dark corner so that no little nasties can leap out at unsuspecting moments?

A dreadful foreboding haunts me as I walk down the hallway, more than my usual feeling of doom, more than my familiar level of fear. Something is wrong. As I pass the phone on the way through to the kitchen it rings, shrieking for my attention, and I jump. The phone has been ringing like this all morning, calling me, then going dead before I can answer it. I feel as if I'm being warned somehow, given the message to run while I still have a chance. The phone stops and I take a second to catch my breath, but there's no rest for the wicked. It rings again, and this time it is insistent, demanding me to pick up the receiver. I do.

"Hello," I say, sounding very tentative.

A voice replies. If you could call it a voice. It's neither male nor female, young nor old. It is a thick, sticky tar that runs from the receiver into my ears, filling me with its putrid, chemical bile, and I wish I'd taken the warning. It is a voice of evil, spilling onto my clothing, spoiling me, uttering five words that can't possibly be true.

Five words. Barely a conversation.

"I know about the napkins."

And whether the words are repeated, or backed up by threats of proof, I do not know because I have let the phone drop from my hand. It bounces onto my foot before rolling comically onto the carpet, jiggling like a demented tea bag.

My mind is held—a rabbit in a fox's death grip—I'm paying attention.

JOHN WAYNE

O'GRADY

"People, listen to me," said John Wayne O'Grady, self-styled revolutionary and hostage taker. "Listen to every command and you won't be hurt." He looked at them, huddled against the walls, each one of them frightened for their own lives, and allowed himself a satisfied smile. This was a great moment in history. He knew they couldn't take the time to savor it as he did. That would come later. They didn't know that the hand of kindness had been held out to them. They would learn the truth, and one day even laugh at how scared they'd been. That was how O'Grady saw it.

Even the girl would laugh.

For the past few minutes there had been a persistent rattling outside, and the gunman assumed it was the girl's parents trying to get in through the locked front doors. He would have to deal with it. Locked front doors might hold back desperate parents, but they'd never stand up to a determined police force.

"You people, lie on the floor! Now! Bunch up in the middle here," he ordered.

Nobody moved, so O'Grady poked his shotgun at the closest male, who happened to be the cook. The hostages shuffled into a tight group in the middle of the restaurant, like cattle.

"Lie down!" shouted the gunman, kicking at them indiscriminately. Reluctantly they lay on the floor.

"I have planted a bomb in this restaurant," said O'Grady.

Some of the hostages started crying, and others tried to sit up, to see the bomb.

"Shut up!" yelled O'Grady, marching over to the tall man and kicking him in the back. "Stay low or you'll all die. Down! Down now!"

They obeyed his command, lying face-first on the floor.

"Nobody move. I have a remote. Don't speak. Don't do anything!"

He ran into the kitchen and pressed the "call" button on the dumbwaiter. The tiny wooden elevator was set into the back wall. A groaning noise sounded above, as it slowly descended from the ground level. It was nothing more than a poky box that was used to carry supplies down to the restaurant, and rubbish back up to the alley above. But it was also big enough to hold a man and a weapon. Once the dumbwaiter was at the underground level, O'Grady wedged the doors open with a metal pole that was used to prop the fridge doors when they were loaded. This rendered the dumbwaiter inoperable, as it could not be recalled with the doors open. For safety's sake, O'Grady removed the fuse for the elevator, then attached a small electronic device to its roof. He gave the dumbwaiter a shake, and a high-pitched screech emitted from the device. Resetting it, O'Grady walked back into the restaurant. The hostages were still in their prone position.

An insistent whispering nagged at the air, and O'Grady looked around, trying to locate its source. Eventually he saw that it was the cook, arguing with a burger-queen. He marched up to them and grabbed the young man by his hair, wrenching his head back. "Shut the hell up!" yelled O'Grady. "You talk anymore and you all die. You move an inch and *you* die." He released the boy's hair, and his head fell forward, banging onto the ground.

A hush fell over the restaurant. O'Grady nodded, satisfied that they all knew now who was in charge. He picked up a second bag that had been lying harmlessly in the corner and said menacingly, "Not one of you move or whisper or even twitch. I'll know." Then he went back up the stairs to the street level.

This was the weakest part of O'Grady's plan. A dozen or so people lay on the floor behind him, the telephone a few feet away, yet they did not move. The threat of a bomb kept them bunched together, barely moving, let alone speaking.

The stairway leading up to the doorway was the only entrance or exit to the underground restaurant, one of the reasons O'Grady had chosen it as the venue to begin the revolution. He made his way up the steep stairs to the double glass doors. The footpath beyond was empty. Whoever had been rattling the locked doors had gone.

Behind O'Grady was a large wall and a blind left-hand turn into the restaurant. All that could be seen from the street was the landing wall, covered by an enormous advertisement depicting a hamburger with a glitzy price tag. For all any passerby knew, someone had accidentally locked the doors to the restaurant.

O'Grady carefully removed a square block of plastic explosive from a wrapper and weighed it in his hand. He worked the gray Semtex explosive into a spot between the two doors, kneading it like dough until it stayed in one spot. He made sure it was visible from the outside so that the police would know that any attempt to break into the restaurant would be met with instant death. He taped the plastic into place with cloth tape, then took a tin box from his bag. O'Grady removed a detonator from the box, his hands shaking slightly. He didn't trust explosives, and had heard that these electrical blasting caps could be unstable, especially those bought illegally on the black market. He wouldn't be the first revolutionary who'd died from his own bomb. Pushing the detonator into the Semtex, O'Grady breathed a sigh of relief that he was still in one piece. He sat back to admire his handiwork. So simple, yet so deadly.

Two schoolkids stopped and watched intently as O'Grady took two rolls of thin wire cord from his bag and attached the end of each wire to the detonator.

"Watcha doing?" they asked, but O'Grady ignored them. "Is that a bomb?"

O'Grady carefully unraveled the wires, keeping them apart to avoid any possibility of a static charge setting the detonator off.

He laid the wire rolls on the ground, then stood on shaky legs and bent to pull a thick chain from the bag. Wrapping it around the two doors' push handles, he locked the chain tight with a padlock. This measure was merely to keep curious onlookers out. The bomb was for the benefit of the police.

Next O'Grady taped a small handwritten note to the door with electrician's tape. *Do not attempt to enter the restaurant, and nobody will be hurt. This bomb is armed. I have no demands.* The note was signed, *"The Commanding Officer."* He stuffed the electrician's tape roll back in his bag, slung it over his shoulder, then picked up the two rolls of wire. O'Grady was about to leave when a man started violently rattling the glass doors.

"What are you doing?" shouted the man. "My daughter is in there."

O'Grady shook his head at the man, saying, "You're too late."

"Please," shouted the man. "I don't know what your problem is, but please just pass my daughter through."

Avoiding eye contact with the desperate father, O'Grady checked his shotgun, gripped it in one hand, then carefully unraveled the two rolls of wire as he walked backward. It was an awkward method, and took forever, especially with the father bellowing and rattling the glass doors above him.

"Shut the hell up!" yelled O'Grady when he reached the landing at the bottom of the stairs, sweat pouring from his forehead. "And stop rattling those doors or you'll be blown to pieces."

The father saw the bomb for the first time and stepped back in panic.

O'Grady backed into the restaurant and looked at the hostages. All was silent, nobody had moved. He taped the ends of the two wire rolls to the restaurant wall, then pulled a large battery out of his bag. For a moment he debated about connecting one wire to a battery terminal, and leaving the other free. In the end he decided that this was too risky. A hostage might get caught up in revolutionary fervor and detonate the bomb. He put the battery back in the bag, then he walked over to his hostages.

"Sit up!" he yelled, the shotgun in his hand. "Sit up or die young!"

Slowly they moved, looking about them as if they might see a large bomb hidden somewhere.

Some rubbed their faces, others bothered to brush dirt and muck from their clothes. Most wore expressions of helplessness and panic.

O'Grady counted them. They were not people to him, but numbers, abstract entities in his overall equation. He defined them by what he saw. They were an old woman, a tall man, a red-haired woman, two burger-queens, a cook, two kitchen hands, a middle-aged man, a mother, her son, the manager, and the young girl. Thirteen. Whether they knew one another or were related or had come here in family groups to celebrate a birthday or an anniversary was irrelevant to him. Those details belonged to their past, and they were about to be shed. Soon these frightened entities would become soldiers, a band of fighters that would call one another "comrade."

He noticed that the girl still seemed distressed, and realized that she would not last very long without somebody to guide her through the early, confusing stages of his reeducation process.

"You," said O'Grady, pointing to Theo Constantine. "Your task is to care for this child. Seeing as she has no parents here, you'll become her prime comrade—"

"Prime comrade?" said Constantine, a confused expression on his face.

"Yes. This is your road to reeducation," said the gunman. He turned to the rest of the group of hostages. "Nobody else is to take care of this child. Only the manager. He will care for her, comfort her. He will see to her needs. Is that understood?"

They nodded, and O'Grady smiled. "Good."

The girl pushed herself up against the restaurant manager, who looked at her for a moment as if he couldn't quite figure out what she wanted. Then he remembered his orders, and patted her awkwardly, before ignoring her.

"Let me make this perfectly clear," said O'Grady, pacing up and down before the frightened hostages. "If any one of you gets in my way, or tries to be a hero, I will kill you. I don't care if you're young, old, infirm, or healthy. I will shoot you dead. Do not disobey me. Do not cross me. Do as I say and you will be able to take part in one of the most exciting moments of history."

The phone started ringing on the kitchen wall, but O'Grady ignored it.

"I am not here to gain money," said O'Grady. "Nor am I a member of any religious sect or political group. They are all illusions. I am here to change the world . . ."

The phone stopped ringing.

"Over the next few days you will change from weak, mindless citizens into hardened soldiers. You will become a revolutionary cell, with one purpose only, to spread the truth around the world until the corporate puppet-masters are overthrown."

Some of the hostages exchanged glances. There was hope that the gunman might not be a murderer after all.

O'Grady counted the hostages again, then subtracted the manager from the equation, figuring that the buffoon was too far gone to be converted. Twelve were left. An even dozen. He enjoyed the symmetry of the number.

"I will educate you 12," he boomed. "Help you shake off the lies and deceit of the puppet-masters that control you, until you know the truth. Then you 12 will each go out and individually educate another 12 people. That will make 144 revolutionaries roaming the streets. And those 144 will each go out and individually educate 12 others, so that in no time 1,728 soldiers will be ready to overthrow the corporate puppet-masters."

Following this equation through to its conclusion, in a matter of months O'Grady envisaged that an overwhelming majority of people would know that they'd been fed a steady diet of lies by the corporations. They would see what the multinationals were up to, and they would act.

"Time to form study circles!" shouted O'Grady. "Time to pay attention!"

The hostages slowly moved, unsure of who should be in which circle, and what size they should be.

"Do you see how you have forgotten to think for yourselves?" shouted O'Grady. "The puppet-masters have used the school system and the media to turn you into mindless morons. You must change your ways now! How do you expect to overcome the multinationals with this sort of enthusiasm?" He didn't wait for their reply. Taking the shotgun by the barrel, he prodded the men with the stock, shoving them roughly with orders to form study circles.

"But . . . what do you mean?" asked Theo Constantine, his arms held in the air with an exaggerated gesture of confusion.

"Do you question a direct order from your commanding officer?" shouted O'Grady, pushing the stock of the shotgun up against Constantine's throat.

"No," croaked the manager, leaning back from the force of O'Grady's menace. "No . . . I . . ."

"Study circles, you fools. Three study circles. Come on! I haven't got time to waste."

Three rough circles were formed on the floor. The elderly woman tried to sit in a seat, but O'Grady barked at her to get down on the floor with her comrades.

"But my back . . ." began the woman.

"You're a soldier now!" shouted O'Grady. "And soldiers do not have bad backs. Get on the floor with your comrades."

Theo Constantine helped the elderly woman onto the floor, muttering comforting words in her ear.

"I don't understand," said the woman. "What's he want us to study?"

"The truth!" shouted O'Grady.

He paced up and down between the circles. "Your lives," he boomed, "have been based on lies. Your teachers have lied to you, the media has lied to you, your parents have lied to you."

Somebody started sobbing, and O'Grady paused. It was the girl. The manager leaned over to comfort her, laying his meaty palm on her back, and O'Grady shouted in frustration.

"Must you always be a fool?"

"But . . . I . . . You said I was to comfort her . . ."

The telephone started ringing in the kitchen again. Several of the Family Value workers shot glances at one another.

"Leave the girl be," boomed O'Grady, still ignoring the insistent ringing of the telephone. "Her crying is a sign. The truth is breaking through."

"But . . . she . . ." stuttered the manager.

O'Grady waved his hand at the manager as if he were swatting a fly. Looking intently at the girl, he called out, "Why are you crying?"

"I want my mom," she sobbed.

Suddenly the phone stopped ringing.

"Do you think she cares?" said O'Grady. "She's not here. Your father's not here. They're not even on the phone. Your parents left you behind. All you have now is me. John Wayne O'Grady. I am here and I represent the truth. Do you want to hear the truth?"

The girl did not reply. She continued her sobbing, face in her hands, shoulders heaving, body bent double. O'Grady walked up close to her and knelt down, speaking in a kind, soft voice.

"I am John Wayne O'Grady. That's all that matters. You wanted a Wild West sticker when you came in. Well, I am the Wild West. I am John Wayne and every other hero you could ever imagine. I am your future. You're smart, you're bright. Put your head up and say it with me. 'John Wayne O'Grady is the future.'"

The girl shook her head and croaked out a defiant "No." O'Grady knelt down and put his arm around her shoulder. "I know this is hard," he soothed. "It always is at the beginning. But you're not alone. Everyone here is feeling the same as you, and they want you to say it for them. They want you to say, 'John Wayne O'Grady is the future.' Don't let them down. They're counting on you."

The girl lifted her head, tears streaming down her face.

"Go on," said O'Grady. "Look in their faces. They want you to say it."

She looked around at the tormented faces in her circle, but each and every one of them turned away or looked at the ground. All except the manager who had shouted at her earlier. He nodded his head to the girl, encouraging her to do as the gunman said, and the girl nodded back.

"John . . . Wayne . . . ," began the girl in a quiet voice.

"That's it," said O'Grady. "You're getting there."

"John Wayne O'Grady is . . . ," but her voice cracked and she started sobbing again.

"I know you can do it, honey. I just know it," said O'Grady. "Make me proud."

The girl looked up again, wiping the tears from her face. "John Wayne O'Grady is the future," she said, staring straight ahead.

"That's the way," boomed O'Grady, his voice so loud that the girl jumped with fright. O'Grady laughed, and patted her on the back. "No need to be frightened," said O'Grady. "You did good. No one need be frightened of John Wayne O'Grady if they do the right thing."

O'Grady stood up and pranced around the room.

"Do you see that?" he shouted. "From the mouth of babes comes the truth."

The girl looked once again at the manager, a desperate, pleading expression on her face, but the man was embarrassed and found it difficult to meet her eyes. Eventually he put his head down, staring intently at his shoes, and the girl's shoulders slumped.

"This is destiny," boomed O'Grady. "You have all been shown the way, now we can move forward . . ."

He was interrupted by a noise, a low whooping cry that sounded more animal than human. It was the girl. She was holding on to her chest, her face red with exertion, making the most dreadful sound.

"What's wrong?" asked O'Grady. "What's wrong with her?"

"She's choking," said the old lady with the bad back.

"Help her," called someone from the next study circle.

Nobody moved, afraid of acting without permission. Each stared at the girl as she whooped and gasped for air.

"What the hell are you doing?" shouted O'Grady, pointing the gun at the manager. "Get her the hell out of here!"

The manager stood up clumsily and grabbed the whooping child under her arms, half carrying, half dragging her into the storeroom where he shut the door. They all listened as her muted whoops seemed to grow worse and worse, before finally coming to a halt.

None of them knew if she was alive or dead. All they could see was the shut door of the storeroom and the ashen face of John Wayne O'Grady. Then they heard the sirens, from up on the street. One after the other, screaming, answering a call for help that seemed so far away it could almost have been in another world.

N A P K i N

Sunday. My name is Theo Constantine. I'll try to write down what's happening. I got some time with a kid who's sick or something. There is one gunman. He is a crazy bastard called O'Grady. He has a shotgun and a bomb, I think. He claims he's a revolutionary. He hasn't got any demands so far. O'Grady seems unbalanced. He hates me. He hates Family Value. If I get a chance I'll write again.
Theo Constantine

If I move, will it make this phone call real, or just another nightmare? If I get up and walk back into my room, then pretend to come out again, will that mean these last few minutes didn't happen? What am I supposed to do now?

I forget so many things.

I forget that every single waking moment is an opportunity for something bad to happen. Phone calls can come at you when you least expect them. Horrible voices, devoid of body and humanity, can make claims that simply are not possible. If I think of a logical explanation, will that help? Was that caller a telemarketer in a bad mood asking what napkins I have at home? Or was it really someone who knows about the napkins?

I forget how you make words do what you want them to.

Why do you always watch me?

I know . . .

I just want a moment's peace . . .

. . . about . . .

Don't you ever tell that bastard about these napkins. Understand?

. . . the napkins!

How is it possible? They were written by a dead man, rescued by a frightened girl, and hidden forever under the orders of a desperate mother. Standing on wobbly legs, I head back toward my bedroom. They were there only a few minutes ago. I saw the box. Unless someone broke into our house and stole them, but that is preposterous. Nothing can get into Fortress Opperman.

N.O. is not around. That is good. I shut the door behind me, reaching into my undies drawer to remove the small wooden box. My hand is shaking. The box is locked, of course, and I retrieve the key that is taped under my bed. Such simple devices, keys and boxes, ordinary pieces of functionality. Then I open the box, the sickening, hurtling feeling from before heightening to a point where it threatens to spin me to the floor.

I look inside. They are there.

The napkins.

Squashed flat over many years, but still showing the creases and rips from when I clutched them in my filthy little hand as the policeman carried me from that restaurant. I take the top napkin from the pile and glance at it quickly, just to verify that it is still the real thing. *My name is Theo Constantine. I'll try to write down what's happening.*

I hold the cheap paper in my hand, see where Theo's pen ripped through, where his feverish scrawl tore apart the medium of his record keeping. *My name is Theo . . .* Such a simple thing to bear witness, to record facts for those who will come later. The idea first came to him when we were in the storeroom, after my breathing attack. He'd dragged me in there, panicked, saying, "You all right?" over and over. "Do you need medicine? What's wrong?"

Eventually my panic subsided, and I held my hand over my face, instinctively calming my breathing. Theo just stared at me as if I was about to die on him, then he breathed a sigh of relief when he realized I wasn't. It was so comical, his palpable release of tension, that I smiled. He started searching around the storeroom and I asked him what he was looking for.

"Paper," he said. "Gotta tell them what's happening."

Theo, the manager, bumbling about, knocking boxes of polystyrene cups to the floor until he found a packet of napkins. "Perfect!" he said, then he started writing. I found it fascinating to watch. His meaty hand on the napkin to hold it steady, his childlike grip of the pen, his tongue almost poking out of his mouth as he wrote.

"What are you going to do with that?" I asked.

"I don't know . . . maybe show the police."

For a brief moment I thought he had a plan to get us out. My "prime comrade," the man who'd been charged with my care, the "hero" of the siege was going to show his napkin to the police and somehow they would know exactly what to do to rescue us. But when he'd finished writing, Theo picked the napkin up, looked at the closed storeroom door, then stuffed the napkin into a wastepaper basket, muttering that O'Grady wouldn't think to look there. My heart sank.

The carved wooden box in my hands is only half filled by these napkins. There wouldn't be more than a dozen of them. They are placed here in chronological order, from Sunday afternoon to the crazy hours of early Tuesday morning. I place my hand on the pile, wondering if I should read the later ones, when there is a polite knock at my door. N.O. breezes into the room, stopping short, taking in the whole scene—me, the napkins, my face, the fear.

"What are you doing, Freda? Why have you got those?" asks Mom.

"Oh, I don't know," I say dismissively. "Just wanted to look at them . . ."

Nancy gives me her worried look, her cheeks squeezed in, her eyes hard and sharp. "I heard the phone just now," she says.

"Hm?" I mutter.

"Have you got those out because of the phone call, Freda?"

"No," I answer. "The phone just stopped ringing. It's been doing that all morning."

"Oh," says Nancy, a bit put out. "I thought I heard you speaking."

She carefully takes the box of napkins from my hands and holds it as if it were a dead cat. "I wish we'd burned these . . . we should have burned them . . ."

"No! You can't burn these," I hiss.

"Yes, Freda, I know," says Nancy, her face a frantic scribble of emotions.

I stare at her, breathing hard, my train of thought lost. "You can't burn them," I repeat, then I go silent.

Nancy shoves the box back into my undies drawer and closes it, but she can't make it "crack" the same way I can. "I hate these things," she says. "And I almost think . . ."

I roll my eyes, this part of the conversation is very familiar to me. "You almost think they're holding me back," I sigh, finishing her sentence.

"But surely they are, Freda . . ."

"Are we late, Mom?" I ask.

"What?" she says, fazed by my interruption.

"The interview?"

She stares at me, blinking, a hurt expression taking over. Damn it. I hate it when she looks like this. I've seen her demolish experienced lawyers for less, yet she always holds back with me. It's too personal when she does this, too bound up in night after night of needing her to come into my room to calm my panic. I don't want to hurt her, I never do.

Now she's rearranging my room, straightening what doesn't need straightening. It's a surefire sign that she's angry. She'll speak again soon, ask me a question in a rational, reasonable tone.

"Is it this newspaper interview?" she asks. There it is. "Are you worried about it?"

"Not really," I say.

"It concerns me when you're like this, Freda . . ."

"I *am* capable of giving an interview."

"I just don't know what he'll make of you if you're in one of your strange moods . . ."

What is William to make of me? I am strange. A creature who holds on to a pile of tatty paper napkins for dear life. I'm a weird teenager, an alien.

"What is most like thee?" I mutter.

"Shelley," snorts N.O.

She doesn't like it when I quote from Shelley. N.O. has never had much time for the poet, or more accurately his poem, "To a Skylark." It's become a sticking point between us over the past few years. At first I used to think she couldn't respect a man who puts forward a simple argument in such beautiful language. She is naturally suspicious of inspiring language, being a lawyer. And yet, I wonder if there isn't more to Nancy's disdain? I wonder if she's looked at my face when I've read the poem, seen me sitting at my desk, taken away with that "blithe spirit," lifted to a place where a bird's song can reveal to mere mortals that the world is full of grace?

"So, you really are fine then?" she asks, a brisk note now. N.O. has swept away unnecessary emotion.

"Yes. I shall give the usual answers to the usual questions . . ."

And never have to reveal the private Freda Opperman. Never have to say what is most like me. Because, whatever it is, I am sure that William has not met it in his entire life. I had not met it until I read about Shelley's bird.

"I still think you should probably give some thought to what you might say in this interview, Freda," continues my mother, straightening my already straight quilt cover.

What am I to say? That I am a teenager who's never even lived a proper teen's experience? That I'm so used to locking up behind me that I've forgotten where I put myself? That I hear voices? No, I definitely won't be telling William about that. After all, what would he write? That Freda Opperman hears the impossible? That she has conversations with disembodied callers who seem to know about something that nobody else in the world knows about? That would require quite an explanation. Even a story.

A young girl is carried from a restaurant. It is early in the morning and the air is freezing. She is lifted into the backseat of a police car where her mother waits to hold her. To clutch her as tight as is possible. Then her mother sees something in the girl's hand. The napkins. She reads snatches of what is written there and says, "Freda, my darling. Give those to Mommy now . . ."

I remember how much my hand hurt after I'd let them go. The ache I felt as I watched Nancy stuff them into her purse.

That is a story that no living soul has heard.

I suppose I *do* have to think about what I'll say to William. If you're not prepared, you can be led into awkward situations. Anecdotes are always an alternative to stories, amusing little bits of froth that don't reveal much. My problem is that I am not very practiced when it comes to anecdotes. My few attempts at this art form have elicited embarrassed silences. The young survivor should accept as many invitations to dinner parties as she can in order to hone her conversational skills. If these are not forthcoming, she should practice on family members, trusted pets, or her reflection in the mirror.

Take the time a teacher asked my class to write an anecdote down, in the guise of a short story, about an embarrassing incident from our lives. She gave me this apologetic look when she said this. All I could think of at the time was the "speech" incident.

N.O. had organized for me to talk to a bunch of snotty, rich girls in a snotty, rich-girl's school. This was a month or two after the siege, because I remember I'd just returned to school again. The principal suggested I might like to tell the girls how I never gave up hope throughout the siege.

But when it was time, I strode to the front of the stage and spoke in the most strident, politic-speak voice I could muster.

"You are gullibles!" I bellowed.

As far as beginnings go, I thought it wasn't half bad. I certainly had their attention. What did a little pronunciation matter?

"There is no value in Family Value," I thundered. "Grown in the tropical rain frosts where cows are cut down by the moldy nationals, the puppet-masters pray each night . . ."

My audience stared at me, the smiles frozen on their faces.

"Death to the parasites!" I yelled.

My mother stepped in and led me from the microphone, thus saving Family Value from any more of my twisted syntax and mispronounced abuse. Two days later she filed five separate lawsuits on my behalf, all of which were settled out of court one way or another. And the teacher never read my story out loud.

I wonder, would William publish it? Or perhaps he might be a ruthless journalist and question the veracity of such a tale. "How do you expect me to believe such crap? A nine-year-old girl giving a speech so soon after the siege?" Maybe he'd be right. Maybe it didn't happen. Nobody was there with a tape recorder, so we have no real way of knowing.

Nobody wrote it down.

Nancy has finished straightening my already straight room,

and she looks at me for a moment, perhaps trying to read any telltale signs of imminent mad ranting. "I won't be at this interview with you," she says.

I stare at her, shocked, unable to even let out a squeak. She's always been at my interviews.

"I think it's time. You've done hundreds, and you're old enough . . . and you know how to handle questions."

"Do I?" I say eventually.

"Freda, you're nineteen. I really think it'd be best this way. I can't be there forever. It's time to go solo a bit. Don't you agree?"

I'm nineteen. It is such a horrid fact. Why is it only me whose heart jumps about at the mention of my age? Nineteen. Kicked from my nest, with a footprint on my backside. Falling overboard.

"I'll be waiting in the car," says Nancy sadly. She leaves.

As soon as she has gone I reorganize my room again, fight off a dizzy head, stare at my undies drawer with a touch of muted outrage in my eyes, then make my way to the car. The phone has the decency not to ring again. It is raining outside, and a cold wind lashes water against my cheek, stinging and numbing me in one action. I climb into the passenger seat of the car and glance quickly at my mother. She is cold and unfriendly, so I gaze steadfastly out the window as we drive away. No whistling on this trip.

Gray patterns of rain-dropped tones blur the scenery out my car window. This view calms me. It is a safe view, a world devoid of color and contrast. A world muted and hidden behind veils of water and cold air. A world withdrawn.

Even Nancy is withdrawn. The silence that spreads through the car is absolute. My mother is worried that I will let the team down. She's passed the ball to me in front of the goal, hoping that I score a victory for all that is right. And what is right? Her causes, of course. Nancy Opperman, secretary of the Anti-Violent Crime Group, president of the Victim Care Support Network, honorary secretary of the National Council for Gun Control.

I study her face, watch her clench her jaw muscles with ferocious force. She's showing signs of age, which startles me, given that she has always been a constant in my life. There are extra lines around her eyes and a slackening of skin around her mouth. Is there any refuge from inevitability?

I sigh, and Nancy glances at me. Every thought I turn to today seems to depress me.

"Are you thinking about those napkins?" she asks.

I wonder if I'd ever *stopped* thinking about Theo's napkins. That voice, the phone dangling from its cord, spinning at my feet. When does a frightening moment in your life change from incident to story? When does it become something you can write down or tell or never tell . . . ?

"What the hell am I supposed to do?" I ask. It's a question directed at no one in particular, but Nancy takes up the cudgel.

"Just answer his questions," she says, assuming that I was referring to William's interview.

"What will I tell him?"

She clenches her jaw again, grinding a hundred answers into a pulp before finally conceding with, "Whatever is appropriate . . ."

And the dead weight of silence fills the car again.

Perhaps William will want to hear about John Wayne O'Grady. How he kept us seated for hours during his education sessions. Like the one not long before he locked the men in the toilet. It was eerily quiet outside, late Monday afternoon. After twenty-four hours of trying to contact O'Grady and negotiate with him, the police were finally putting a rescue plan into action. They now knew who their gunman was. They'd trawled through all the employment records of Family Value for workers who might have a grudge against the company, and came up with his photo, which my father identified.

O'Grady didn't like the silence outside. It made him nervous. He took two large metal bowls and held them in his lap. Bowl one and bowl two, musical instruments. He scraped them together, back and forth, around and around, perfecting the most irritating, high-pitched metallic sound you'd ever want to hear. And we were to remain silent and listen.

Scrape! Scrape! Scrape!

At the whim of John Wayne O'Grady.

It's a dumb story, and I toss it away, watching as it bounces and rolls into the gutter, coming to rest inside a discarded soft-drink can. Perhaps it will leap out at an unsuspecting can collector and vex his delicate ears—all for the sake of a lousy deposit.

Since my anecdote strategy is out, I search my mind for some conversation starters. But the young survivor is once again lacking in experience. Had I been invited to more morning teas, book groups, decoupage classes, and charity letter-lickings, I would have a number of starters to get any rollicking conversation going. I don't even know how to engage in idle chitchat. Everything I say seems to startle people. Perhaps comments on music would work. They'd be a safe option. Everyone knows at least something about music.

That is what I'll do, then. William might even think that I am up to date with my popular culture. All I have to do is listen to whatever is playing through the café speakers and say, "I hear that this song is quite popular," and he will raise his eyebrows slightly, jot down a few notes, and nod vigorously. I should practice now, but there is no music playing on the car radio, and the last thing I want to do is encourage Nancy to whistle.

But now our car has reached Grange Street. N.O. is pulling up near the café, causing a traffic snarl behind her. "We're running late," she says, ignoring the blast of car horns from behind us. "You go in, I'll park." I nod once again, wondering why she would need to park the car.

"I'll come in, too," says N.O. in answer to my unasked question. "In case you need me." I catch her words through the insistent noise from the impatient driver behind us.

"Come on, Freda," says N.O. anxiously. "He's waiting."

I climb out of the car and straighten my clothing in the spitting rain, then close the door. The driver in the car behind pokes his head out and yells in a sarcastic tone, "Take your time, why don't you?"

I turn to the man and nod, thanking him. He's reminded me to take my time. "Freda Opperman" time. Hours to prepare for any sudden movement. Days to get used to the idea that I'm about to walk into that café.

But all I have is seconds.

My life is continually pared back to the merest tick of a heartbeat, the shallowest pause between intention and action. I live within these tiny spaces, squeezed in to the silences. It's quiet in here, a nice tight fit for a thin girl like me. I do not move north, nor south, nor east, nor west. I live within the shaving of a frozen frame, hoping that the cacophony will pass me by.

I live here with my one wish. That I be nobody. That I be nothing.

That is the bargain I have made with life.

THE GOOD LIFE

OF FREDA O,

AGED 13

Thirteen. A bonus of four extra years. Freda, thirteen, out there in the world, walking, talking, learning. Nine plus four. A number, an age, a point in time that Nancy Opperman, in her darkest hours, thought she'd never see. Her young teenager daughter, trying so hard to be normal, to fit in. Doing what all teenagers do. Bringing home a friend after school.

Doing something she has never done since the siege.

"This is Rani," said Freda, standing awkwardly in the hallway with a dark-skinned girl who had the most beautiful brown eyes that Nancy had ever seen.

Nancy smiled and said hello, and Freda shuffled, as if she might be waiting for approval. Is it all right to break the routine? Nancy was on the verge of saying, "Would you like something to eat?" when Freda tapped Rani on the shoulder and took her into her bedroom, shutting the door.

Oh no, thought Nancy Opperman. She could not deal with shut doors. Not ever. After a short but decent interval, she knocked on the door and entered with a tray of afternoon snacks. Everything seemed fine inside the room. The girls were on the bed listening to Indian music. The mood was calm.

The friend had a red dot on her forehead.

Later, Nancy tried to ask Freda about the girl.

"She has such beautiful dark skin."

"Her mother is Indian. Her dad's Irish. Rani says she's half spiritual, half crazy."

"Rani is a lovely name. She reminds me a little of Andrew Crushmam."

"Who the heck is he?" asked Freda.

"You don't remember Andrew? He was your best friend in kindergarten . . ."

"Oh . . . yes. He was really brown . . ."

"Indian. A lovely boy. He came over here to play after kindergarten once, and you two took it upon yourselves to go shopping."

Freda smiled, a private delight showing on her face. "We weren't shopping," she said. "We were looking for something else."

"Where are these fairies?" whined Andrew.

They were down this way. At the end of the street. The little Freda had seen them once, on a walk with her parents. Bright, flickering, flying in the sunlight. Their wings a blur, their flight so wild and unpredictable.

She turned quickly to her friend. "There's lots," she reassured him. "One will be yours, and ten will be mine."

"I can't see any . . ."

"They will be there. Honest. They will. Lots and lots of them."

"Can I name mine?"

"Yes. But it has to be a proper fairy name."

"What's a proper fairy name?"

"Something sweet," answered the little one.

That evening, after Rani's visit, Nancy went into her daughter's room to retrieve the pile of clothes Freda had stuffed under her bed. This was where she put her laundry, shoved away so that she wouldn't wake and see their strange shapes in the middle of the night.

Nancy shook the clothes individually. Something fell out of Freda's school dress. A card. There was a picture of a man on the front with a red dot on his forehead. The same she'd seen on Rani.

Nancy held the card in her shaking hand.

"You banished Andrew after we ran away, didn't you?" called Freda from the living room.

"Banished him?" replied Nancy, flustered. She walked over to her daughter. "No . . . I remember he came around a few more times . . ."

"Uh-uh," said Freda. "He got the boot."

The phone rang. It was that girl again. Rani. Freda took the phone into her bedroom. Nancy Opperman listened to her daughter's half of the conversation, catching words like *guru* and *ashram*. When Freda hung up the phone, Nancy counted to twenty, then went into her daughter's bedroom after her. She didn't even get a chance to say her first sentence.

"Just let me live my own life, will you?" shouted Freda.

"I'm not trying to interfere," said Nancy. "You're young, so there's things you can't see. I just want to protect you from being hurt."

"I'm sorry," said Freda, turning her back on her mother. "I forgot the golden rule. We can only believe in Nancy's way of life . . ."

"That is so unfair!"

"Fairies!" shouted Andrew.

She shouted, too, calling out, naming each one of them. Their own special fairies. One, two, ten . . . a hundred of them. Swirling around at the end of the street, flying in and out of the sunlight.

The little one reached her hand out to touch the insects as they danced through the sunlight, and she felt a few flicker against her skin. They were real. They were hers.

"This one is called Chocolate," she cried. "And Lollies. And Fizzy!"

"Chutney!" shouted Andrew.

She stopped to look at him.

"It's really sweet, and it's really yummy!"

Nancy tried to put her arm around her daughter's shoulder, but Freda shrugged her away.

"Leave me alone!" she shouted.

"You naughty children . . ."

"Chutney!"

"Andrew! Freda! How dare you leave the yard. Whose idea was this?"

"Chutney!"

"Children! Come back at once."

"No, Mom. We haven't named them all, yet."

"Chutney one and Chutney two and . . ."

"Named what?"

"The fairies . . ."

"They're not fairies, Freda. They're insects. Now get inside."

There was only one more get-together with Rani O'Hara. Once again the girls had shut the bedroom door. This time Nancy stood and listened, amazed to hear the sound of singing coming from the room, a sort of chant-song. It had been so long since she'd heard Freda sing that a small tear formed in the corner of her eye.

As a little child Freda had always sung, making up her own words. Songs about cooking or her dolls or helping around the house. She'd even made up a song about a rat. Little Freda squeezing the life out of the rat, singing her heart out.

After that there was no more Rani. Freda wouldn't talk about what had happened. Nancy only found out by accident. Some months later, she came across Freda's diary lying in the living room. Nancy opened it, glancing at the writing, catching the word "Rani."

When we did the chant I felt so stupid. Rani said we chanted our love for God. But not God in heaven. She said that God was inside yourself. I laughed when she said that, but she was serious. She said, "You are God." I shook my head, got angry. "You are God," she said. I didn't want to hear that stuff. "No," I said. "You don't get it. I can't be. Not me."

She doesn't speak much to me now. I think I scared her.

Nancy closed the diary and shut her eyes, refusing to cry. After all she'd been through, how could she let a silly teenage infatuation unsettle her?

But an image came to her, a vivid memory. Little Freda sitting on a swing, the wind blowing her dress all about. Laughing so much her face was red, her cheeks alive. Laughing until she was in danger of falling off. Shouting at the top of her voice, "I'm the best swinger in the whole world!"

Flying.

JOHN WAYNE

O'GRADY

The air was stale, oppressive, filled with unwanted words, the leftovers from the gunman's endless diatribes. He had talked and talked, never once looking at the storeroom door. The manager and the girl were still in there. Talked and talked until his only recognizable phrases were the ones he liked to repeat. Then suddenly O'Grady stopped and told them to get something to eat. Some were desperate for the toilet, and O'Grady gave them sixty seconds to relieve themselves or he'd burst in on them shooting. Some were hungry and ate bread buns. Some tried to get meat out of the fridges to cook until O'Grady bellowed at them. "That is the poison of the corporate Fascists! Peasants have died for those hamburgers. Put them away!" Some stayed seated on the floor of the restaurant, too tired to move. Others settled for cups of black coffee from the machine. John Wayne O'Grady walked among them, noticing their glances at the storeroom door.

"A fallen comrade must not slow the group down," he said, his voice low and soothing. "The group is paramount. It must push on toward the enemy lines. That is the only way to achieve victory. That is the new way from now on. The truth will make you strong."

The phone rang on the kitchen wall again and some of the hostages jumped. They looked at their captor, who seemed oblivious to the sound. It had rung all through his education session, a shrill reminder of their freedom.

O'Grady broke out of his thoughts and marched to the kitchen, picked up the phone, and shouted, "I have no demands.

I want no money. I am not here to negotiate . . ." There was a pause, as the police negotiator on the other end of the line tried to say something. O'Grady pulled the phone away from his ear, then shouted, "Shut the hell up and listen! I will *not* negotiate! Stay behind your cordon and the people here will walk free. Attempt to enter this restaurant, and they will die!" Then he ripped the phone from its socket. He held it in his hands, staring at the set as though it had personally offended him. Somewhere on the other end of the line the police negotiator cursed and began barking orders.

"The police," said O'Grady to nobody in particular. "They'll be the first to go. Once you're all educated and I release you into society, puppets like the cops will collapse . . . they'll die from the disease of truth." He smiled, enjoying his metaphor. "That's exactly what you are," he announced cheerily. "You're a virus, and I am the virus man."

The storeroom door opened and John Wayne O'Grady looked up to see the manager, Theo Constantine, emerge. Some of the other hostages moved to stand, then looked toward O'Grady and stayed in their positions. After a beat, the girl emerged from the storeroom looking none the worse for her earlier attack. The old lady with the bad back whispered, "Are you okay, dear?" but the girl didn't hear her. She shuffled along the wall adjacent to the storeroom, looking at her feet, avoiding eye contact with O'Grady.

"So, you are all right in the end?" said O'Grady. The girl nodded. "You see that," he shouted. "It was nothing. See how you mistake yourselves for mere humans? You're not humans . . . you're revolutionaries, and revolutionaries are invincible. Isn't that right, honey?"

The girl ignored his pronouncement, her whole attention on her polished shoes.

"Come over here, hon," said O'Grady, cradling the shotgun in the crook of his arm. The girl didn't move. "Come on, I won't hurt you. I'm not mad, honest. I'm just glad you're okay. You had me worried for a moment there." She shuffled hesitantly over to where O'Grady stood. "What's your name?" he asked.

"Freda," answered the girl in a tired, almost inaudible voice.

"That's a good name for a revolutionary," said O'Grady, and he patted her head in an encouraging way.

"Thank you," muttered the girl, then she smiled back at O'Grady, allowing her face to light up for a brief moment.

"Now there's a smile," said O'Grady. He responded so warmly and openly to the girl's smile that she visibly relaxed, releasing the tension in her shoulders. "You should show the comrades that smile," said O'Grady, and the girl screwed her face up into a frown. "The comrades," said O'Grady, pointing to the hostages seated on the floor. "They could use a bit of encouragement right now . . . a bit of sunshine, eh?" The girl nodded, and O'Grady put his hand out to her, but the manager arrived at that very moment and almost became entangled with O'Grady's arm. The gunman's face darkened considerably, and he gave the manager a suspicious look.

"Medicine," said the manager, a foolish smile creasing his face. "She . . . ah . . . needs asthma medicine. I had some . . . in the storeroom . . . which I gave her. She gets attacks, just like me. So I gave her my medicine . . . in the storeroom."

O'Grady frowned at the manager, who seemed to be growing more uncomfortable with each second of silent response from the gunman.

"So . . . ah . . . I'll give her medicine now and then . . ."

Constantine's words trailed off into nothing, silenced by the piercing stare of the man with the gun. They stood looking at each other for many seconds, until O'Grady pointed his finger at Constantine and said, "Your turn to check on the doors."

"The what?" said the manager.

O'Grady spoke in a slow voice, as if he were addressing an imbecile. "Go to the stairs and check to see if anyone is trying to get in. Got it?"

"Yes . . . sure," said the manager. He bustled his way to the entrance and vanished into that unknown place, the landing. John Wayne O'Grady knew that it was, by now, a place of certain death. Outside on the street, police sharpshooters had their sights trained on every inch of the stairway and landing, ready to take down the enemy—him.

Many long seconds passed, then Constantine shouted, "There's nothing here!" before returning to the restaurant.

"What kept you?" asked O'Grady as Constantine took up a position next to the cook.

"I'm sorry?" said Constantine.

"You will be if you lie to me. What kept you?"

"Nothing . . ." Constantine was sweating now.

"Do not lie to me!" shouted O'Grady, and beside him the girl jumped, edging away from his loud voice.

"It was . . . they . . ." He couldn't finish his sentence.

O'Grady stared at him for a long time, then asked in a low, barely audible voice. "Did they hold a message up for you?"

The entire restaurant grew quieter, allowing the distant rumble of traffic to fill the space. A siren sounded outside and several of the hostages jumped with fright. Most were now looking at Constantine, waiting for his answer. Some seemed more nervous than others—particularly those who had already been out on the landing.

"Speak," said O'Grady. "Did they hold up a written message?"

"Yes," muttered Constantine.

There was a general murmur of disappointment.

"Shut the hell up!" shouted O'Grady. "How dare you defy me? How dare you?" He waved the shotgun in the air. "Do you think I'm playing games here?"

They remained silent, unsure of what this madman was playing. All they could see was the Barrett, and the fierce look in his eyes.

"What did the message say?" shouted O'Grady to Constantine.

"It was . . . I couldn't read it."

O'Grady marched over to Constantine, raised the shotgun, and pushed it against his chest, edging him back toward the wall. Speaking in a deliberate, yet menacing voice, O'Grady said, "Answer my question within three seconds or you're a dead man."

Constantine coughed, then answered the question. "The note said, 'How many gunmen?'"

John Wayne O'Grady lowered the shotgun and laughed, sitting back down in his plastic chair with the gun barrel of the Barrett waving perilously around the room, pointing randomly at the hostages.

"The fools!" he eventually shouted. "They have no idea. 'How many gunmen are there?' Well, answer them."

He waved the shotgun in Constantine's direction and the manager pointed to his chest like a nervous schoolboy. "Me?" he asked.

"Yes, you bumbling idiot. How many are there?"

Constantine looked around the room, as if he might have missed a gunman or two who'd snuck into the restaurant when he wasn't looking. Feeling satisfied that there was indeed only the one gunman, he answered, "One."

"Wrong!" boomed O'Grady, and the manager jumped. "You are a fat, useless, fool. Look around you, what do you see? Your comrades! The future of the revolution. They don't need guns, they have something even more powerful growing in their heads and in their hearts. They are the gunmen that the police lackeys will truly have to worry about in the future."

O'Grady laughed again, enjoying his joke, even though it was totally lost on the rest of the "comrades." He pointed the shotgun at a tall man standing near the back of the group. "Here, you!" he called. "Take a piece of paper and a pen and write this down for me. Write: 'The invisible man plus twelve!'"

The tall man hesitated for a moment. "The invisible man?" he asked.

"Yes, you idiot. *I* am the invisible man. Now write that note."

Paper and a pen were found, and the tall man wrote the message out, holding it up for O'Grady's approval.

"Well, go on then," said O'Grady. "Take it out there. Hold it up to the doors. But you've got fifteen seconds. Take any longer than that and I kill your girlfriend here." He waved the barrel of the shotgun airily at the red-haired female hostage standing beside the tall man.

The man ran from the restaurant and onto the landing, his heavy footsteps echoing through the restaurant as he bounded up the stairs. There was a brief pause, then he ran back down the stairs and into the restaurant, a wild-eyed look of terror on his face.

He'd taken no more than seven seconds.

O'Grady seemed to be oblivious to his return, not even looking up as the man stood before him panting heavily. "I'm back," said the running man eventually. There was a brief nod from O'Grady, but still he would not look up. The young girl took a few steps away from O'Grady, uncertain of her captor. The shouting, bellowing, bullying man with the gun had gone eerily quiet.

Suddenly the silence was broken by an amplified voice, the police negotiator talking through a megaphone from up on the street.

"This is the police. It is in the best interests of everybody if you pick up the phone and talk. All we're after is a peaceful settlement to the situation. You will receive fair and just treatment . . ."

O'Grady sat up, his head cocked to one side, listening intently to the voice from outside.

"There are children in there. And there are people who may need medical attention. Show us a sign of your good faith and let them free. I'm sure you don't want anyone to get hurt. I repeat, we *all* want a peaceful resolution. If you allow the children to go free, you will be proving to us your good intentions . . ."

O'Grady laughed out loud, slapping his side in an exaggerated show of mirth. "Did you hear that?" he shouted. "They think you're in danger. They think I'm gonna hurt you . . ."

The girl, who had listened to the voice talk about allowing the children to go free, glared at the gunman.

"None of you want to go free, do you?" he asked.

She was about to step forward and say, "Yes," when she felt an anonymous hand on her shoulder. She held back.

"Let the children go free from the restaurant. They are young . . ."

O'Grady grabbed Constantine by his shirt and pushed him toward the entrance to the landing.

"What? What?" said the manager.

"You get them to shut up, or they watch you die."

He shoved the manager out onto the landing, poking the barrel of the shotgun at his head where it would be clearly seen by the police. There was an audible gasp from outside, and the police negotiator stopped talking. O'Grady still remained hidden from view to the outsiders.

"He says shut up!" yelled Constantine, glancing at the gun near his head. "Please! Don't talk to him. Just be quiet. He's got a bomb in here, too. He means it."

O'Grady nodded, then said, "Get back here."

Constantine stumbled back into the restaurant, his face dazed and shocked. He joined the others as the gunman sat on a nearby chair, lost in thought. Eventually he spoke in a low, menacing voice without looking up. "Do you want to know how I locked the doors?" he asked.

As the question was directed at nobody, nobody answered.

"You!" said O'Grady, looking up at the manager. "Do you want to know?"

"No . . . It's not really my business . . ." muttered Constantine.

"Oh, but that's where you're wrong. It *is* your business. Your Family Value business. You see, I had my own key."

"Your what? But . . . how?"

O'Grady laughed. "That's got you baffled, eh? The invisible man strikes again. How did I have my own key? Because I was a manager of a Family Value restaurant once. Because *I* was down to be the manager of *this* restaurant."

John Wayne O'Grady stood, waiting for the full effect of this information to sink into the slow brain of Theo Constantine. For its inherent betrayal of trust to rattle the manager right down to his Family Value socks.

"But why are you doing this?" asked Constantine.

"I am the invisible man," answered O'Grady. "I'm the neighbor you thought was friendly. I'm the guy on the street you didn't give a second glance to. I'm the manager who thought if he did all the right things he'd get a promotion. I'm the jerk that everyone thought they could walk right over. I was *nothing* to them. *Nobody!* I am invisible because you don't have the eyes to see the real me. I am John O'Grady, who took on the middle name of Wayne. I am the gun-toting cowboy who rode into town to take out all the bad guys. You won't ever see the real me if you still believe in the system. Only the true believers can see me. Only they know that I wear the badge of truth, that I am the good guy, and out there, waiting behind those doors, is the posse of black hats all waiting to shoot me. I *am* John Wayne O'Grady! I'm your way out of here. Can you see me now?"

Not one single soul who stood before him answered. Not one of the cowering hostages let on that all they could see was a man gone crazy, and if he were indeed a cowboy, he was riding slowly into their sinking bleak future.

But there was one who stood beside him. Who looked up at this impossibly tall man with the large gun and saw a neon halo around his head. And in her fear, in her heart-thumping state of terror, she thought she saw the faint glint of a badge on the man's chest, caught in the neon glow. There a gun holster . . . here a pair of boots . . . there a dusty vest. The girl looked into an impossible light and imagined, wondered.

What dreams may come of this man?

FREDA OPPERMAN

He stands eagerly as I enter the café, no more than a year or two older than me, clutching a pencil, his notepad sitting on the table before him. This would have to be William. He looks like a badly assembled teddy bear, with a slightly portly tummy and a head that no matter how you look at it appears to be a size or two too large.

For a brief moment I think I know him. His face is not familiar, it's something else. The way he looks at me, the "William" I see behind the wall of his eyes. I *know* that person, without ever meeting him. It is the strangest feeling, a recognition I've never experienced before. It disarms me, weakens me. I could sit with him, relax, be myself . . . Then his face changes, his smile becomes a bit more rigid, his eyes bright. He's a bit *too* pleased to see me. And I admonish myself. How could I fall for such a foolish, girly trap? That wasn't recognition, that was charm. This is just a journalist-student. Just a young man trying to win me over so I'll reveal more. He is a nodding teddy bear with a notebook and a pencil.

Nothing more than that.

William holds his hand out to me as I approach and asks, "Freda Opperman?" Considering that he's just spent the past thirty seconds grinning at me as I walked in, it seems a rather dumb question. Perhaps he likes to be certain of his facts. I nod in answer, then sit, noticing how his rather large head bobs as he takes his seat, how his portly tummy disappears so compactly behind the café table. William's body behaves so well for him. He asks what I would like to drink, and I answer, "Water."

"Mineral?"

Oh, dear, choices. It's bizarre how the simple act of ordering water these days has become a complicated dance. Mineral? Soda? Carbonated? Spring? So many shades of water.

"Ordinary," I say, just to confuse him, and he nods to the waiter. I half expect him to order a "spray from the tap," but he has the good manners to order a "glass of water for my guest." As if this is his café, his table, his little corner of the world.

And so we wait. He appears to be nervous, which is a new one on me. I don't normally make people nervous; alarmed perhaps, or concerned, confused, but not nervous. There's a pause now, a silence that very quickly becomes embarrassing. I'm quite an expert on silence. I search for an opening line, but all my rehearsal and preparation has been in vain. I can't think of a thing to say, so I listen in to the speakers, hoping that the music they're playing will give me inspiration. Some kind of Latin rhythm is playing, and I'm not sure what to say about this "cha-cha-cha."

At last William speaks, stumbling into our gap with a jumbled introduction. "So glad you could make it . . . A real privilege to meet you . . . I've read so much about you . . . and, of course, when I was growing up you were in all the newspapers . . ."

The young survivor will have many such conversations, where members of the general public establish how she fits into their world, how she is a signpost on their personal highway. She should remain polite and attentive, enduring this conversation with good humor. She should try not to be too distressed at being reduced to nothing more than a symbol.

"If you don't mind," he says, "I'd like to establish the theme for this interview."

I'm a little shocked by this. Have we come to the business already? Too soon, William. Too soon and too fast. Be patient, be gentle and kind and caring. Don't fumble with the clasps of my outer defenses yet. We should be talking about the weather, about the café, about music. What *is* this song that is playing?

"I've given it a lot of thought over the past week or so . . ."

And to think, for a brief second there I might have loved this boy. He reminds me a bit of my first, and only, sexual encounter. Not that it was too sexual, and not that it was an encounter in the strictest sense of the word. More like an assault. It was at an end-of-year party for my school, and as it was organized for all of the students, they had to invite me.

For the most part of the evening I was ignored, but one boy did come and ask me to dance. He was a portly boy, not dissimilar to William, with a sea of acne on his face. Perhaps he thought that I was desperate enough to take on a deformed face such as his. Or perhaps he had a deeper understanding of the situation— he knew that we were both marked.

After our obligatory few dances, he led me outside for kissing and groping. I was curious enough to play along for a while, feeling the push and pull of his clumsy hands as he scored mini-victories over my body. First the kiss, then the squeezing of my breasts over my dress, then the plunge down my front to claim a feel over my bra. It was as he moved toward his next moment of glory that I decided I'd had enough and put an end to it all.

But the strange thing is, the boy wasn't surprised or shocked that I'd ended our encounter. He seemed almost relieved, and stepped back, mumbling, "Sorry." I felt such tenderness for him then that I held his hand, and we sat among the groping couples saying nothing much at all.

"What I'm interested in," says William, launching into his theme, "is how the different players in a siege situation impact upon its outcome."

Isn't that sweet? He's called us "players." John Wayne O'Grady with his brutal regime and his even more brutal shotgun was just a "player" in a game. I suppose this is what you get when you agree to be interviewed for a university magazine.

"In a sense," continues William, "you can understand when people are caught up in a natural disaster, such as a landslide or earthquake, that they are truly innocent bystanders. They can't possibly have any impact on what is happening to them. But a siege situation is so different."

He pauses to check my face for reaction. I start to panic a little. Should I be having a reaction? Luckily, the waiter arrives with my glass of water, dressed in a paper napkin, which I remove immediately and start to tear into little shreds. William looks around the café; perhaps he's lost his train of thought. That would be a relief.

I see N.O. walk into the café discreetly and sit a few tables away, calling the waiter over in that definite way of hers. Should I acknowledge her now? Or should I ignore her presence? I forget what the rules are. William looks like he's about to grasp his theme again, so I leap in and distract him.

"How old are you?" I ask.

"Pardon?"

"How old are you?"

"Twenty," he mumbles.

"We're almost the same age," I say, and he gives me a narrow-eyed look, as if he's checking for some hidden trick to my question.

"I'm just interested, that's all," I say. "You're in college, and I'm not. What are you studying?"

"Journalism," he mutters. "Politics . . . that stuff. Getting back to your siege," he says, leaping onto his train. "It's kind of fascinating how some people withdraw in a siege situation, others try to fight their way out, and others . . . you know . . . they sort of join in."

He fumbles with his pen, unable to meet my gaze, which is fine by me because I'm not looking at him, either. Has he finished? I hope so. This is becoming altogether too sticky for me. I wrack my brain for an interjection, but my bearlike companion beats me to it.

"How many days was the siege?" he asks. "Two?"

"Thirty-six hours," I answer. Sunday afternoon to the early hours of Tuesday morning, William.

"And then there was what? An inquest that lasted for fifty-odd days of evidence?"

"I suppose so," I say, a vague, uneasy feeling washing over me. This "chat" is not behaving normally.

"You see, that's what fascinates me," says William, his head flicking about in some kind of nervous agitation. "It's the aftermath, the long, drawn-out consequences that are almost more important. Don't you think?"

"I . . . I really don't . . ."

William doesn't wait for my opinion. "All sorts of issues like retribution, compensation, readjustment . . ."

"They're very long words," I say, attempting to divert him away from his lecture with a little bit of humor.

He stares at me for a moment, then shrugs his shoulders. "Sorry. I guess I mean . . . like . . . what do they, the hostages, what do they do with all that stuff?"

Stuff? What stuff? This is the strangest interview I've ever had. He seems more interested in his own opinion than mine. Before I have a chance to ask him to clarify himself, he speaks again.

"Don't worry about it. You know . . . I was just wondering,

that's all. So . . . Um . . ." He looks at his notebook. It's reassuring, I suppose, that he's prepared *some* questions. "The inquest. Don't you find it interesting that after all this time, that huge inquest, they still can't say for sure what the events were that led to Theo Constantine's death?"

I squeeze the napkin in my hand until it is a flat, bunched-up thing, then I let it go. "It was a shotgun blast," I say. "The coroner gave a cause of death . . . Look, really . . . I don't think this is working out." I go to leave and William talks fast.

"I'm sorry," he says, holding his hand out to me. "I was just going off at the mouth . . . you know . . . just wondering about it all. It was insensitive. That must have been such a painful time for you. I mean, you yourself were questioned for so long at the inquest. I think they had you on the stand for almost a day, overall. But then your mother had that psychiatrist speak on your behalf and they took you off. So, after that there was what? Six more days without you, trying to fill in the missing last hours of the siege?"

I glare at him for a full ten seconds, then shoot a glance at Nancy. Why isn't she waving her arms at me, signaling that it's time to get up and walk away? This "chat" is fast becoming horrid. William sees the distress in my eyes and changes tack.

"Look, forget about the inquest, okay?" he says. "I expect all those hostages are like family to you, now."

Where is all this heading? He is flitting from one topic to another, but there does seem to be a theme here. I just can't get a hold of what it is. Now he wants to know if the other hostages are family to me? "Um . . . not really," I say.

"But you shared so much together. Haven't you kept in contact? Haven't they helped you remember?"

There's some kind of in-joke here I've missed. I shift uncomfortably in my chair and avoid William's gaze. No, my fellow hostages are not my family. If I never see them again in my life I will shed no tears.

William is searching my face now for something . . . for me. I don't like it and try to distract him by turning to the café speakers and asking, "Do you know this song?"

He shakes his head irritably, then continues with his questioning. "It's almost bizarre, don't you think, that after six days of evidence, the commissioner was happy to write off those last couple of hours of the siege as lost?"

You couldn't leave it alone, could you? You had to poke at it again, even when I told you to stop. This conversation has quickly become downright rude and nasty. There are no rules to play by now, and I feel myself becoming angrier with this teddy bear and his questions. Six days of evidence at the inquest? What a joke. Six days of guessing what happened after O'Grady had locked all the hostages away in the toilets and allowed Theo and myself to roam the restaurant. Six days of probing thin air and the faulty memory of a nine-year-old girl.

I smile at William, because I can sense it makes him uneasy when I do it. Inside I feel close to panic. The young survivor should never panic. This can only lead to awkward emotional outbursts or horrible memories jagging back at her when her defenses are low. The young survivor should reach, instead, for the last straw, the tool to be used in desperation. Her mother's rhetoric.

"I have spent the best part of my life devoting myself to helping victims of crime, to supporting networks against gun violence, to . . ."

"You mean those organizations that your mother runs?"

I nod.

"Lead a good life," he mutters.

Ah, he recognizes my famous last command. We're on safer ground now. I have steered his probing little mind into *my* theme.

"Yes," I say. "I may not have stayed in touch with the hostages, but I have spent many years making sure other people such as them are given a better chance. I could have faded away, but I didn't."

"You know," says William, scratching the base of his neck. "What's interesting to me is that the tactics that your mother's organizations have used . . . the litigation against corporations . . . the use of the legal system to bring governments into line . . . wouldn't you say that the resultant purpose of those actions is similar to what was being advocated during the siege?"

I drop my napkin, and bend to pick it up, wondering if I shouldn't just stand and run. This obnoxious little boy beside me has somehow drawn the energy out of me. I have a sick feeling, as if the entire café is in on a private joke and I'm the only one who hasn't got it yet. Mr. William, the journalist-student, is staring intently at me, gauging my reaction to his thesis. If he doesn't watch out, I'll "react" all over his shirt!

"You don't like interviews much, do you?" he asks eventually.

"Is this an interview?" I say, an edge of hurt and anger in my voice. "I thought it was a chat."

He's confused by my use of the word *chat,* trying to work out what I meant by that. As he ponders, I listen to the cha-cha music on the café speakers. Damn William, I won't let him carry on with this sordid little probe. Whatever the heck this music is, I'll use it to break his headlock.

"Is this Suntanna?" I ask, waving my hand as casually as I can at the café speakers.

"What?" Now William sounds annoyed.

"The music," I add for explanation.

He corrects me. "Santana. You mean Carlos Santana, and no, this is not his music."

He looks a little sullen, sitting with his body slightly turned away from me. He *was* after some kind of specific reaction out of me, after all, but I've let him down by talking about music. Perhaps he'll give up now and sulk away? I have to keep up the pressure, make sure he doesn't find his train again.

"To tell you the truth," I say, "I don't care much for music at all. What about you? Do you like songs and all that?"

"I like the saddest songs," he answers quickly, his voice far away.

Oh, William. The saddest songs? Really? He sees the look on my face and starts to defend himself.

"I don't mean that I'm into sad stuff," he explains. "I was just thinking of a quote, that's all. *Our sweetest songs are those that have the saddest thoughts.*"

Shelley. He's quoting Shelley at me, or rather, he's misquoting Shelley at me.

For a brief moment I panic, thinking that this teddy bear has been snooping around in my past, digging up dirt on me from my old teachers. *Oh, yes. She read that Shelley poem all the time . . .* How else did he come to the quote? Unless he pulled the words out of his memory as a party trick. That's more than likely what's going on. There are a couple of telltale signs. Like the fact that he has misquoted the lines from "To a Skylark."

Our sweetest songs are those that tell of saddest thought.

But even more damning is the fact that he has decided to truncate the quote, to cut off the last line of the stanza and present it as the popular, more digestible version of Percy Bysshe Shelley.

I close my eyes and allow my favorite stanza to come back. It was written for me. Who could possibly understand that?

We look before and after,
And pine for what is not;
Our sincerest laughter
With some pain is fraught;
Our sweetest songs are those that tell of saddest thought.

We look before and after, and pine for what is not. Now there's a theme for you, William. There's a hearty, strong, direct theme of life, played out in the way I sit and speak and smile and answer your dumb questions. Played out in my everyday life, my aftermath as Freda Opperman, icon of a nation.

"I really don't think you wanted to interview me at all, did you?"

"You have no idea what I want," he says. "Do you? No idea at all . . ."

That's it. Interview terminated. I turn to Nancy and give her an urgent look, and she nods, standing.

"There's my mother," I say.

"What?" says William, almost knocking his cup over with fright. He shoots his wobbly head around, trying to locate my mother, eventually spotting her. "Why . . . What's she doing here?"

"Must be a coincidence," I say, standing up. "I'm so glad we had this chat about music."

It takes an enormous effort just to walk toward Nancy, and not run, not fly to her in panic. This has gone so badly. Something has been opened up here, in this neat little café with its neat little napkins wrapped around its glasses. Some horrible smell has been released, and no matter how much I tried to push and shove it back where it belongs, it is out now. I don't turn to look at

William. I can't. I just take my mother's arm and say, "Let's get out of here."

She glances over my shoulder, then walks me out the door. As we step onto Grange Street I remember the rules that I'd struggled to recall. Don't speak. Don't reveal. Don't tell them anything. Don't even look at them, because they can see, in your eyes, what you really are. The truth is as simple as that. They can see it in your eyes.

THE **GOOD** LIFE

OF FREDA O,

AGED 14

His daughter was looking at him, waiting, expecting an answer. Standing in his workshop in her school uniform. Hugh Opperman returned her gaze, wondering what answer she was looking for. Her young eyes flicked over his face. He wasn't used to answering anyone in his furniture workshop. Normally he enjoyed long periods of silence, in deep concentration, lost in the smells and the feel of the wood.

Freda had been coming to his workshop the past two months, ever since her fourteenth birthday. Skipping school lessons, defying her mother. He supposed that if he'd remained a lawyer there'd be no place for her to get away from being Freda, daughter of Nancy.

He'd bought her some soft wood to carve. It was just a small thing to distract her, except it wasn't working right now. "I'm sorry," he said, shrugging, deflecting her question. "I forget."

Then he turned to his piece, expecting her to do the same behind him. He was a private man, and never more private than when he ran his hands over a piece of Huon pine. Smelling the richness of the timber, the ancient resin and rain-forest odors seeping from the history of the wood. He could almost see the tree that the timber had come from. An old corpse perhaps, left over from the heady days of logging when the Huon was open season. Its long, slow story hidden for decades.

Freda was busy behind him, sanding out another strange shape. These carvings she made never seemed to resemble anything much. What did it matter? It was the running of her hands over the wood that was most important. The regular, rhythmical sanding and carving that offered the truest moments. He fancied that her breathing behind him was synchronous with his own. That her rhythms and movements matched his like an accompanying musical instrument.

It made him think of her when she was young, a little girl with high-minded ideals and a will of iron. Her demanding moments, her precociousness that was lost in that place. He paused. Breathed deeply. Hoped that the smell of *this* place would anchor him to the spot. Not take him back to those dead hours. Waiting outside the restaurant. Waiting for a glimpse of her.

"I asked you what you were making," said Freda. "Before."

Her voice broke into his thoughts and he glanced back at her. She had sawdust on her school uniform and a fine spray of white over her chin. There was a line on her cheek where she'd wiped some of the fine dust away. A mark like war paint.

"Hm?" he said. "Um . . . I'm making a chest of drawers."

"Out of . . . ?"

"Huon."

"I love the smell."

"So do I."

She wasn't normally talkative, but this day was different. Something was on her mind. He tried his best not to sound irritated when he answered her questions. That would be a most dreadful thing to do. To be irritated by his daughter when every waking second he shared with her was a second stolen from fate. During those long hours of the siege he'd dreamed about what it would be like when she finally emerged. How he would embrace her. How he would hold her so tight she'd have to say, "Daddy! You're squeezing me!" And in his dream he'd laugh because it meant she was alive!

When she was eventually set free, he was elsewhere, keeping the media pack at bay. Nancy took the girl into the backseat of a police car. He told himself he'd get to her in a minute, that she needed protection. And when at last the media pack were sated, a young police officer passed him and said, "You must be so relieved, sir." He'd realized at that moment that he felt empty. His daughter was free, and he was numb.

"You haven't asked me what I'm making," said Freda, her serious face somehow made comical by the braces on her teeth. Braces she'd fought against having because she didn't think they were worth it.

"I thought you'd tell me when you were ready," he answered.

"Hm," she said. "Then I'm not ready."

He nodded, returning to his work, trying to shake off the awful image he'd seen that cold morning. It would not leave him. He'd stood outside the restaurant, almost unable to move. The officer had returned and pointed to the police car. "She's in there," he'd said. And Hugh was about to go to the car when for some unknown reason he'd glanced back at the restaurant.

That was when he'd seen the girl in the doorway.

"Miss Dumbleton in our religious education class said that when we make things it brings us closer to God," said Freda, still in a chatty mood.

"Really?" he muttered after a pause, busying himself with measuring.

"But I think that was just a dumb thing to say. Which makes sense, 'cause she's Miss Dumbleton."

"Right," he said.

Even today he still wondered what his brain had meant by showing him the girl in the doorway.

"I mean, how do you suppose God made a human heart?" asked his daughter, pausing yet again from her sanding.

He didn't answer. This timber was expensive. Too beautiful to make a mistake with.

"Dad?" she said, her voice insistent.

"What?" he asked.

"Did you hear me?"

He nodded, vaguely aware of her question. He put his pencil down and turned to her, hoping that they could put a quick end to the conversation.

"I don't know how God made a human heart," he said. 'Probably similar to how someone would make a pump."

"But . . . that's exactly what I mean. There's more to it," she said. "A pump works on electricity. Something starts it in the first place. What starts a human heart beating? I mean . . . don't you think that's amazing? There's no answer . . . not a scientific answer, anyway."

"I'm sure there is," he said. "Science would have a theory about how the heart starts beating."

"Well, I'm not so sure," she said. "How could we ever match that sort of thing?"

"I don't suppose we can match such a creation," he said. "We're not even in the same league."

She watched him for a second, hoping perhaps for an elaboration. When none came she sighed and said, "No, we're not."

He went back to his wood then, hearing her activity starting up behind him a few seconds later. He didn't notice his daughter pause behind him, staring around the room with a glint in her eye. Didn't notice her gaze flicker from corner to corner, as if she were watching strange movements in the shadows.

"We're sponsoring a girl from Indonesia at our school," she said, almost to herself. "Up until a few months ago she was working sixteen-hour days for a monthly wage that wouldn't buy her a cup of coffee in most cities."

He turned to her and smiled. "That sounds like you got it from a brochure."

"I think I probably did," she said, smiling broadly at him. "Sixteen-hour days. I don't think she was feeling all that close to God."

"No," said Hugh Opperman. "I expect she was feeling closer to exhaustion."

She appreciated his joke, nodding her head. He was about to return to his work when she muttered in an almost inaudible voice, "She's only nine years old."

He froze, unable to look at her lest he register the pain he'd heard in her voice. Eventually, the sound of her sanding filled the workshop. He returned to his Huon, putting it into the vice and taking up his saw.

Within minutes they were synchronous again. He thought about that police car. Young Freda in the back, her mother holding her so tight. He never did go into the car, too shaken by his crazy head to take the few steps to his family.

"Do you think if I made things for other people," said Freda from behind him. "Do you think it would mean I could be . . . that I was . . ."

She let the sentence hang there, in need of only a single word to be complete. Both of them knew the word, both heard it in their heads but refrained from speaking it. In all truth he didn't know what would make this daughter of his take a step closer to that prize she should so rightly claim. He hadn't been able to do it all those years back, how could he advise her now? Instead, he turned and took one of her hands.

"You've got sawdust under your fingernails," he said.

She looked down at her hands and smiled. "So?" she said.

"Ever wonder how it gets in there?"

She shook her head.

"Neither do I," he said, then turned back to his Huon, knowing that the distractions would be over for now. As he worked in sync with his daughter, their sanding blending into a long, fading afternoon light meditation, he thought about the silence, about the deep peace he could feel in this place.

And he knew it was true.

It was . . .

Good.

FREDA OPPERMAN

Imagine for a moment a scene from a movie, set in a car. A daughter and her mother, driving through the rain. Perhaps the scene starts with the daughter in the passenger seat turning slightly toward the window, looking for a comfortable position. Or perhaps it starts with the mother speaking . . .

"So, how did the interview go?"

"Not very well."

The car seemed to be sitting heavily on the road, like a barge making slow progress through hostile tides. The daughter tried to hide her agitation. The mother tried to negotiate the crazy traffic.

"Why not?"

"He didn't ask any questions."

Even the windshield wipers had a hard time fighting off the torrents of water that flowed down the glass. The mother bit her lower lip and glanced at her daughter sitting so quietly.

"What did he do, then?"

"Got angry with me. Wanted me to say things for him. Questioned me about my memory . . . It was really stupid."

The engine labored against the tide, pushing tons of metal and rubber and upholstery down a watery highway. The mother was no longer consciously aware of the road, or the traffic, or the streetlights ahead. Her mind was reeling with a myriad of ugly possibilities, and a dead feeling that everything was getting out of hand.

"Your memory? What did you say to him?"

"Not much."

"Oh."

The daughter glanced at her mother, and saw the hint of worry in her eyes. She wanted to ask her what was wrong, but at that moment the mother took the corner into their street just a little too fast. For a second the car fishtailed in the wet. It was out of control. Before the daughter had a chance to cry out, it righted itself and the car cruised sedately toward their drive.

Nobody could hear the mother's heartbeat as she pulled on the handbrake. Nor could they feel her daughter's tremor as she opened her door.

Both responses to a fright that had nothing to do with wet roads or sliding cars.

In reality, my mother and I have a short, sharp conversation after the debacle of the café interview with wobbly William. She asks, "How did it go?" and I reply in an angry voice, "Don't ever do that to me again."

It was a very taciturn drive home, each of us locked away in our thoughts. I can't help but think that growing up has been nothing short of a disaster. Nancy's tactic of throwing me into the interview solo left me to trip and stumble over William's clumsy feet. We were like bumbling fools on a dance floor, spinning wildly, crashing into one another with no time to offer any apologies.

Not that I think William is sorry.

Others have tried similar tactics to his, unsettling me, throwing questions from a non sequitur. But they were always diverted by N.O., grabbed by the scruff of the neck and had their snouts pushed back into their notebooks. "Ask a decent question, or we shall be leaving . . ." In the nicest possible way, of course. Because Nancy has always had a friendly relationship with the media, seeing them as her allies in the ever-continuing struggle to maintain the public image of Freda Opperman. The relationship has grown into a mutual position of exploitation over the years.

And now my mother is asking me to take over the reins. To grow up. I have studied so-called grown-up people, watched them on the train as they go off to their jobs. They sit contained within themselves, their minds occupied by quiet thoughts. They know exactly where they're headed, and where they've come from. I can see it in their eyes. Not one of them is a seeker. The train takes them to a predictable destination. They do not hope for an unexpected moment to create light or grace in their lives.

I suppose I have a lot in common with these creatures. Look at me now, sitting in my own seat with the bends, the twisted metal, the rough patches tossing me from side to side. It just seems like such a disappointing way to end it all.

Nancy pulls the car into the drive and turns off the engine. She holds the steering wheel for a moment, then turns to look at me. "You all right?" she asks.

"No," I say.

She closes her eyes. I have stung again. Even when I had no intention of doing so. "Sorry," she says, then she opens her door and allows the air to slap my face.

I follow her inside, heading for my room where I flop on my bed. The phone rings. God. Please leave me this next minute. That is all I ask. This next sixty seconds. I will offer up anything. My past, my present, my future. Let me lie here knowing that my mother is only a wall away, an open door and a short walk down a hallway. Let the old ways prevail. Cease this intrusion. Stop asking your questions. They cut me, break open my binding, and unravel me to the world.

The phone rings out.

I breathe a short sigh, lay my hand on my chest, and feel it rise and fall. Then the phone resumes its summons. Nancy calls for me to answer it. She's in her office. If I don't answer then she will. Would the voice speak to her? I can't risk that possibility, so I get up from my bed, go out to the hallway, and pick up the receiver and say, "Hello?"

"Why didn't you tell anyone about the napkins?"

I listen. Allow the question, and the accusations behind it, to sink in. I am not compelled to answer this time. I can just listen. Listen as I always have. Eventually the voice ceases, and I hang up, going back to my room. I remove the box from my undies drawer. A quick inspection of the contents tells me that all the napkins are still there. Theo's handwritten account of hell. It is an enormous task, the role of record keeper. To see horror unfolding, to accurately take note of numbers and events and times. Count the frightened people. Thirteen. Count the hours. Thirty-six. Recount the number of times he terrified us. To show that we forgot what it felt like to be safe. To be the voice of the oppressed. To remember what we left behind and hold it up to us like a window with a view so that when we look out we know the deep regret that comes with never being able to visit that place again. Yes, the responsibility of the record keeper is great. To tell it for us all.

For us *all*.

I remove the napkins, stash the empty box in my laundry basket, and go to my curtains. With a bit of cutting and pulling, I'm able to separate part of the backing material from the curtain, and I slide the pieces of paper into the cavity between the folds, closing it up with a safety pin.

Deception.

I stand up and look at my room, once my sanctuary against the madness outside. I'll never feel the same in here again. I have lost the crack between time, the space that held me between the points of the compass. It is not the mysterious caller who I have hidden the napkins from. I have hidden them from Nancy Opperman. She will test me. She will wait until I am relaxed, then slip her interrogation into the conversation. She has heard the phone calls. She has seen me take out the napkins, something I never do. She is thinking. And she is waiting.

It seems that I am losing everything.

I settle my room and lock the door behind me. The phone rings again. I stop. Stare at it. What would the question be this time if I answered? What is your game, Freda Opperman? Why do you deceive? Are you good? Nancy promised me she'd always be there. That if they asked me awkward questions, all I had to do was squeeze her hand and she'd step in.

The phone stops ringing. Nancy is still in her office and I go there, holding the door on the way in so I don't fall into the room, don't rush to her desk and grab at her skirt hem. She looks up at me, startled.

"What?" says N.O.

Am I imagining it, or is there a hint of furtiveness about her expression?

"I thought we could go out," I say.

"Out? Where?"

"For dinner. I really want to go out . . ."

"Who called before?"

I stare at her, like a small child caught red-handed. "I don't know . . ."

"You don't know?"

"Can we go out?"

She looks down at her office phone, a separate line, debating something in her head. Perhaps she is waiting for her own call? Eventually she nods. "Okay, I'll get the keys."

Once we are in the car we decide to go to the restaurant on the mountain. It is nearly an hour's drive there, but we have the time as it's still only late afternoon. This is my favorite place, high up on the side of the mountain, the city spread out below me. I like the distance from up here, the reminder that there are thousands and thousands of other lives down below, going about their own business, stuck in their own moments.

Nancy's not talking again. Perhaps she's too busy concentrating on the road. It is wet and slippery, and it seems that every driver coming down the mountain has decided to race against the clock. A white car rounds a bend on our side of the road and Nancy brakes, not even having time to call out in shock. The driver of the white car moves back onto his share of the road and is gone in a flash, a blur of danger vanishing behind us.

"That was close," says Nancy after a while.

I nod.

The road is making me sick, and I concentrate on staring straight ahead. When we arrive at the restaurant, Nancy goes in to reserve a table. She emerges to say we couldn't get a window seat but we'll have a table in forty minutes. We go to the observation platform to take in the view while we wait for dinnertime to arrive.

As we look out at the flat expanse of city and suburbs below us, Nancy speaks. "You haven't really told me much else of what happened at the interview."

"I thought I had," I say. My fingers start tingling with nervous anticipation.

"No," she says.

"Well, you're the one who said you didn't need to be there."

"Freda. You were clearly upset . . ."

"He asked stupid things and didn't even wait for my answers. He had no idea what he was trying to do, and in the end he was so clumsy that he ended up being plain offensive. That's all there is to it."

"Are you sure?" asks Nancy Opperman, almost casually.

This is the moment, then. For years I have watched my mother draw her victims in with that slightly bewildered, fair-minded voice she adopts. Watched her smile as they answer, only to turn their replies into scythes and cut them down with their own words. And now I am the recipient. How did we get to this?

The young survivor must remain calm and cheerful. She must not cry or hold her mother's arm desperately. The young survivor cannot be young forever.

"He really was fairly stupid and boring," I say, deflecting. "I thought college kids would be more intelligent."

Nancy looks at me. She has that sad look in her eyes again. "Freda," she says evenly. "What's going on with all the phone calls?"

I can't stand her doing this. Not to me. "Come on, Mom," I say. "Just come out and ask what you want to ask."

"This is not a game, Freda," she says. "Has it got something to do with you getting those napkins out? Is that it? Won't you please tell me what's wrong?"

"I can't," I reply. "I'm afraid of what you'll do."

"But, Freda. I'm your mother."

A bus pulls into the parking lot behind us, its brakes hissing. I turn to look, seeing windows fogged, raindrops streaked along its side. "Do you know that O'Grady whispered to me all through that last night?" I mutter.

"Freda!" She is genuinely shocked. I have brought up *that* subject. "That was so long ago now . . ."

"He did whisper!" I say, turning back to her, my voice firm. "I remember. You hate it when I do that, don't you? I remember his voice. 'You can't do bargains with the truth. It'll bite back and destroy you in the end.' That's what the bastard said to me."

"He was a crazy man," says Nancy. "Don't think about him." She reaches out to touch my hand. "He was insane."

I like her touch, I always have. It calms me. From behind we hear the sound of the bus doors opening, and the late afternoon air is filled with voices. Nancy gives me a worried look as the tourists crowd our spot, pressing in. We are surrounded. I breathe heavily, staring at the vacant distance, controlling myself. Nancy moves closer, knowing how I am in crowds. Eventually the Japanese tourists move away to one end of the platform, talking animatedly about the view. As I return to a relative calm I watch them, so happy, so full of conversation, and I almost feel sorry for them. Perhaps they got a package deal, forcing them to come here during the coldest part of winter. They don't seem to mind much as they line one another up for photos, the older members stiff and unsmiling, the younger ones holding their fingers up in peace symbols.

"Do you remember how you used to get me to imagine kicking O'Grady out of my room?" I say.

Nancy looks alarmed.

"I don't think they can hear us," I say, nodding toward the tourists.

"I wasn't even thinking about them . . ."

"Do you remember?" I ask.

"Yes," she says.

"Well, what I never told you was no matter how much I tried he always came back. He seeped back in under the door. He soaked his way through the walls. That he was always there . . ."

"Oh, Freda."

She puts her hand out to hold me, but we are interrupted by a young man with a camera. He offers it to us, saying "Eka-scuse me . . ." in a strong Japanese accent. I jump slightly, and he apologizes profusely in Japanese. The only way to get him to stop is to take the camera. He stands with his friends against the railing, back to the view, and they look solemn as I take their photo, recording the fact that they once stood at this place, the wind whipping around them, the clouds threatening to burst open, the air so cold it turned their cheeks red.

The group take in the view for a while longer, until the tour guide speaks. Their allotted time at this destination over, the bevy of Japanese tourists file back onto the bus.

"We've still got half an hour before our booking," says Nancy.

We walk to each end of the platform, as if the view might substantially alter by doing this. It doesn't. We are higher than the moon, and no matter how much we adjust our position, the world refuses to change.

Later, as we sit in the restaurant foyer waiting for our table, the warmth so welcome I almost feel sleepy, Nancy tells me about her mother. She tells me the crazy, funny stories about crockery and plates and the quest for mosaic color. She tells me how her mother once received a plate for her birthday from a dear friend and was so excited about the pattern that she "accidentally" smashed it a few days later. It ended up on the garden table.

"She had a dreadful childhood," says Nancy. "Her mother was killed in a train accident when she was six or seven. Do you know what they told her? They said that her mother had gone to live among the stars. Truly. Mom used to look up at the sky at night and try to imagine which of those stars was her mother. In the end she decided it was all of them. That was how they treated children in those days. "Gone to the stars." Sometimes I think all those mosaics she did were somehow trying to put her own mother back together again."

"Like Humpty Dumpty," I say.

She nods. "I guess we all have our own ways of coping."

The waiter informs us that our table is ready, and even though we don't have the view, we can still catch the city lights from where we sit. The meal is hot and filling, and Nancy and I steer the topic toward safer subjects, the earlier intrigue left aside for now. As dessert arrives, I ponder little William and his botched attempt at an interview. Nancy says that all interviewers have an agenda, and when you work out what it is you can answer safely without falling into their preconceptions. It is hard to imagine what William's preconceptions were, other than I am a bad person. And it's even harder to imagine what he'll write about me.

I ask Nancy if she thinks he'll still write the article, given that he only asked me a few questions. She pauses, her spoon caught in midair, ice cream hovering.

"I never thought about that," she says. "Perhaps you could ring him?"

"No," I say. "No, I won't."

She looks down at her plate. I have disappointed her again. Every move I make . . . everything I say . . . We leave the topic alone, finishing our desserts, the fire crackling behind us. It is raining again by the time we leave, and we dash to the car, our coats over our heads. Nancy drops the keys in her rush to get the car door unlocked, and she curses out loud. We drive home in silence. No nausea for me this time. Nancy goes straight into her office when we arrive, shutting the door.

I go to my room and lie on my bed, thinking about William. About Nancy's request that I see him again. It was she who broke the rules, who thrust me into the big wide world alone. What did she expect? That I'd get it right? I look at my curtains and close my eyes. I want to say something to her, but I don't know what. Ask her to pull me back from this wide, unknown, grown-up world? Seek her approval of my curtain deception? Tell her I've never felt so alone? She would raise her eyebrows at that one.

In the end I go to Nancy's office under the pretext of talking about William. I knock on the door, hearing her end a conversation before telling me to come in. She seems relieved when I enter, and tells me straightaway that she has been talking to William.

How alike we are, mother and daughter. "Why?" I say.

"Don't be like that," says Nancy. "I was worried for you. He's very apologetic. Says he wants to talk again."

I shake my head, taken completely off guard. "I don't get it," I say.

"I was worried about the article," says Nancy. "What he'd write. Look, he really wants to make amends. He agrees that he did a terrible job. I think it would be a good idea to talk to him . . ."

"Why? So your good causes will get their plug?"

"No," says Nancy, genuine hurt in her eyes. "No. It's not anything like that, Freda. God . . . I'm doing this for your sake."

"He was a little turd, Mom."

"Which he admits. Please, Freda. I'll come along, too. It will be different, trust me on this one."

I feel the bindings that were flapping loosely behind me tighten a little, rolling back into their familiar formation. Trust my mother.

"Will you do this, Freda? Please?"

"Give me his number," I say, holding out my hand. "I'm not saying I'll call him. I might, that's all."

"Of course, darling," says Nancy, scrawling his number on a piece of paper, which she hands to me. Her face is beaming.

"Please, Mom," I say. "Don't be proud."

Her face drops. "It'll be better next time," she mutters.

"Maybe."

I return to my room, a piece of paper in my hand. It will be different next time, according to Nancy Opperman. She'll be by my side, stepping in, reminding William of facts and figures and manners . . . A dark, ironic smile crosses my face. For something so different, it feels depressingly familiar.

I straighten my room for the last time today, get undressed, switch off the overhead light, and climb into my bed. Where do you sleep now, Freda Opperman? Here. Upon a bed unguarded. In a room tainted by events. Your sheets and blankets drawn military tight. But they won't protect you.

Half awake. Half asleep. I dread this state. Caught between two worlds, between two certainties. Visions come to you here.

Insights.

I see William, asleep, lying on the ground, his head on a dark pillow. On a red pillow. Spreading like blood.

I wake. Startled. My heart racing. After a while of staring at my ceiling, I close my eyes again, drifting.

I see the Japanese tourist on the viewing platform. Smiling at me. "Eka-scuse me," he says. Then he falls backward, as if blown by a furious wind. I run to the edge. His body is below. There's a stain on him. Colored.

I wake. Jolted back from the dark of my dreams. Outside my door the phone rings. I will not answer it. It rings out, then starts up again. Eventually, I hear Nancy emerge from her bedroom and answer the phone.

"Hello? Hello?" she says, but the voice doesn't want to talk to her. She tries one more time, "Hello? What do you want?"

What does it want, that voice? And how far is it prepared to go to get it? Nancy paces outside in the hallway, up and down, her soft, birdlike steps like butterfly kisses. She's thinking. Making connections. Eventually, she finishes her sentry duty and goes to bed. All is still in my family home, Fortress Opperman, with its electronic alarm system and locks. But there's one thing I can't lock out, no matter how many barriers I put in its way. *He* knew all about it, that's why he whispered his deranged thoughts to me in the dark those ten years ago.

JOHN WAYNE

O'GRADY

"I will break you," said John Wayne O'Grady, his voice weary. "I *will* break you. I will be in your every waking moment, your thoughts, your responses, your prejudices and your passions, until all you can see is the clear light of my vision."

He was holding yet another education class, talking endlessly. The muted sunlight from the landing behind him had long since faded, allowing the cold glare of the neons to fill the void. The "comrades" were close to exhaustion, having endured hours of his command. Some swayed as they tried to sit upright on the floor, most sat with their heads bowed, withdrawn into themselves. Some found comfort in well-disciplined thought modes, repeatedly assuring themselves that everything would be okay, that this would not last. Some literally "shut down" their minds, keeping them as empty and as blank as humanly possible, constantly aware of the flood of terror and panic that beat endlessly against the outer walls of their sanctuary. Some gave way to despair and defeat, repeating to themselves that all was lost, until it became a silent mantra and offered some sort of comfort in itself. Some formulated impossible plans of escape, working out minute details in their tired brains, constantly wondering if this was the right moment, or if it would come later.

Of the two children inside the restaurant, one clung to his mother, burying his face against her shoulder, taking in the fine detail of her wool jacket, enthralled at how uneven its surface was with its peaks and valleys of woven fabric. The other, the girl, supposedly in the care of the manager, slipped quietly into a private fantasy world, making up games in an attempt to bring order to the chaos around her, imagining rescue from magical forces that she was sure would come. Police officers who could slip through the crack in the doors above and float down the stairway.

The police had not tried to make contact again. O'Grady had bragged about how he could control the cop puppets after the incident with Theo Constantine on the landing. The gunman had pranced about, saying he knew all the tactics the police would use.

"First they cordon off the area," he said, sounding like a belligerent schoolteacher. "And that's because they don't want the disease of truth to spread any further."

He squatted next to the girl and placed his hand on her shoulder. "Then they contain this place and they wait. You know why they do that, honey?" he asked.

The girl shook her head.

"Because they're afraid of you. Those big police officers out there. Contain and wait. Contain and wait, because they're afraid of what good old John will turn you into."

He stood, laughing at his statement.

"And then they'll try to evacuate you. Get the children out, the old people. They'll do *anything* to stop you from listening. Can you see how dangerous this is to them? How much those puppet-masters fear what I have to say?"

He continued in this way for some time, talking about the police strategies as if the hostages had no emotional involvement in them. They were the comrades to him, the eggs opening up to reveal the fledgling revolutionaries under the shells. Why should they fear for their lives?

But the prancing and the bragging about how he had foiled the police soon gave way to more lecturing, more ranting about the system, about the corporate puppet-masters, and especially about the hated Family Value chain of restaurants. The day slipped quietly away outside, and the cold neons buzzed overhead as John Wayne O'Grady paced around their large circle, repeating familiar phrases and messages. "Let go," he said, his voice as tired as they were. "Let go of the old ways. See the truth. See what is in front . . ."

He was midsentence when the restaurant was plunged into darkness.

Something, or someone, had cut the power. All the lights were out, and the muted background roar of the heater had been silenced. Several of the hostages cried out, and a child started sobbing in the darkness.

"Probably a fuse," came the voice of Theo Constantine.

"I'll fix it," came another voice.

Even though they sounded so decisive in the dark, none of them moved, conditioned now to wait upon the whim of the man with the gun. He stood, seemingly motionless, but those close to him thought they saw him shiver slightly. The hamburger cook made to stand, saying in a careful voice, "Shall I check that fuse?"

O'Grady snapped out of his repose, waved the shotgun at them, and shouted, "Stay where you are." There was perspiration dripping from his face, and his voice had a dangerous quiver to it. The cook sat back down onto the floor as the rest moaned quietly.

"All of you," shouted O'Grady, his voice squeaking slightly with hysteria, "move closer together. Closer! So you're touching. Move!"

They shuffled along on their bottoms, huddling together into a tight-knit circle, their bodies pushed up against one another.

"Now bow your heads," shouted O'Grady. "Bow them down to the floor."

They bowed their heads and waited, but no further orders came. All they could hear was the heavy breathing of their captor and his steady pacing around and around their circle.

One of the burger-queens glanced up and saw the gunman go over to the wires taped to the wall. She'd already guessed they were connected to a bomb, and she started to cry.

"Shut up!" yelled O'Grady.

He pulled the battery from the bag, held it up to the wires as if he was about to connect it. Then he paused. Waited.

Suddenly a high-pitched alarm sounded from the kitchen, and O'Grady dropped the battery and ran toward the dumbwaiter, knocking a chair flying on his way through.

"Get the hell out of that elevator shaft!" shouted O'Grady. "Now!"

A thin burst of light from the shaft was poking through the crack around the dumbwaiter. It was extinguished immediately.

"Move now!" shouted O'Grady, the alarm piercing the air. "Get away from my restaurant. Leave me alone. Just leave me alone! Now! Now!"

A muted radio voice could be heard, followed by strange scrapings from above the dumbwaiter. Whoever was in the elevator shaft was making their way back to the top. O'Grady reset the alarm, then ran back into the restaurant. The cook was standing, and the gunman pushed him backward onto the ground, then kicked the nearest hostage, the Vietnam veteran, and shouted for him to report on the status of the doors.

The veteran ran to the entrance, then paused, peering around cautiously. They were under attack, and he didn't want to give anyone cause to start shooting out there. Logically he knew they'd be unlikely to shoot with a bomb taped to the door, but the heat of the battle didn't always hold true to logic. He watched the doors for a few seconds, then said, "All clear."

"Walk up there and tell me exactly what you see," shouted O'Grady.

The man walked up the stairs, slowly, licking his lips nervously. "Police marksmen," he called. "Three . . . four of them. Automatic weapons trained on the stairwell. I see tactical response officers, also armed . . . with assault rifles. They are behind a barrier. There are some civilians . . . that's all."

"Tell them," said O'Grady. "Tell them to pull back now from the elevator shaft and the doors or they'll watch you fall dead."

"I understand," said the veteran. He yelled up the stairwell. "Fall back! Fall back from the entrances now! Lives are in danger here."

"What are they doing?" said O'Grady, his breathing hard and fast.

"They're conferring by radio."

"It's taking too long," said O'Grady.

"They have to wait for orders from their commanding officer . . ."

"It's taking too long!" shouted O'Grady.

"Be patient," snapped the veteran. He looked back up the stairwell. "They're giving the signal. The tactical response unit is pulling back. You've succeeded."

The veteran didn't wait for orders from O'Grady. He walked back into the restaurant and joined the rest of the group, flopping to the ground exhausted, his hands shaking visibly. O'Grady paced around the restaurant, checking the dumbwaiter and the entrance repeatedly, getting other hostages to walk up the stairs and report on what they saw. For another thirty minutes he made them sit on the floor, their heads bowed. Some fell asleep, some leaned against their neighbors, and some had their own struggle against headaches and nausea. They could hear little, aside from the quiet sobbing of the girl and the insistent wheezing of the manager.

Finally O'Grady spoke, breaking the ring of silence with orders for them all to make themselves as comfortable as possible and get some sleep.

The hostages slowly arranged themselves into small groups on the restaurant floor, sticking to those they knew, those they worked with, those they felt comfortable with, or those they thought might protect them. Their preparations were silently watched over by O'Grady. An eerie quiet filled the place, allowing the outside noises to amplify in their heads and in their hearts. They talked very little, breaking the silence only to say a short "sorry," or "do you mind . . . ," polite little utterances that belied their fear at having to sleep the night in this miserable place.

The girl wandered around aimlessly, no home to go to, no place to sleep. O'Grady, seated with his back to the landing, snapped out of his state to shout at the manager, "What are you doing letting this child alone like that? Find her a place to sleep."

The manager nodded his head. "I'm sorry," he said. "I . . . um . . . forgot my orders."

"Never forget your orders," boomed O'Grady. "They will keep you alive during the armed struggle."

Theo Constantine arranged a spot for the girl next to one of the exhausted young burger-queens who served behind the counter.

John Wayne O'Grady watched the comrades as they tried to sleep, but the uncomfortable floor and the misery of their situation made them restless.

"The dark is everywhere you look," he said. "But you must not let that disturb you. It's just a tactic used by the police lackeys. They are trying to stop you from hearing the truth. They're not interested in saving you, only in making your life a misery. No electricity means no light, no heat. They think the cold will stop you from concentrating, comrades."

O'Grady counted the thirteen shadowy lumps of the comrades, reassuring himself that none had moved, that all was well.

"A good soldier has to be prepared for anything in a war zone," he said. "And this is war. Your enemies are outside, never forget that. The police marksman, ready to shoot a bullet down those stairs. A decent family man who'd kill you the minute he recognizes that you know the truth. Shoot a ripping hole through your body and watch you fall, watch you die in a pool of your own blood. What sort of man does this kind of thing?"

The hostages remained as still as they could, hoping that the gunman would think they were asleep and stop this evil version of a bedtime story. But O'Grady had ceased talking for their benefit. He was completely caught up in his soliloquy.

"Outside, the police negotiator is working on his tactics," continued O'Grady. "What master does he serve? His commissioner? Or the corporate bosses of Family Value who want you all crushed before you have any further impact on their profits. Then there's the TV news reporter out there, trying to keep it cool and professional. She feels outrage because she thinks you've all been cruelly imprisoned. What a hypocrite. She is a puppet, working for a medium that deliberately incites emotions in its viewers to drive the profit margin higher. More emotion, more viewers, more ratings, higher salaries. This is a woman who trades in the pain and suffering of human beings, of you, comrades. If you fall in this battle, she will rejoice."

O'Grady sighed, and a sudden wave of immense exhaustion washed over him. The comrades were silent and still now. In the midst of the darkness, he fumbled through his pocket and pulled out a small packet of tablets that he'd bought from one of the truck drivers who supplied his restaurant. He popped it into his mouth and swallowed it whole, without water. It was a trick he'd taught himself in case he ever had to take his own life during a combat situation.

As the effects of the pill started to grip his system, his heart rate rising, his mind snapping into a new zone of alertness, John Wayne O'Grady rubbed the barrel of the Barrett and smiled at his charges.

"Tomorrow we will begin in earnest," he mumbled. "Tomorrow the lights will be switched on forever."

N A P K i N

It's late Sunday night. O'Grady keeps waking us up and talking to us. We aren't allowed to complain. He just put the men in the toilet for the night. But not me. He said they were not listening. He's not scared of the women. Everyone is so tired. And he gets angry. O'Grady has some kind of alarm on the dumbwaiter so he knows if anyone is coming. And he keeps waking us to look at those doors. O'Grady is poison. He points that gun at us. I'm in here with the kid again. I said she was sick. She smiled at him today. I ~~couldn't~~ ~~didn't~~ *Shit. What's he doing to us? I think he has taken*

pills or something. He doesn't seem to sleep. If I
have a chance, I will slip one of these under the
front doors.

Theo Constantine

FREDA OPPERMAN

It's a well-used doorway, unremarkable in design. A few scattered leaves roll around nearby, a welcome mat at its feet, telling you to "Watch Your Step." This was once a place where marksmen waited, where police lines were drawn. Once a doorway belonging to Family Value, before Nancy Opperman brought down this franchise. She filed a crippling lawsuit that saw them jumping into a sea of bankruptcy. And she didn't stop there. Next in her sights was the Family Value chain. They paid up fast. Now this doorway is the most hated image in the Family Value boardroom.

The stairs still lead down to the underground, but there's no wall blocking the view of what's inside now. It's been ripped away, revealing a surf shop with racks of shorts and tops. Bright product logos are everywhere, waves the predominant feature. It's a happy place, full of sunshine and sand. The new owners have obscured the events of the past, wiping away vestiges of bad planning and ugly memories so that the unsuspecting shopper will make no connection to this place and that *other*.

There are no mysteries beyond the wall. I do not like mysteries. Either you try to solve them, or you choose to ignore them. This seems to be the way. I tried and failed to come up with a logical explanation for the phone calls about the napkins. So I opted for ignorance. It is said to be bliss. But when the phone calls continued—fewer and fewer over the days—and I practiced disregard, neglect, even contempt, they still tormented me. Then one day, when Nancy was out at a meeting and the phone rang again, I had a revelation. Which led me, in part, to this doorway.

The city is in prelunch mode, more relaxed than usual. There are a few scattered shoppers, and the footpath stretches out before me. I can see William approaching on my side of the street, wobbling toward me from a distance. I'm not very good with anticipation, and I wonder if I should sit down on a seat, turn my back and pretend I haven't seen him yet, or stare openly. Neither seems like much of an option.

William is close now, and he smiles at me, just as he did when I first walked into the café for the interview. I want to wave to him, to say, "Over here. Can you see me?" Why does his smile do that to me? I was thinking of that smile when the phone rang during Nancy's absence. When I had my revelation. I was recalling William's glassy-bead eyes, how they offered me something in that café. How they made a brief connection. And how quickly they were shut off. Then I realized something, not to do with William, but Fortress Opperman. We have an unlisted number. Nancy's office line is listed, but only trusted people are ever given our home number. A complete stranger could never ring and say what has been said.

I called William right away and made a time to meet him. Then I told N.O. that I would go meet the teddy bear alone. We did not discuss the meeting place because she would not have approved of my choice. But I am an independent young survivor now, and we will sometimes make inappropriate decisions, such as coming to this doorway. This perfect place for abandonment.

And now William is here.

"Hello," he says as he arrives. "This is a good place to meet."

"This is not a good place," I mutter.

"Actually, I wish we'd met here last time," he says. "It would have made a great start to the article . . ." He looks down the stairwell, then back to me. "Ever been down there? Since . . . ?"

"No," I say. "Not down there."

"Would you ever consider it?"

"For your article?"

"Oh, I've written that."

He has already written the article, yet he comes. He stands at this doorway and asks in an ever-so-casual voice if I've been down there since, yet he knows this. He knows so much. Too much. I sit at a bench that faces the traffic, my back to the doorway and the hideous opening beyond it. William joins me, but he doesn't ask me what's wrong. He doesn't say a word. I look at him. His eyes are blank.

"Isn't there something you should be telling me?" I ask.

He is startled. "Me? Oh . . . I . . . um, no. Why?"

I hold on to the seat. A yellow van passes by, flashing a wall of color. Then a red car, its driver singing along to the radio. William doesn't speak. After a while he tells me that he likes to count cars when he's waiting for a bus. I don't comment. Then he tells me that something bad once happened to him. Something that keeps him awake at night.

"Happened to you?" I say.

He thinks about his statement, then corrects himself. "Something I did."

"Do you remember all of it?" I ask.

He nods.

"Does that make you lucky or unlucky?"

A car swerves in front of us and nearly hits a cyclist. The driver blasts the horn, laying blame, and the cyclist retaliates with a rude finger gesture. The driver of the car hesitates, contemplating his next reaction, but the cyclist has already pedaled away down a side street.

"Do *you* remember all of what happened to you?" he asks, his voice faint. "Imagine being able to clear up what really happened . . ."

"Clear up!" I shout. "You idiot!"

Some people stop, and a man asks me if I'm all right. I ignore him. William mumbles something about having a dispute. The man pauses for a while, then joins his companions.

"That day you called me for the interview," I say. "What phone number did you use?"

"Yours. Why?"

"It's unlisted," I say.

His eyes move about as he processes this piece of information, the wheels turning, the cogs clicking. Then his face becomes a mask, but he can't hide from me.

"Nancy never told you that, did she?"

"No," he says.

"What's it going to take to get you out of my life?"

"I'm here to help you . . ."

"You can't honestly believe that," I say.

"I am. Ask your mother."

I turn on him. "What?" He is smug, grinning. Scoring points. Hinting at a conspiracy with my unsuspecting mother. What sort of game is this?

"She reckons," says William, "that I can help you feel . . . I don't know . . . better about yourself?"

I would laugh, if my throat weren't so tight. I would howl with derision, if I didn't feel this awful betrayal. So this is my mother's plan. Send me out into the big wide world with a job and a friend to hold my hand. A damaged teddy bear that she picked up off the shelf somewhere and asked to be kind to me because I'd been through so much. She thought we'd be good for each other. Nancy Opperman, who has been so careful until now.

"I *can* help," says William. "You've got to believe that. I know what it's like to be afraid of things that have happened to you. That's why . . . why your story means so much to me. To lots of people my age. I really want you to trust me, to be able to talk to me . . ."

As he talks, as he rolls out words like *trust* and *story,* I feel my head lurching forward, as if someone has taken me by the back of the neck and pushed me with all his strength. It's making me sick. This has happened to me before. In the dark. A polished floor underneath me. Head bowed as a man paced above us. So afraid I thought I would throw up.

"I don't have stories," I whisper.

I feel a cold rush of air from behind me, on my neck, on the base of my hair. It curls its fingers around me, whispers to me, *"If you are good, then he will be good, too. If you are bad . . ."*

"Look at that doorway," I say, shivering. William cranes his head around.

"Yes?" he says.

"Sometimes I see the bomb there."

William turns back to me and his eyes are urgent. Watching me. "The bomb? But how did you . . . ?" He is shocked, this boy who has read the inquest report, who thinks he knows everything. Yet here is a fact that was kept from public knowledge, suppressed in the interests of a young girl's sanity.

It's intoxicating, watching his shock. The smug little game player reeling backward, flailing his arms to regain his balance. I close in on him, wanting to push and push and push until he is on the ground and I can shout in his face, "Leave me alone, you little turd!"

"O'Grady sent me up the stairs," I say. "Very few people know that. He sent *me* up there, and the police nearly went into a panic. I stood before a bomb that could have ripped me to pieces. A child in a fragile mental state. Can you imagine that?"

There they are. His eyes. They do not move from mine. Only his breath betrays the fear. My heart is racing, but this is not something I'll try to forget later. This is not a dark, horrible moment. This is exhilarating.

"Such are my stories, William," I say, jabbing him with my voice. "Such is my history. You have no idea what you're playing with. It is the cruelest thing. Can you handle that? Have you got the guts?"

"I . . . I . . . Yes," he says.

I turn to look at the doorway, spiraling away to the underground. If I remember more, if I tell him about those stairs, will it trap him in that awful hole?

"I stood on those stairs," I say. "And I looked up to see everyone watching me through the chained glass doors. The police so tense. The emergency crews grim. The reporters eager. And my parents . . ."

"What did you do?" he whispers.

"Would you write it down if I told you?" I ask.

"I've finished the article . . ."

"Would you write it down?"

"No."

No, he wouldn't write it down. Instead, he would drink it in, my story, use it as a salve for his own wounds.

"John Wayne O'Grady had sent Theo Constantine to check on the doors," I say. "I remember that."

I close my eyes. Has this moment always been with me? Or am I calling it from a far-off place? Late on Monday night. Everyone else was locked in the bathroom. Constantine had been gone for some time, so O'Grady sent me out to check on him. Slowly I reconstruct my nine-year-old self, walking out of the dim interior of the restaurant into the harsh police lights that flooded the landing. I can see details. Fine close-ups of a decade-old memory. I can see Theo Constantine slumped against the wall, his face pushed into its painted surface. I can see his skin squeezed, his mouth forced into a half smile. I can see the little trail of saliva running down the wall from his lips.

And I can see up there. "It was bright on the stairs . . . my eyes were squinting. So when I looked up . . . shapes . . . All I could see through the doors were shapes."

A car passes us, close, its radio so loud it's an assault. William shifts his position. I remain still. Whispering.

"The shapes were people. On the other side of the glass. Moving toward me. I see them . . . holding out their arms . . . like they were swaying . . ."

Remembering is more than sight, more than sound. It's terror. It's the words of John Wayne O'Grady in my head. He said things to me that night. Things I hadn't allowed myself to recall for years. They weren't police officers out there waiting for me. They weren't my mother or father. They were the puppets.

"What did you do then?" asks William.

"I saw my mother, do you understand that?" I say. "I saw her only a few feet away. There was a glass door between her and me. Just a thin glass door. Can you possibly conceive of what that would be like?"

"Yes, I think I ca . . ."

"You can't!" I shout. "You have no idea. I put my hands up to make her go away." My voice is a husky whisper. "And when she moved closer to the door . . . God, I can see her face . . ."

"What did you do?"

"I was scared of her, you moron!" He cringes, and I want to hurt him more. "I yelled at her to 'Go away!' again and again. 'Go away!' but she didn't."

William is staring at me. He wants to ask "Why?" To know. To feel it himself but something holds him back. I lean back against the seat for a moment. This isn't release. It isn't a clearing or an easing. It is the unluckiest thing in the world. Ten years ago I stood on those stairs behind me in a state of blind fear because I thought my mother wanted to hurt me.

This is wrong. I have to get out of here.

"Where are you going?" asks William as I stand.

"I can't . . . sorry . . . I can't tell you this."

"This is important," says William.

"Is it?" I hiss. "How could it be important? You've made me step down those stairs, you bastard. You've made me go down there, too."

"It *is* important," he says, "because it's the truth."

"The truth?" I shout. "The truth doesn't matter. Whatever people say at your inquest, or what they write down, it's not the truth. You want to know what I did? I screamed at them to go away. I screamed so much I was hoarse. And when they still wouldn't move, I spat at my mother. I spat at my father, the police . . . I stood on those stairs and spat and spat until my mouth was dry. I spat so much that I was wet all down my front, then I marched past the drooling Theo Constantine and poked him in the ribs. 'He wants you again,' I shouted, before stomping back into the restaurant like a spoiled child."

Back to John Wayne O'Grady, who looked as terrified as I

felt. But that is another story, one partly told in scratchy detail on a napkin that nobody was supposed to know about.

I look at him, at the shock on his face, at the sadness in every corner. Oh, William, will you take another step with me now? Down to that place? Down to where the lights will suddenly go out, to where the people around you will cry and whimper and a man will place a gun in your hand and teach you how to shoot? Will you come with me now, William?

I don't think so.

"This is evil," I say. "To remember. To dredge this up again. Don't you see that? It is nothing but evil."

And I leave him behind to ponder the stairs and the long way down into the past.

NAPKIN

This is Theo Constantine. He nearly killed me. I nearly died . . .

JOHN WAYNE

O'GRADY

"Comrades! Comrades! Wake up! Your lives are in danger!"

The women, children, and Theo Constantine woke from their improvised sleeping places and stared wildly around them. Daylight was coming in through the landing, filling the place with a softness that belied their rapidly beating hearts. What was the danger? Where did it come from? As they adjusted their eyesight to the gloomy interior of the restaurant, all they could see was their tormentor, John Wayne O'Grady, grinning at them.

"Yes! That's right!" shouted O'Grady, waving the shotgun about. "Your lives are in danger because you have swallowed so much of the puppet-masters' lies. But I am here to save you." He threw the bathroom key at Constantine and ordered him to release the men. Then he shouted, "Form one big study circle. Now!"

A few groans emerged from the group. They had been woken constantly by O'Grady during the night, forced to listen to more lectures in the small hours. Their bodies ached, their heads ached, and they felt nauseous. The men shuffled bleary-eyed into the restaurant and took up positions on the floor. An argument broke out again among some of the kitchen staff, and O'Grady marched right over to them, singling out the young hamburger cook.

"What is your rank?" shouted O'Grady.

The hamburger cook shook his head in confusion. "Huh? My rank . . . ?"

"Your rank!"

"I'm just the hamburger cook . . ."

"Wrong! You are nobody, and I am your commanding officer! Up until now your life has been meaningless, but when you follow my orders you shall see the light. Now, get into that study circle with your comrades or I shall exit you from the program."

The hamburger cook didn't bother to ask what this last cryptic comment might mean as he sat on the floor with the others. He watched the old lady pull her cardigan around her, complaining about the cold.

"That's because they've turned the heater off," whispered Constantine.

"The cold is nothing, comrades," shouted O'Grady.

Each and every one of the hostages completely disagreed with his statement, but not one of them dared to utter a sound. The girl curled her legs up under her dress and rubbed her eyes. She watched the young boy snuggle closer to his mother, protected by the woman's arm. Looking up at the adults around her, the old lady, the hamburger cook, her guardian manager, Freda pulled her skirt down over her legs as far as it would go and waited for the words of O'Grady.

Their "leader" walked around the inside of the circle, pointing the barrel of the shotgun at them, asking the same question over and over: "Are you ready?" Each of the hostages nodded their heads, or answered "Yes," hoping this would please the madman enough for him to leave them alone. There was a worrying edge to him this morning—he seemed hyped-up and aggressive, barking at anyone who said the wrong thing. O'Grady reached the young girl and pointed the barrel of the gun in her direction.

"Are you ready?" he asked.

"What for?" she replied, trying not to look at the gray metal of the barrel as it swayed carelessly near her face.

"At last!" boomed O'Grady, and the girl jumped with fright. "Here is a comrade who truly is ready. Do you hear? She is curious. She wants to know what's next. She wants to hear the truth!" He knelt next to the girl and placed his arm around her. "You're not that cold, are you, honey?"

She nodded her head, shivering slightly in the arms of this strange-smelling man.

"You are? Well, that's because the puppets have turned off the heat. Those police out there, those firemen . . . even your parents. They want you to feel cold. They want you to suffer so that you won't listen to the truth of John Wayne O'Grady. But you're ready for the truth, aren't you, honey?"

The girl nodded her head.

"You see," boomed O'Grady, "she knows that those people out there don't really care about her. What does she need police or ambulances or even parents for now?"

The girl stared straight ahead, her eyes locked on an anonymous pair of shoes—anything to take away the horrible feeling in the pit of her stomach.

"She's got *me,* now," said O'Grady, shuffling over to the manager and pointing the shotgun at his chest. "Isn't that right, Theo?"

"Oh, jeez," moaned Constantine.

"Isn't that right?"

Constantine nodded his head.

"Tell her."

"Tell her?"

O'Grady pushed the barrel of the shotgun harder against his chest.

"That hurts," gasped Constantine, but O'Grady was not moved. "Please . . ."

"You're her closest comrade here. So, be comradely and tell her!" shouted O'Grady.

Constantine sucked in a deep breath and said in a terse voice, "You don't need your parents, okay? You've got . . . him."

The girl flinched, as did others in the group. Some shook their heads, some refused to look at the farce being played out before them. Tears started rolling down the girl's cheeks.

O'Grady laughed, prancing around the restaurant like a crazed harlequin. "Are we all ready now? Huh? Like my little girl here?

Ready for John Wayne? Well, pardners, yesterday was your introduction. Today we're gonna get right down to it."

The cook put his hand up and O'Grady stared at him, incredulous that anyone should interrupt him. "What the hell do you want?" asked O'Grady.

"There are elderly people here," began the cook.

"I know that."

"Couldn't you at least let them and the children sit out of all this?"

"Sit out of all this?" said O'Grady, as if the cook had just proposed the most ludicrous thing imaginable. "Sit out of the truth? What sort of comrade are you?"

"I'm not a comrade . . ." began the cook.

"Oh yes you are!" shouted O'Grady.

Many of the hostages openly glared at the cook, furious with him for starting this ridiculous argument. The young man seemed oblivious to their disapproval.

"Why aren't you negotiating with the cops?" asked the cook. "What's the point of all this? What are your demands? What do you want?"

"What I want," said O'Grady, speaking slowly in a voice that promised more menace than his bellowing. "Is for you to sit back like a good young man and listen to me speak."

The cook opened his mouth to continue, but one of the burger-queens nudged him in the ribs and he finally got the message.

O'Grady stood in one of his still poses, eyes half closed, swaying slightly. The hostages shifted uncomfortably in their places as they waited for him to do something. Finally he broke into action again, pointing at the cook and smiling.

"I was like you, once. I was blind, my mind was clouded by the lies and deceits of the puppet-masters. That was back when I wore a badge like this fool here." He pointed the shotgun in Constantine's direction. "But I changed, and you can change, too. Look at this kitchen behind me, look at what goes on in there. They churn out thousands upon thousands of processed meat burgers and buns, and vegetables that have had every single living vitamin cooked out of them, until you'd get more nutrition from the cardboard box they serve it in. I was responsible for feeding this poison to my fellow citizens, but I wasn't happy about it. You see, deep in my heart the truth was trying to work its way in. Deep in my heart I knew that I was playing a role, dancing to the strings of the puppet-masters. So I fooled myself with puny justifications. I told myself I needed a change of scenery, that's all, a new challenge. I even put myself down for the position of manager for this restaurant. I thought that if I climbed up the corporate ladder it would make me happier. I was a fool."

O'Grady paused again, nodding his head slightly as if he were continuing the conversation in his head.

"Imagine that," whispered O'Grady. "I actually thought that what I was doing meant something. Ever stopped to think how insane that is?"

None of the hostages answered, more inclined to think that the insanity lay with the man rather than any situation he might be in.

"We started getting some of those pamphlet people outside my restaurant," said O'Grady. "I thought they were just nutcases, sprouting some rubbish about the quality of food we served and the cutting down of the rain forests. I was blind! You hear that, comrades? I was blind, too, and I believed what the puppet-masters wanted me to believe. Then one day an amazing thing happened.

I was on my way home for the day when I decided to take one of these pamphlets . . . and I began to see the truth."

Constantine stirred. He'd heard about this man. It was in the manager's newsletter, although they didn't name him. An article about a manager who'd been demoted by the Family Value senior management for inappropriate behavior because he'd been seen taking the pamphlet outside the restaurant. There were rumors that he'd been acting increasingly strangely, mistreating his staff and even bullying some of the customers.

O'Grady continued with his story. "To this day I cannot tell you whether it was a man, woman, or child who gave me the truth, but whoever that person was, they opened my eyes forever! And now I'm gonna do the same favor for you. I will open your eyes to the truth, comrades."

He walked over to Constantine and stood before him, staring at the manager with open hatred. Constantine shifted uncomfortably in his place, avoiding O'Grady's gaze. Then the gunman shouted orders for the hostages to cook up some breakfast and check on the doors. He slumped into a nearby chair and closed his eyes. O'Grady was exhausted, the effect of the pills had worn off hours ago. He tried to stay awake, but inevitably he drifted away on the strong surf of sleep, the white noise covering and covering his head until he could no longer resist . . . no longer . . .

He woke with a start.

Arguing.

He could hear someone arguing, and was that also sobbing in the background?

Reaching instinctively for his gun, O'Grady looked around wild-eyed. The arguing had died down, but it seemed to have come from the girl and the manager. She looked upset, and the fat man had an exasperated expression on his face. O'Grady frowned at the pair, and without moving from his chair, he held his hand out to the girl and asked, "What is it, honey?"

She looked up at him, tears running down her cheeks, but did not answer.

"She won't take her medicine," said the manager, holding his arms out in a helpless gesture.

"Medicine?" asked O'Grady.

"For her breathing . . . you know . . ."

"Are you sick?" asked O'Grady, and the girl shook her head. He indicated for her to come to him and she walked over, shooting Constantine an angry glance.

"Now, what's the fuss about, honey?" soothed O'Grady when the girl reached him.

"I don't want to take medicine," she said, eyes on the ground.

"Why not?"

"I don't know."

"Are you scared of him?" asked O'Grady.

The girl shook her head again, eyes still locked on the floor. O'Grady rubbed her back in a kindly gesture.

"Come on now, honey. You can tell John Wayne all about it. Are you scared of him?"

"A little," the girl muttered.

O'Grady leaped up from his chair and pointed the gun at Constantine. "You! Fat man! Did you hear those words? You are failing in your duty as a comrade. Everybody! Form one large study circle."

It took nearly five minutes for the hostages to drag themselves away from their breakfasts and sit once again on the floor. O'Grady placed Constantine in the middle of the circle and paced around him, a satisfied look on his face.

"Look at you," he sneered. "You're a failure, a nobody. Look at that badge you wear. I bet you even feel proud of it. Imagine that. Actually being proud of your dumb badge and your dumb life. I bet you go home every night to your whining, piss-poor family, your mean-mouthed wife, and your filthy kids crawling all over the furniture like ants."

O'Grady paused, lost in some recollection in his head, and Constantine took the opportunity to shift slightly from his uncomfortable position.

"Stay the hell where you are!" shouted O'Grady.

"I wasn't moving, I was . . ."

"You were what?" demanded O'Grady.

Constantine seemed to be debating something in his head. Then he spoke up in a meek voice. "I . . . I don't have a family . . . like you said . . ."

"Shut up! You're nothing but a trained dog, begging for any tiny morsel the puppet-masters throw at you. How many times have you been Employee of the Month? Five, ten? And I bet each time you thought you were doing real good, huh? Oh, what a good boy is Theo, the puppet-masters have praised the way he sits up and begs. You'll never wake up to the truth, fat man. You are a clown, a buffoon. The only reason I still keep you alive is to show the comrades here just how low you can sink if you swallow the puppet-masters' propaganda. Now get up and parade around the room, let them see what a pathetic nonsense you are."

Constantine stood reluctantly, moving slowly around the room at the insistence of O'Grady and his shotgun.

"Yes, yes, that's the way. Look at the fool. Look at the fool."

"Please . . ." said Constantine.

"Don't you have the ticker for it? You're like the Left. You think puny little PR victories in the courts are scoring telling blows. Idiot! The courts are the tool of the puppet-masters. The media are the lackeys of the puppet-masters. They are pulling your strings. Dance like a puppet, fat man. Dance like a puppet."

"I . . . I can't . . ."

There was a chorus of shrieks and gasps as O'Grady raised the shotgun and pointed it at Constantine's head.

"Dance like a puppet now!"

The manager danced about on one foot, a halfhearted effort that did not please O'Grady one bit.

"Can't dance properly, puppet? Then how about I shoot you?"

"Put the gun down!" pleaded Constantine in a high-pitched voice.

A woman screamed, another voice called, "No!" and several voices joined a chorus of crying. In the midst of this escalating madness a discordant note was struck. A weird, unnatural sound, like a dog, or a seal perhaps, whooping and gasping and clutching for air. It was the girl. She clutched at her throat, bending slowly in the middle, head almost touching the floor.

"Not again!" shouted O'Grady.

"Her medicine," said Constantine. He picked the child up in his arms and carried her into the storeroom, shutting the door firmly behind him before the madman could offer a word of protest.

Behind them, all was still. The hostages sat stunned, their faces distorted with fear. The gunman sat back in his chair with his head bowed, thinking or praying or lost to exhaustion. Then with a sudden burst of laughter he put his head up and pointed at the storeroom door, shouting, "Did you see that? Did you see what just went in there? It was a dead man. A dead man walked in there. How about that." And he shook his head, repeating over and over in a low voice, "How about that? A dead man."

NAPKiN

This is Theo Constantine. He nearly killed me.
I nearly died. Shit. That was close. It was the
girl's fault. Then she helped. Shit. Shit. She's
crying a bit. It's like she understands the bas-
tard or something. It's so freakish. That prick
is calling me "dead." This could all end soon.
Please, N. If you read this. I'm doing my best.
Now the girl is calm.

FREDA OPPERMAN

My father keeps the company of ghosts—aged cabinetmakers with leather aprons and stained hands who crowd him in his workshop, nodding at his choice of tool, at the sureness of his hand. They lurk in the smell of the varnish, playing with the stacks of lumber, sniffing the ancient stains on his workbench, mouthing the names of his well-oiled instruments. They mimic his long, smooth strokes with the plane before leaning back against the bench to sip on mugs of ghostly tea and lend half an ear to our conversation.

Most of all, they watch me, noticing how I move through the narrow spaces, how I negotiate the material world with deft ease. How my thin body seems to fit so casually between the sharp obstacles of my father's workshop. They wink at one another in a knowing way because each of those ghosts recognizes me for what I am—another ghost, here in this workshop.

My father's ghost.

For as long as I remember I have looked into Dad's eyes

and seen my own death. My own passing away from the bright, colored world of possibility to the gray, muted shades of loss. I have seen it in his deep, sad eyes. Seen the hidden span of two long nights played out in his every expression toward me. Even though I was carried alive from that restaurant into the cold early morning light, wrapped tightly in a blanket . . . to him I was lost.

My father's workshop, a place where I shimmer among the ghostly builders of tallboys and dressers, where I flicker in and out of two realms, mortal and spiritual. A glorified garage, with its roller door that is only ever opened when he has to remove a piece of furniture for delivery. This place among the ancients. I cannot float as they do. I cannot hover above my father and tenderly touch his balding head with fingers of light. I'm unable to bump up against him (only to pass right through him) in a warm show of affection. So I haunt him in my flesh and blood body.

I step in through the small cutout door that never closes properly, my eyes adjusting to the gloom inside, and find my father at his workbench, which sits like antiquity under a brace of fluorescent lights. I love this place where he rips and planes and machines the finely crafted furniture that has been his life for so many years now. He isn't surprised to see me, but then again, I never announce my visits to him. He looks up at me, a weary expression on his face, and says, "Hello, Freda."

Hugh Opperman, once a lawyer, now a crafter of handmade furniture for a tiny client base. He works at a troublesome piece of wood, his fine-boned shoulders hunched with exertion, his high forehead showing a sheen of sweat, his hair all dusty and gray.

He sweeps across the wood with his plane, its blade sharpened and resharpened on an oiled stone by his very own hands. Hands so stained that it is difficult to know what his true skin color ever was. He works as the ghosts watch him. At least he can be sure that *they* are dead, if he even knows that they exist.

We all have our secrets.

"How have you been doing?" asks Dad.

I don't answer him right away, because there's too much detail that I can't, or won't, tell. Instead I opt for a cryptic answer, something I could never do with Mom. "The past seems to be creeping up on me lately," I say, and the ghosts ripple in the background, shooting alarmed looks at one another. They do not like references to the "past," it brings up too many memories of flesh and blood and happier days. I have this urge to repeat over and over, "the past, the past, the past," just to get up their ethereal noses, but I resist.

Hugh Opperman, though, has a strong interest in the past. He attends to history as if it were a piece of lumber, examining its grain, seeing early growth and faults and strength of spirit. It's in this way he can make the right cut, send the unwanted parts to the workshop floor to bounce and roll among the sawdust. The kept piece he caresses, he sands and strokes and cleans, bringing out its best.

I wonder, then, what I should tell him of my recent events. As far as I can tell, he doesn't know about the napkins, which strikes me for the first time in my life as rather curious. Hasn't he ever been suspicious of the conspiratorial whisperings that went on between Nancy and his daughter? Surely when I was younger, and not as schooled in the N.O. method of concealment, I must have made the odd reference to the napkins? Or my medicine? Or Mr. Constantine's scribbling?

Hugh puts his plane down and blows some sawdust from his

hands. "Have you read it?" he asks, nodding toward another bench against the wall where a university magazine lies opened.

"No," I reply.

William's article has been published at last, released today, of all days. My growing-up day. Nancy Opperman woke me early this morning, helping me to choose a suitable outfit for my first day of work at Guardian Angel. Today is the day I was to begin my life as a file sorter, coffee maker, and general gofer for all the earnest and socially just lawyers who make up the Guardian Angel team.

The mail arrived as Nancy and I were eating breakfast, and I saw the unmistakable university logo on the large envelope. The magazine was inside. The article. But Nancy folded it away for me to "read later," lest I be distracted by what William has written.

She read it, though, when she thought I was dressing. I stood at the door watching her face. It fell. He is a disappointment to her, is William. I did not tell her what I'd said to him at the doorway. Fear, I guess. She had been eager for details, asking what we talked about, hedging the conversation into strange corners. I think she thought that William was somehow going to soothe my troubled psyche.

I told her nothing because I can't, or won't, see how much she is mired in William's dirty little game. So I let her think she's still in control. I let her drive me to work. My mother, who forbade me to read about myself. I let her drive me to be grown-up on my growing-up day. The young survivor must resign herself to certain contradictions in her life. Nancy's mind would have been working overtime, thinking up what she was going to do about William and his article.

"Just let me off here," I said as we neared Guardian Angel. Grown-ups do this sort of thing. "I'd rather go in alone."

She hesitated, but in the end she let me off without coming in. She really thought I was going to let it drop at that. To simply go to work like a good girl while she tried to make everything all right in the background. Nancy waved good-bye, watching me for a while. When she finally sped back to Fortress Opperman, I ran down the street and caught a bus.

I can see a photograph of the Family Value restaurant staring back at me from the open pages. Dad sniffs, turning his back on the magazine. "I wouldn't bother with it," he says. "It's all crap."

"Nancy read it this morning," I say. "Over her coffee. She wouldn't let me see it."

"That'd be right," sighs her ex-husband.

"I started a new job today," I announce. "She didn't want me to be . . . 'disturbed.'"

"You *started* a new job?" He looks at me, hoping for more of an explanation.

"Tell me about that article," I say, changing the subject. "Is it as bad as Mom says?"

"It's bad," says my father. He goes over to the bench and retrieves the magazine. "I could throw it in the trash and we'd be done with it."

What is it with my parents that they want to get rid of every single thing that's been written about me? Are they so careless with the truth? John Wayne O'Grady said that the truth was the simplest thing, yet we do our best to hide away from it. We fool ourselves, we justify, and we burn . . .

"Show it to me," I say, and Dad hands the magazine over. The first thing I notice is the cheap recycled paper and the poor photographic reproduction. So far William has not let me down. There is the usual "blah" at the head of the article, the background briefing, a story I have read over and over in so many different versions of this very interview.

I skip over the introduction and come to a part where William is being "colorful," speaking, as it were, to his reader in a friendly, direct way.

Remember Freda Opperman? That girl on the front page of the newspaper? For a few days the entire nation was gripped with her plight. Was she all right down in that restaurant? Would she come out unscathed? Those grainy photos of her were flashed across every news bulletin, followed by shots of the police with high-powered rifles in vantage points around the restaurant.

You joined in from your living rooms, became part of the big media Brady Bunch as you waited for the little girl to come home.

Brady Bunch? Oh, please. Couldn't he have picked a better metaphor? Oh, well, what does it matter? Okay, where was I? Yes, William is warming up now.

Freda Opperman was the kid down the street. You knew her face but you'd never spoken to her. You knew what her parents did, but your family weren't friends. And then she came out. She was unhurt. Everyone celebrated.

But the kid grew up. She went to school and smoked cigarettes in the bathroom and kissed boys at parties. She became a nineteen-year-old teenager. She's not that smiling girl in the photo anymore, not that clinging little bundle in her mom's arms.

She's not the girl down the street anymore.

I'm beginning to see why Nancy's face fell when she read this crap this morning. William is steering this article into a very troubling corner.

What do you say to someone who's been through something like that? All through my preparation for this interview I wondered what she'd be like. Would she be timid, afraid of her own shadow? Has she been a wreck since her trauma? Or maybe she's corporate-smart and high-powered, a spokeswoman for her mother's many organizations and lobby groups.

What I met was nothing like any of those descriptions. Freda Opperman is, to put it simply, weird. Not weird in a geeky, pimply, strange-behavior sort of way. No, she's weird because she seems caught behind in a time that she supposedly doesn't remember.

I stop reading for a moment and catch my breath. A waft of air brushes across my cheek, and for a moment I think it might be the wind, or a glimmer of something else moving about in the workshop. Then Dad speaks.

"Had enough?" he asks.

I shake my head and read on.

Freda Opperman was told to "lead a good life" by the manager of the Family Value restaurant just before he died.

She was given a *purpose* for her survival. The others who walked out of that siege were left to their own devices, to struggle with the guilt and the horror. She just walked away . . .

I was carried, you fool. Get your facts straight. God, this is all over the place. I skip a paragraph or two, then read on.

So, what's a good life worth? More than the lives of the two men who died in the siege? Theo Constantine was shot by O'Grady, but why? Nobody knows. Freda Opperman was there, but she says she can't remember. Did Theo die because he was trying to save this girl? Was she given that gift?

I feel a horrible tightness in my chest, followed by a warm touch between my shoulder blades. There's a voice . . . Dad's voice . . . coming from somewhere.

"Give it to me, Freda."

He tugs at the magazine, but I won't let it go. The more he pulls, the tighter my grip.

"I have to read it," I say.

How do you measure goodness? Would all the charitable acts in the world equal the life of a man? Freda Opperman is not a saint. She's just a girl who can't remember.

What went on down there? Did you intervene, Freda? Play the Good Samaritan? Or were you something else?

Good Samaritan . . . or "something else"? The line is like a sly knife in the dark.

My father places his stained hands on my shoulder and takes

the magazine from me. "Leave it now, Freda," he says. "You don't need to give excuses. What happened to you should never happen to anybody. You were just a kid, going down those steps . . . Just a kid. You're the victim here."

I wince at the word victim—take it out of my heart and try my best to grind it into my father's dusty workshop floor.

"Dad," I say, holding my hand out for the article. "Let me read the rest."

I have met Freda Opperman. I have seen the pain of her suffering, the dreadful effects the trauma has had on her. But what is there to hide? Isn't it time you came out from behind the protection of angels and stood by yourself?

As a young boy I believed in you, Freda Opperman. I wanted you to grow strong, to become normal, to lead a good and healthy life.

I want to stay believing.

"Why did he make it so personal?" I whisper.

"Put it out of your mind, Freda. He's just a little prick."

A pinprick, perhaps? One? Three? A thousand little pinpricks that continue to prod at me? I feel dizzy and clutch hold of my father's arm.

"Dad," I say, my voice so thin it could join the vapors that swirl around his workshop.

"Freda, come and sit down."

He leads me to a chair and gets me a drink of water, which I leave untouched on his workshop bench. William's words roll around in my brain, but they don't make any sense no matter how many times I repeat them. What is a good life worth? What is a good life? What?

Dad is looking at me, worried, hovering between anxiety and concern. My father, awkward in his own space. He doesn't wonder why William's article has upset me so. Quiet, patient, never curious about what else might be going on. I'm his well-behaved little ghost.

"Why don't you ever ask me questions?" I say.

He stares at me, confused, then shrugs as if that might put aside this awkward non sequitur. I hold my gaze on him, not allowing his shrug to end it. Dad raises his eyebrows, then says, "What would you want me to ask?"

I smile. "Don't you think I'm worth a question or two?"

"Look, Freda," says Dad. "That snotty little bastard has no right to treat you that way . . ."

I interrupt him before he gets into any more William bashing. He can leave that department to me. "William hardly even knows me," I say. "Yet he's full of questions. Why can't you find one thing that excites your curiosity?"

"Freda, I'm sorry," says Dad, that helpless look on his face. "I know I've just stood by and let your mother arrange your life . . ." And he shrugs again.

For a curious moment I see John Wayne O'Grady in that careless shrug, the way he tried to absolve himself of all responsibility. It is such a bizarre comparison to make, because my father has nothing in common with that madman, yet there it was like a flickering neon. Perhaps it's the same light that I sometimes see in William, the flash of recognition before the snotty little shit takes over.

"Come on," says Dad. "Cup-o-tea time."

He goes to his little wood-burning stove and places a kettle on it, then stokes some more wood onto the coals. I pull my chair closer, warming my hands. The kettle doesn't take long to boil, spilling water onto the stove top where it hisses and bubbles before vanishing into steam. Dad pours water into two chipped mugs, then hands one to me. I jiggle the tea bag absently, soothed by the ritual. This is Hugh Opperman's genius. His ability to provide quiet spaces for me to calm down and stop spinning.

Sipping his tea noisily, Dad grins at me through the steam from his cup. Perhaps he avoids questions because answers can be tricky things. Like unraveling a beautiful scarf to see how it is made, only to find you have a handful of tangled wool. Perhaps he'd rather appreciate the beauty of something. Like the way he holds a piece of wood. There's no mystery in the lumber, it's all there for him to read in its grain. I doubt if he'd be much of a poetry person, either, rather like his ex-wife.

"Do you read much poetry, Dad?" I ask, curious.

"Can't say I do," he says, skillfully removing his tea bag and tossing it into the trash.

I nod, then try to copy his tea-bag technique. All I achieve are wet, burned fingers. Dad is watching me, thinking. Then he says, "Do you like poetry?" with a grin on his face. He's so proud of his question.

I sigh. "There's one poem I like . . . by Shelley."

"Didn't he write *Frankenstein*?"

"That was his wife," I say.

"Oh," says Dad, a sly grin on his face. The association of Frankenstein and wives has tickled his fancy.

"Mom hates this poem."

He glances at me. "Does she? Recite some for me."

"No."

"Go on. You can't just bring up the subject of poetry and not recite some."

"I can do what I like," I say, a hint of huffiness in my voice.

He sulks now, in that way my father has, drifting off into his own world, looking so peaceful and serene that you itch to get in there with him. His sulks drove my mother to distraction, and for a moment I share some of her annoyance. There's only one way to break this.

"Higher still and higher," I recite, doing exactly what I said I wouldn't. *"From the earth thou springest/Like a cloud of fire;/The blue deep thou wingest,/And singing still dost soar, and soaring ever singest."*

"That's nice," says Dad, reducing Shelley's words with his description. *"Like a cloud of fire . . .* Is that you, then? Soaring and singing into the sky?"

"No," I snort, blushing a deep red. "It's about a bird."

"Oh . . . right."

We finish our tea quietly and sit in the rarefied atmosphere of the workshop. Suddenly I feel closed in, suffocated, as if staying in one place too long will leave me with no air. I stand up abruptly, dizzy but on my feet, and Dad stands, too. He puts his hands out to steady me. I push them away. "It's okay," I say to my father's hurt expression.

"Come on," says Dad. "I'll drive you home."

I don't protest, but simply follow my "old man," my father, who has aged too fast over the past few years. Dad ducks his head through the little door, and for a moment he's burned out by the brilliant sunlight before him, reduced to a stick figure. Then, as I step out into the light, he becomes the cabinetmaker again, the diffident man leaving his lumber and tools behind. He pushes his thin frame up the hill toward his truck, walking on the incline as if he's leaning against an almighty wind. Dad always seems lost to me out in the real world, away from his workshop. Incongruous, even.

As we head for home, mute partners among the oil rags and saw blades and rusted tools on the floor of his car, he looks at me and smiles.

"When you were little," he says over the noise of the engine, "you used to be so stubborn. I remember you in kindergarten refusing to wear some frog hat for a concert."

I shrug. "I am an Opperman, after all," I say. "We don't like decoration."

"Maybe," he says. "It was just that . . . that poem . . . it reminded me. You were like a kid on fire. Every issue was a *burning* issue for you. You could never be lukewarm. God, you gave us hell. Like when you decided that you should be allowed ice cream for breakfast."

"I didn't . . ."

"Oh yes. I never knew a little kid could wake up so early. We had to stop buying ice cream."

I smile, thinking of a younger Freda with a chocolate mouth and grubby pajamas, caught brown-handed in a corner somewhere.

"You sometimes used to drive your mother to distraction," he says. "That's probably why she hates that poem."

"And what about you?" I ask. "Did I drive you to distraction?"

"Hm?" he says, negotiating a tricky patch of traffic.

He doesn't say any more, just watches the road, glancing in his rearview mirror, checking behind him as he changes lanes. I look at him, a tall, thin Opperman, his shirt covered in sawdust, his hair sticking out in strange places, his face covered in a fine, gray stubble. Stained hands hold the steering wheel on an unerring course, not too fast, not too slow. No burning here, no rushing headlong into the unknown.

My kind, patient, ineffectual father, stepping back to allow his wife to "handle the child," biting his tongue, his attitudes, his reason for being around. I don't think I *did* drive him to distraction when I was young. He would have been amused by me. He would have seen it as a sign of life.

No, the distraction for Hugh Opperman lies elsewhere, in another time, when the unknown quality of life gave way to the certainty of disappointment and pain. When the fire in the sky became nothing more than a thin wisp of vapor, and the clouds refused to release their secrets and allow the bird to come back again.

JOHN WAYNE

O'GRADY

Monday afternoon had begun with the usual noise from above, but gradually the background hubbub had receded to an eerie quiet. No cars could be heard, no moving about or voices. It was as if the police had driven away. Hostages were sent to the stairs to check out what was happening. They reported that there was still a vigil of law enforcement outside. John Wayne O'Grady was clearly unnerved by this silence. He kept looking up at the street level, interrupting his speeches. Then he retrieved two large metal bowls from the kitchen and started rubbing them together, making an irritating noise that grated on everyone's ears.

"Have I got your attention, yet?" he kept saying. "Have I got your attention?"

Eventually he dropped the bowls and returned to his rant

about corporations and profits. At least that was familiar, and the hostages could slip into their own sort of routine.

The mother could play quiet little games with her son, getting him to draw pictures on a notepad she'd retrieved from her handbag. The girl could lose herself in her fantasy world, imagining vast, detailed scenarios where good men on tall horses rode past and whisked her away to a land that had light, that smelled nice, that was safe. The old woman could lean against a wall and close her eyes, drifting into sleep. The cook could wonder how he would get out of this, the burger-queen next to him could worry about the old woman.

John Wayne O'Grady had started the morning with plenty of enthusiasm, mocking the manager after he'd emerged from the storeroom with the girl. The threat of death no longer an issue. He'd made them all form study circles again, pacing among them, talking, talking, talking. But the morning wore on in this fashion, with the tired hostages battling the cold and their resistance to the madman's rants. Lunchtime came and went. Still he talked. Then all grew quiet outside.

Some of the hostages hoped that O'Grady would give them a break after the metal bowls, but he continued his monologue, becoming increasingly disjointed, pausing for long periods where he seemed to be either in conversation with voices in his head or trying to remember something. He slipped into a low mumbling that none of the hostages could hear. Then he snapped back to reality and said, "Do you read me?" They nodded their heads as enthusiastically as they could, hoping he wouldn't single them out.

O'Grady went over to the wall where the wires were taped and picked the battery up from the ground. Those who recognized what it was intended for exchanged alarmed looks as the gunman seemed to contemplate hooking the wires up and blowing the door bomb. He didn't. The hostages visibly relaxed when the man put the battery back onto the ground and paced among them once more.

This went on for hours, with no pause. The old woman fell asleep, while other hostages slumped against chairs or table legs, lost in the deep exhaustion of despair. And still O'Grady walked among them, still he ranted and raved and berated corporations and Family Value and puppet-masters in a voice that had become so tired his words were almost unintelligible.

Then O'Grady, his brain fried by a potent mix of chemicals, exhaustion, stress, and hallucination, stood in the middle of the room, broke off his rant midspeech and shouted, "No, Caitlin! You're wrong!"

The hostages exchanged glances, raising their eyebrows to indicate that they weren't Caitlin, and they didn't know who she was.

"Oh, so you have protocols, do you?" sneered O'Grady, looking at no one in particular. "Your Anti-Corporation Group doesn't believe in violence. You cowards! The only effective method of change is armed struggle. Symbionese Liberation Army! The Weather Underground! Baader-Meinhoff. They knew all about it."

He fell silent again, and the boy whispered to his mother, "Who's he angry at?" His mother shushed him, holding his head against her.

The cook watched the gunman carefully, counting how long he was silent for. He'd been doing this for the past hour, hoping that there might be some kind of pattern to the madman's slumps.

"Bullshit, Caitlin," shouted O'Grady.

The hostages all jumped.

"They deserve to feel my revolutionary sting! Look what they did to me!" O'Grady's voice broke into a high-pitched squeal, spittle flying from his mouth, eyes wide with anger. "They hurt me!"

Once again he fell into an abrupt silence, staring at nothing in particular. The cook started his counting. The pauses mostly lasted between twenty to thirty seconds. Something had to be done. Earlier that day, O'Grady had seemed to fall asleep, and the cook had debated rushing him. When the gunman woke, the cook realized that a perfect opportunity had passed him by. He wasn't going to let that happen again.

Twenty seconds. The pauses were long enough to rush the man and disarm him. The cook prepared himself. He didn't whisper his plan to anyone else because he knew they'd try to talk him out of it. There was a three-meter gap between himself and O'Grady. He looked at it. It seemed as wide as a football field. Luckily there were no obstacles in his way. O'Grady had turned slightly away from him, which meant he wouldn't notice the attack immediately.

O'Grady started talking again, his words even more slurred, and the cook slowly raised himself on his haunches. This was the moment to make a move. If he had been a man trained in combat, as the gray-haired, quietly spoken Vietnam War veteran opposite him was, then he would have known that the odds were against him. First, the gap was too wide to be able to make any surprise move. O'Grady, as strangely as he was behaving, would still be alert to any danger. Second, O'Grady was facing the wrong way. He had his right side slightly turned away from the cook. As he was right-handed, it was a natural move for the gunman to swing around and instantly defend himself. Third, O'Grady had just finished a "pause," and going by his recent pattern, he would be alert now for at least a minute or two.

Having raised himself up on his haunches without detection, though, the cook wasn't going to go back. He counted slowly in his head. He intended to jump on "ten" no matter what, like a child at the edge of a swimming pool on a cold day.

One, two, three . . .

O'Grady was staring at the old woman, aware for the first time that she was asleep.

. . . four, five . . .

He raised his shotgun slowly and pointed it at her, causing a general chorus of alarm from the hostages that surrounded her.

. . . six, seven . . .

"Why is she asleep?" he asked in a slurred voice.

. . . eight, nine . . .

The hostages beside her shrugged, unaware that the cook was just a second away from acting. He should have bailed out. O'Grady was alert now, was waking up and preparing himself to launch into a tirade against the comrades for being so slack.

. . . ten!

At the precise moment that the cook lunged into a run, O'Grady swung around to address the group and caught sight of the man out of the corner of his eye. It was a simple maneuver to raise the shotgun and catch the oncoming man under his chin with the barrel.

The cook staggered back from the blow, clutching at his bleeding chin. O'Grady flew into a rage, advancing on the cook, shouting a string of invectives. He raised the shotgun by the barrel and smashed the stock against the side of the cook's face. There was a sickening crack. Every single hostage cried out in horror as the cook crumpled into a heap on the floor, his chin wound slowly bleeding onto the floor.

Some hostages stood up, some took an instinctive step toward O'Grady, wanting to stop him from hurting one of their own, but they were impotent, held back by the threat of the shotgun. "You bastard!" shouted the tall man who'd been the messenger the day before. "You bastard!"

"You want some, too?" replied O'Grady, raising the shotgun into a shooting position.

The woman next to the tall man screamed, and O'Grady swung the gun around the group. "Everybody stand up!" he yelled. "Get on to your feet now! All of you."

They rose quickly, terrified at what an angry O'Grady might do. Someone shook the old woman awake and she slowly raised herself, aided by the Vietnam veteran.

"Huddle into the middle here. Now! All bunched up! Move." They shuffled into a tight group, bodies pushed up against bodies, breathing in each other's staleness.

"Is this how you repay me?" shouted O'Grady. "Huh? Is this it? I educate you . . . open your eyes to the truth . . . and you want to hurt me? Is that it?"

They stood like naughty children before a ferocious headmaster, wincing at the force of his attack. The young boy sobbed into his mother's stomach, the old woman moaned quietly, the burger-queens looked at their friend the cook, bleeding on the floor, and cried openly. All they offered were noises—frightened, terrified, angry, sad—their only freedom, their only allowed response. Noises that were joined by a strange, musical sound, like something scratching away at the carpet tiles. They looked around and saw that this last noise came from the girl, her eyes locked on O'Grady, a steady stream of urine running down her legs.

"I have given you a precious gift," bellowed the man, oblivious to their plight. "A precious gift, and all you can think of is deceit! Lies! How dare any of you betray me? After all I've done for you. How dare you?"

The gunman seemed genuinely hurt and upset by what had happened. Pointing the shotgun at the tall man who had called him a bastard a few minutes earlier, O'Grady shouted, "You! Step forward. What are we here for?"

"I don't know," mumbled the tall man, unable to even bother with a reply that might please. All he could do was stare at the unconscious cook on the floor, at the lurid purple bruise swelling on the side of the man's head.

"What the hell do you mean you don't know?" shouted O'Grady. "What have I been telling you? Huh? Are you a comrade or not?"

"Yes," answered the tall man.

"I want you to say it louder. I want you to say 'I am a comrade,' just like that."

The tall man shifted uncomfortably on his feet, glancing at the men around him, at the stricken cook. He cleared his throat then said, without any conviction in his voice, "I am a comrade."

O'Grady reacted instantly, shoving the barrel into the tall man's stomach, sending him crumpling to the floor in pain.

"You stay down there!" shouted O'Grady. He turned his attention to one of the kitchen hands, a shy boy of about seventeen. "Come here!" shouted O'Grady. The boy took a step forward. "Now you say it."

The kitchen hand spoke in a clear, loud voice, "I am a comrade."

O'Grady was not satisfied with this reply, and he shoved the barrel of the shotgun against the boy's throat, ordering him to drop onto his stomach. The boy fell to the floor without any protest. O'Grady turned then to the Vietnam veteran, and held the shotgun against the man's chest. There was a slight twitch in the corner of the veteran's eye, otherwise he showed no emotion.

"Say it," whispered O'Grady.

The veteran locked eyes with the gunman, silent, just staring the man down.

"Say it!" shouted O'Grady.

The veteran said nothing, instead he lay down on the floor next to the other men with his hands behind his head.

"Get up!" shouted O'Grady. "Get up now!" The veteran refused to move. "You ungrateful bastard. You're all ungrateful bastards. I am showing you the way out of your shitty little lives and you repay me with this. I will have discipline, you understand me?"

The ragged and exhausted band of "comrades" that were gathered around him made no response.

"Men should have the internal discipline to readily become soldiers," he shouted. "But you lot are weak, piddling little pissants who can't take the heat. Get up all of you."

The tall man raised his head to look at the other prone hostages, but as they did not move, he stayed where he was.

"I want all the men over by the bathroom," said O'Grady in a calm voice. Still they did not move immediately, so he shouted, "Now!"

"Why should we?" said the veteran.

"Why should you?" said O'Grady slowly. "Because I've got this."

He pushed the barrel of the shotgun against the back of the man's head. The veteran lifted his head against the force of the gun, looking around the group, at the women and children and prone men who lay on the floor beside him. A terrifying "arm wrestle" was being played out between the man's head and O'Grady's shotgun.

"This is more than a gun," whispered O'Grady. "This is the enforcer of the truth. Anyone who follows me follows the rule of this gun. No amount of talk is going to change the puppet-masters. They have to feel the cold steel of your resolve. And I've got resolve, cowboy. You wouldn't want to test me on that."

The veteran craned his neck around further to look O'Grady in the eye, the barrel of the Barrett rubbing against his nose. Several of the hostages made tiny movements toward him, their faces showing a glimmer of hope.

"Yes," said the veteran. "I can see that. You have resolve."

He sighed, then stood slowly, followed by the other men. There was a faint murmur of disappointment as the veteran and the tall man helped carry the stricken cook to the bathroom.

"He needs help," sobbed one of the burger-queens, but O'Grady ignored her. Once the men were gathered by the rest-room door, the gunman bellowed at them, "Get the hell into that bathroom." Pointing the shotgun at their chests, O'Grady pushed them back into the restroom, his eyes wide open and white, his movements jerky and twitchy. He barked, "Move!" over and over, becoming increasingly hysterical. When the last of them had filed into the bathroom, he said, "You are all lost to me now," his voice breaking with emotion. Constantine, who had stayed back from the drama with an uncertain expression on his face, began to walk toward the bathroom, and O'Grady held the barrel of the Barrett up against Constantine's chest.

"Where the hell do you think you are going?" said O'Grady.

"To join the men . . ." said Constantine.

"Don't be stupid. You're not a man."

Constantine blushed deeply, staring at his tormentor in disbelief. He seemed to be frozen on the spot, caught between wanting to save his dignity and save his life. "But you said you wanted all the men in there . . ." he stammered.

"And I also said you're not a man. So you aren't. Got it? You're whatever I tell you that you are."

"Then . . . what am I?" asked Constantine, a confused look on his face.

O'Grady looked past the manager at the frightened women and children who were huddled in the middle of the restaurant. "For now you're a woman. So go join the ladies."

Constantine opened his mouth to protest, but O'Grady seemed to have grown bored with the conversation. He took the keys from his pocket and locked the restroom door, then rejoined the women and children.

"I won't give up," said O'Grady. "Even if only one comrade goes out into society with revolution in his heart, I have managed victory."

Then he saw the boy.

He was pushed up against his mother's stomach. Terrified.

"What is he doing here?" asked O'Grady, an awful menace in his voice.

"He's just a boy," hissed the mother.

"And he can join the men like the rest of them," said O'Grady, marching up to the boy.

"You let him stay with me last night. Please . . . you can't . . ."

"Don't you tell me what I can't do," shouted O'Grady. "Now get away from your mother, boy."

"Please," sobbed the mother.

O'Grady reached forward and grabbed the boy by his skinny hand, yanking him free from his mother's grasp.

"No!" screamed the boy, but O'Grady paid no attention.

"Leave him be," pleaded the mother.

"I'll go in his place," offered Constantine, but O'Grady just gave the man a withering look before dragging the boy to the men's room, unlocking the door, and pushing him in with the others. He locked the door again. The mother collapsed onto her knees, sobbing loudly as the boy's cries broke through the door. She was joined then by the young girl, who started crying loudly, calling out, "I want my mommy and daddy," over and over.

O'Grady put his hands over his ears, shouting, "Shut up! Shut the hell up all of you." But they would not be muted, and instead were joined by the younger of the burger-queens who had formed a strong bond with the hamburger cook. The cacophony of crying was raising the mood inside the restaurant to breaking point again. Having lost the men to their punishment, O'Grady was in danger of losing the women also. He marched over to the mother and spoke in her ear. "You've got twenty seconds to shut up or I'll go in there and make an example of your boy."

The mother reacted as if she'd been stung, instantly wiping the tears from her eyes, bending her head low to the ground as if this might help her stem the tide. Then O'Grady turned to the burger-queen and told her to shut up or he'd "finish the job" on the cook. She too managed to suppress her tears, sitting against a wall with her head in her hands. That left the girl. O'Grady pointed toward Constantine and ordered him to comfort the wet Freda.

"I want my mommy and daddy," she wailed, slurring the words into an unintelligible string of sounds. The manager put his hand out to the girl from a distance of half a meter away. It was clear that he did not want any of the urine that soaked the child's dress to transfer to him.

"I wanmymommyandaddy!" Louder. Desperate.

"I will have discipline," shouted O'Grady over the sound of the girl's tears.

"Iwanmymommyandaddy!"

"Harden your hearts . . ."

"Iwanmymommyandaddy!"

O'Grady stopped, unable to concentrate any longer. He turned to Constantine and yelled, "I simply don't believe it. You're a joke as a man, and you can't even be a woman, so what the hell are you? A dog? A monkey?"

O'Grady walked over to the pair and pushed Constantine out of the way.

"Iwanmymommyandaddy!"

"Listen, honey," he spoke over her din. "Everything is okay. Daddy is here. Old John Wayne is here. I just got a little angry back there, but you don't need to be scared. This is a safe place, baby. Real safe."

The girl started sobbing, no words left.

O'Grady scratched his head furiously, his frustration palpable. Here was his shining light, his bright example of the future, given over to the weakness of the others.

"Would you like to touch my gun?" asked O'Grady.

There was a slight break in her sobs, before they resumed again.

"This is a fine gun . . . and you could touch it if you like."

Now the girl looked at the Barrett, then up at O'Grady.

"That's right," said O'Grady. "You could even hold it for a second or two. That'd be fun, eh?"

She did not make any move toward the gun, did not nod or shake her head, yet her crying had subsided considerably. O'Grady stepped even closer to the girl, blocking her from the view of the other hostages. Theo Constantine stepped around as O'Grady held the Barrett out to the girl. She seemed to be trying to gain some control over herself, looking at the fine engraving on the gun's side plate, the fancy scrollwork etched into the metal. It was an abstract sort of pattern, a floral swirl that evoked images of belt buckles or silver spurs worn on dusty cowboy boots. Its delicate beauty served to enhance the romantic image of the gun as a peacemaker, a tool to be used by the righteous, the good guy in the white hat with the flashing smile.

"It's pretty, isn't it?" said O'Grady.

The girl nodded, running her fingers over the surface of the side plate, feeling the fine texture of the etching. Then she wiped the tears from her cheeks.

"Go on, you can hold it for a minute."

She did not take the gun immediately, so O'Grady squeezed her hand slightly, and she responded by wrapping her left hand around the fore end, then taking hold of the pistol grip with her right, the stock bulging awkwardly under her armpit.

"You got it now, pardner," he said, smiling broadly. He took a step back, giving the weight of the gun to the girl who nearly dropped it. She picked the gun up higher, holding it as if it were a large lump of wood. "Look at you." O'Grady laughed. "Like a cowgirl. Go on, shoot some of those bad guys."

He stepped in behind her and guided her hands so that she held the gun in a shooting position.

"That's the way, hon," said O'Grady. "That's the way you do it." Then he prized the gun from her hands.

A loud banging broke out from inside the bathroom, and the boy could be heard calling his mother's name. The girl tensed visibly, and O'Grady stopped to listen for a minute. The boy became silent after a moment, no doubt comforted by one of the men.

"You see," said O'Grady. "We don't need mommies and daddies in the new world. Good comrades look after one another. We are not alone after all." He placed his arm tighter around the girl's shoulder. "You're home, honey. I am John Wayne O'Grady. I'm better than mommies or daddies. You don't have to believe in nothing else, got that? I am the truth. I'm all you got."

N A P K i N

N

It's Monday evening. I feel sick. It's so cold. Shit. What a crazy mess this is. That kid. She held the gun. I saw it. The others think that the bastard made her do it. She wanted to hold it. I saw. Why'd she do that? Is she sick in the head? She held his gun and liked it. Shit, shit. I reckon she thinks she's on O'Grady's side. This is a kid. What a mess.

Theo

P.S. Sorry about my language.

FREDA **OPPERMAN**

Personal apologies, or expressions of regret, should always be handwritten, and where possible, hand delivered. I have so many apologies to make. I am sorry that I did not turn up to work today. I am even more sorry that I attacked my father, who drives me home now in his usual, unruffled way. And I am even more sorry that I didn't make everyone's life a lot easier and get myself locked up in the bathroom with everyone else.

My father stops at a red light and turns to look at me. "God. Freda, what is it? You look terrible . . ."

"Do I?" I say, forcing a smile. "Just tired. It's been such a big day."

"Yes," he says. "It has. That article . . ." And he lets it trail off there.

The light turns green.

There is something potent about written words. They can be held, scrutinized, each reading taking them further into the soul of the reader, planting them deeper.

That is why I try to avoid reading.

I am, of course, a terrible failure at it. I have read William's words, allowed them to burrow into my consciousness and unsettle me. He has wondered what "choices" I made down there in that underground hell of John Wayne O'Grady's making. I was nine years old, dressed in my Sunday cotton and warm tights and my hair done up with a ribbon. I was shaken, and threatened with a twelve-gauge shotgun. I was pushed into corners that no nine-year-old should ever have gone to.

I made the choices that I had to make.

And yet William has seen fit to write about it. To question me. To wonder. Are words enough for him? Will he be satisfied with the writing, knowing that he has joined a very small but elite band of men who have questioned my character on paper? Or does he want more memories, more stories?

I was afraid as hell of O'Grady and his gun. But the strange thing is, he was also the only person inside that restaurant I could rely on. At least, that's how I remember it.

But memory is an unreliable ally. It glues together separate events and makes them seem continuous. It gives words to people who never spoke and makes people forget the things they said. I've read the inquest report and noted how many tiny contradictions there are in it. She was standing here, not there. He did this, no he did the opposite.

William places importance on *my* memory because I walked away with my life. He has asked me, "Did you intervene, Freda?" Isn't it enough that I think about those two men every day? That I wish, I wish, I wish they hadn't died? As stupid as it sounds, I even regret O'Grady's final, lonely little act. I can tell you how he did it, but I cannot recall what led him to it.

It's a strange burden, being the survivor, being a symbol of hope. Hope is filled with air, with emptiness, just like my memory. It's the nothingness that makes it float. I guess that's the whole point. I guess I should shut up and put up with my position in life, maybe even be proud of it, wear a badge. *Hi! I'm Freda, National Symbol of Hope! Watch me float.* Just don't stick pins in me. Don't ask me rude questions, or demand that I come out from behind the protection of angels and tell the truth.

That is a curious phrase for William to use, "the protection of angels." Is he referring to N.O. when he says that? Or Dad, perhaps? Both are such absurd suggestions that I break into a smile. It almost seems a careless use of the word *angel,* as if William was too rushed to think of a better image. Then again, maybe it isn't so careless after all. I have listened to the phone ring, and a strange voice ask me about the napkins. I have sat with William at the very mouth of my nightmare and told him stories I thought I'd never remember.

Everything he has done so far has been deliberate.

"Can you turn back?" I ask suddenly.

We are heading out on the main road that leads to Fortress Opperman, away from the city and Guardian Angel. Dad looks at me sideways, then asks, "Why?"

"That place . . . um . . . Guardian Angel. I'm supposed to start my job thing today . . ."

"Oh."

Dad slows the car, then executes a careful U-turn. There are benefits to having a father who asks you no questions. We head back to the angels, where I may or may not be protected. One thing is for certain, I *will* have to come up with that apology now. Verbal, of course. "I regret that I was unable to attend your place of employment today. In any case, I am unworthy of your organization, which does its best to assist the downtrodden, the oppressed, the stricken, and the poor." That should be about right, not *too* formal.

We arrive at the city, and I direct Dad to the Guardian Angel office, which is nothing more than an old brown building nestled among other old buildings, most of which are deserted or boarded up. This is a very depressing part of the city.

"Thanks for the lift," I say as Dad pulls the car over.

I go to open my door, but it's obvious that Dad has something else to say. He never taps me, or touches me in moments like this, relying as always on his face, his presence. That's my father for you, as still as ancient stone, and just as hard to ignore.

"You know, Freda," he says. "About that question thing . . . I guess I . . ."

He is fumbling, attempting an awkward explanation. I leap in to save us both the embarrassment. "Don't worry about it," I mumble.

"No, I do worry . . . I guess I've always thought you'd break free better without my interference. Like the poem, in a way.

I mean, you have enough of it in your life . . . interference, that is. I'm just giving you space, I suppose."

"Thanks," I say, opening the door hastily.

"But maybe that was wrong," he says, placing his hand on the back of my seat.

I smooth out my work pants, purchased for the big occasion, and he watches my hands. They are thin, milky, long-fingered like his own. But not stained.

"I have no idea about right and wrong," I say. "Only that they never seem to be too far from each other. That poem we talked about? Not every stanza is filled with light and hope and flying birds. So . . ." I shrug.

"Maybe we could talk later?" he says.

"Yeah," I mutter.

Then I leave before this becomes a conversation. He watches me step out onto the footpath and look up at the brown building of hope and angelic fortune. I give him a quick wave, and he drives off. As I open the front doors of Guardian Angel, my stomach thrills with anticipation and fear. This is unusual for me, to walk into the unknown, to go in search . . . to seek . . . to enter that dangerous land where risk comes into play.

Before me is an open-plan office, strewn with too many desks and too many piles of papers. Untidy people walk around with purpose, paying little attention to the important symbol of hope who stands politely at the door. Eventually, a young man with round glasses approaches me and asks if I'm all right. I fumble around for an answer, because I don't know how to tell him that I'm here in search of William and not for the job I so carelessly skipped. As useless words tumble out of me, a careworn man in jeans and a denim shirt approaches us and says, "Are you Freda Opperman?"

"Yes," I answer, and several heads look up at me.

I have this powerful impulse to turn and run, certain that they've all read William's article. Here I am, folks. *Hope of the Nation!* Is my badge straight? Do I live up to your expectations? What do you see when you check me out? A tall gangly girl with slightly hunched shoulders and a badly arranged haircut? An evil imposter who has been deceiving the world for these past ten years?

One of the office workers gives me a casual wave, as if to say, "Oh, hi there, Symbol." I wave back timidly, and the guy in denim holds out his hand and introduces himself, but I'm not sure if he's said "Brad" or "Chad" for his name.

"You were supposed to be here ages ago. What happened?" asks Chad (or Brad).

I shrug, and search again for some kind of excuse. Then he says, "Follow me," and leads me to a partitioned-off corner, which presumably is his office.

"Take a seat," he says, and I sit in the only chair that isn't stacked with files and papers and old coffee cups.

"Your mom's pretty angry," says Chad (I've decided he's definitely a Chad now).

I nod, trying to look ever-so sorry. Chad takes a sip from his coffee cup and gives me a stern look, which might have impressed me if it hadn't been for the milky mustache he'd acquired from his cappuccino. How can a young survivor execute a proper apology when confronted with a white caterpillar crawling up a man's nose?

"Are you actually interested in this job?" asks Chad.

"I suppose so." I shrug.

"You know your mom put in a lot of effort to get you this position . . . we're normally fully staffed here . . ."

I must have my bored expression on my face, because I can see Chad-boy beginning to get hot under the collar with me. If he doesn't watch out, he'll melt that caterpillar and have milk running down his chin.

"I'm sorry," I say. "I know that you people work hard and all that . . ."

Chad becomes even more agitated by my inept apology. "It's not *you people,*" he snaps. "This place is part of you and your legacy. It stems directly out of the court cases your mother fought against Family Value. Did you not know that?"

"Not really," I mumble. "Perhaps you could remind me?"

The last thing I want is for Chad to tell me the history of the glorious struggle against hamburger chains, but it should keep him suitably occupied for a moment or two while I check the place out. He gladly launches into a saintly Nancy Opperman spiel, and for a brief moment I wonder if maybe he *is* a Brad, so easily did he follow my suggestion. I scan the busy workers of Guardian Angel as they flit from one desk to another, answering phone calls, filing documents. No sign of William, just dedicated workers earning a pittance for the cause of social justice. I try to imagine myself working in this place. What would I be then? A grown-up with a purpose? (Other than to "lead a good life.") Who am I kidding? What possible job could a symbol of hope carry out here? Photocopy machines remind us too much of flashing lightbulbs, everything we file ends up under "S," and telephones make us nervous.

"Just trying to imagine the political landscape without your mother's efforts would be almost impossible," continues Chad. I'd forgotten that I'd set him going like a windup toy, churning out a familiar tune. "She's empowered so many ordinary people, given them real clout against governments and corporations, yet most of what she does goes unsung. And it's not as if we're talking about an easy task, either. The struggle to bring justice has become increasingly harder and murkier, the boundaries have blended and merged. What was once a straightforward path is now fraught with all sorts of political and social considerations. You can't just simply set out and assume you are doing good . . ."

My full attention is back, and he *is* a Chad. Talking about doing good. Touching on a topic close to my heart. I nod enthusiastically, agreeing with his sentiment entirely.

"You can see, can't you, the effect she's had?" says Chad.

And I nod again, but this time it's an automatic response, so I check myself. Damn it. I'm tired of being a symbol that tells lies all the time.

"Actually, no," I say. "She's my mother. Sorry. But for as long as I can remember, people have been saying that stuff to me . . . which is fine, I guess. But that's what she is to you. What she is to me is private."

Chad scrutinizes me carefully, then asks, "Are you really interested in a job here?"

I shrug. "I don't know if I can see myself in a place called 'Guardian Angel.'"

"It was a name your mother came up with," sniffs Chad, a little too defensively. "This place is not about being good, do you understand that? It's about change."

"Change . . ." And I whisper the word. It is so powerful. So connected to my past, my present, my future. "I knew a man, once, who was interested in change . . ."

"You can't bring about positive change with brutality, Freda. You'd know that better than anyone. That sort of thing isn't change, it's just another aspect of the problem. Why does everyone have to imagine revolution? Sometimes it is the simplest thing that brings about a better world."

"That's funny," I say. "He said that change was simple, too."

Chad grunts, clearly unimpressed by John Wayne O'Grady's philosophy. "He did what all oppressors do. He denied people their dignity. You were just numbers to him. The irony is, I guess, that in this sense he was similar to all those corporations he tried to bring down."

"But . . . aren't you trying to bring those corporations down, too?"

Chad shakes his head, like he's talking to a six-year-old. "No," he says. "We're not. We're just making sure they play the game fair and square. I leave that stuff to other people. But I'll tell you one thing. O'Grady and I agree on Family Value."

"There is no value in Family Value," I say, repeating O'Grady's catchphrase.

"Exactly," says Chad. "They feed children food that is a nutritional disaster. And as a corporate member of the world family, they are greedy, ruthless bastards. Do you know I met some of the people who were in that Anti-Corporation Group that O'Grady joined after he was demoted?"

I stare at Chad. For some reason I'd always assumed that the Anti-Corporation Group was a figment of O'Grady's imagination. A justification, in a way, for his terrifying actions. I don't know if I want to hear that they really existed. It gives too much credence to O'Grady's philosophies.

"They realized fairly quickly that he was unstable, Freda."

"What point are you trying to make?" I ask.

"That it was the man, and not the ideologies he appropriated, that you should hate."

That I *should* hate. As if I possibly don't hate O'Grady, that man who stole my life away from me. Who stuck his fingers into my brain and messed about until I walked away empty.

"Hatred is too simple," I say.

Chad looks at me. There's something fatherly about his look, although he'd only be about ten years older than me. "Do you know why your mother named this place 'Guardian Angel'?" he asks.

I blink, wondering why he's trying to steer the discussion away from O'Grady. "No," I answer.

"Because that's what drives her. She has a fierce desire to see that no person ever feels alone when faced with oppression, with bullies, with terror. She's always worked at giving people back their power and their dignity. From that terrible incident she's made *real* change, Freda. With no fear involved at all. Are you willing, or able, to be a part of something like that?"

Chad is a persuasive speaker, I'll give him that. His calm, yet forceful argument almost has me swelling with pride. Almost has me standing up and announcing "I'm in." Then I see a familiar face near the back of the office, and my moment of inspiration is brought crashing back down to earth.

It is William.

Ah yes, the conspiracy. William is not looking at me. He's talking to a woman at a desk. He's telling her that I have no right to be in a place like this, where honest people work tirelessly for a good cause. He's telling her I'm a fake.

How can I argue with him? I can't help other people. I once helped a lady pick up the groceries she'd dropped and ended up smashing her jar of peanut butter by mistake. I once intervened in a fight between two little kids and inadvertently supported the bully. I once helped a stray cat over the road, only to have it run back after me and miss being knocked down by inches. I'm a failure as a "good" person. All my changes turn out for the worst.

"What's wrong?" asks Chad, a worried look on his face.

I nod my head toward William. "What is he doing here?" I croak.

"Who?" says Chad, craning his neck.

Oh, please don't do that. Please don't make yourself obvious. "Him," I say, nodding my head in William's direction.

"He's one of our clients," answers Chad.

"Why is he a client?"

"I can't tell you that," says Chad, a hint of indignation in his voice. "We're handling a case for him. He's a friend of yours, then?"

"Does my mother know he's here?"

"How would I know?" says Chad. "We get lots of people through here. We're a legal organization, Freda. We fight court battles for people who can't afford to take on expensive teams of lawyers . . ."

Who the hell would William be fighting? It doesn't make sense. He is standing now, making his way out of the office, past Chad's little corner. He doesn't even give me a glance, but he knows I'm here. Oh yes, he knows I'm here. I stand, too, and Chad asks me where I'm going. I turn on him, a sudden rage in my heart. Has he been a part of this, too? Some awkward conspiracy to help me grow up, perhaps? Or maybe it's a sick joke to capture me in a virtual underground, keep me prisoner with imaginary weapons?

"This is all a bit too convenient, don't you think?" I snarl.

"Pardon?" says Chad.

"What's your involvement in all this? Huh? Did Nancy pay you? Or William?"

"I'm sorry, I don't know what you're talking about . . ."

William is getting away. I don't have time to decide if Chad is innocent or not, instead I huff out as best I can.

Outside. William is here somewhere. What's he going to do? Threaten to shoot me? Threaten me with the truth? Take me back down the stairs? Not today. Not anymore. Watch out, William, I'm hunting teddy bear. Bang, bang, William, I'm almost there. There's a secret that lurks in my heart, William.

Bang, bang.

I'm almost there.

THE **GOOD** LIFE

OF FREDA O,

AGED 16

She sucked deep, as she'd been instructed, and instantly felt the unnatural tightening around her skull, around her kidneys. The smoke burned her eyes. Other than that, she felt nothing. Except for disappointment, which she didn't reveal to her companions. One of them, was it Miranda or Kate? turned to her and asked, "How is it?" She nodded her head and said, "Great," in a thin, weedy voice that made them laugh.

When Sunday came, they drove to the park in their usual silence. It was their regular outing, listening to the orators at Speaker's Corner. Nancy had heard about a new guy, someone interesting, but when she tried to engage Freda in a conversation about him it fizzled out. She looked at her daughter. This silent anger was heartbreaking.

There were precious few parking spots to be had when they arrived. Eventually, they found one some distance away. It was a long trek to the Speaker's Corner. Dodging picnic groups, kids playing ball games, joggers, bicycle riders, couples, and assorted dog owners, Nancy led the way, swerving determinedly through. She glanced over at her daughter constantly. Once she thought she caught a sneer on Freda's face. It made her jump with shock.

The orator was younger than Nancy imagined he'd be. Good-looking, too.

"There's a sickness at the heart of the world," he shouted. "A horrible disease where terror is born . . ."

Nancy looked at Freda. She had a bored expression on her face.

"Think about who creates terror," continued the man. "It's not created 'out there.' It's not the sole preserve of governments who turn to their military to solve problems, of desperate men who turn to their Kalashnikovs. It's a disease that stems from all of us."

"Is that what AIDS is?" quipped an onlooker.

The man closed his eyes for a second, then grinned. "AIDS, my friend," he yelled, "is a disease that comes from the larger disease. The drug companies refuse to allow cheap AIDS medicine into African nations because it might harm their profit. By acting this way, these corporations simply inflict a different kind of violence on fellow citizens in the global village. AIDS is a disease within a disease, a tragedy within a tragedy."

Nancy nodded. And you make choices about how to help. Wasn't that what she'd been fighting for all these years? Freda knew all that. Even so, Nancy turned quickly to check her daughter's reaction. She wasn't there. There was no sign of her daughter anywhere.

"It's good stuff, eh?"

She nodded, even though she still couldn't feel anything. None of the "high" that she'd thought she'd experience. Miranda and Kate looked at each other, sharing some sort of knowledge between them, and she felt a pang of jealousy.

"That's my mom over there," she said, trying to shock them.

"Seriously?" they shrieked.

"Yeah. She's listening to that speaker. I came here with her."

"Shit. You've got guts," said Miranda.

Freda tried to suppress her joy at this compliment, but all she managed to do was make her smile go crooked and awry. "Yeah, she, like, wants to turn me into a good person . . . or something."

Nancy stepped away from the crowd, and instantly her vantage point was swallowed up by somebody else. She walked toward the general park area. No sign of Freda.

"Any belief that is based on fear, on corruption, on lies, on violence, will only ever be a thing of evil . . ."

Was that Freda under those large fig trees at the other end of the park? It looked like her, talking to a group of teenagers. It was more secluded up that end. The trees were denser. The undergrowth of plants and large roots from the trees were easier to hide in.

Nancy looked back at Speaker's Corner. Now and then the crowd burst into applause, and she wished she could be there to listen. They'd come to hear the man speak, not have a social chit-chat with a bunch of strangers. There seemed to be smoke coming from this group of teenagers. Surely Freda wasn't smoking?

The two girls were lost in giggles again, a private joke that did not in-
clude Freda. She felt a dead weight on her shoulders, as if she were being
pushed into the ground. It frightened her. She no longer had legs or thighs
or buttocks. She was grinding into the earth.

"My mom doesn't care what I do," said Freda, trying to break this
giggling pair. Hoping to startle them as she had earlier.

"True?"

"I can, like, do whatever I want to."

"I thought you said she was trying to make you good," said Miranda.

"Trying . . ." said Freda, bursting into giggles. "And failing," she
added, lying back on the ground, laughing so hard she almost choked.

The other two exchanged looks, screwing their noses up at the prone
Freda.

"I'm, sorta like, this totally free outlaw," said Freda. "I can do what-
ever . . ."

"Um, Freda . . ."

"I . . ."

"Hey, look . . ."

"Want . . ."

"Freda! Get up now!"

Freda started with fright, sitting up fast, then swaying with
dizziness. She lay back down again. Nancy bent to tug at her
daughter's arm.

"Freda. Come now . . ."

"Hey," called one of the teenage girls. "It's cool. Freda's just
hanging out with us . . ."

"I can see exactly what she's doing," snapped Nancy. "I'm not
stupid."

"You want some, Mom?" asked Freda, holding up a rolled joint, a stupid grin on her face.

Nancy reached down and half dragged, half pulled Freda from the group. Her daughter didn't protest, just allowed herself to be dragged away. The joint dropped to the ground. One of her companions scrambled to retrieve it. Freda shook her mother off and walked across the park. Her new friends didn't even wave good-bye.

"What the hell do you think you were doing?" snapped Nancy as she marched after her daughter.

Freda didn't answer, just walked on lazily, coasting past the crowd and the speaker and the fresh breeze that blew around her dress.

"Look closely at the evils in the world," yelled the speaker. "Sponsored by governments, or hiding behind faith, or working toward corporate profits . . ."

Freda paused for a second, watching the man for the first time.

"Look at these evils, because when you begin to know what evil is, then you can begin to know the opposite . . ."

She seemed to be listening. Taking in what he was saying. Then she burst into giggles and snorted, "Evil." She staggered her way through the picnics and the ball games toward their car. From behind her the silent rage of Nancy Opperman was a feather's touch, and the voice of the orator as unintelligible as a baby's prattle.

FREDA OPPERMAN

I think I see a wobbly shadow up ahead. I am stalking a cunning prey, a wise young bear who will lead me on until he's got me where he wants me. I seek out William in all his dark, treacherous places. I seek him in the knowledge that I shall force him to reveal his truth. I seek him in places where he has no logical reason for being. I don't feel completed by this task. Instead I feel sick to my stomach, caught up in the queasy nausea of uncertainty.

And still I walk on.

There are tall brown buildings on either side of me, and I listen for footsteps. I scan the alley, breathing slowly and deliberately. What a dull, unhappy little area this is, consisting of weeds, cracked concrete, and dark, foul-smelling puddles. This is a place devoid of love. Before me are two turnoffs, two options, right and left. Where has William scurried? I look left, no sign of him. I look right, and see him sitting on a trash can halfway down the alley.

When I'm a meter from my prey, I catch sight of a dark shape out of the corner of my eye and look up. It's a dead bat, feet fused to the electricity cable that runs overhead, glued to the spot by thousands of volts. But it isn't the feet that have been the downfall of this creature, it is the elegant sweep of its wing, those instruments of flight. Halfway through a graceful wing beat, the bat has brushed lightly against the cruel hum of death and created a current loop. Now it stays here, as if caught by a powerful camera. Its wing fused, bent back in an arc.

William looks up at the bat, then looks at me. "I thought this might be a good place to wait for you," he says. "Under a dead thing."

"That's a very clever party trick," I say, then I look back at the bat. "That poor creature is probably the most beautiful thing I've seen in a long time."

"It's horrible," he says. "Like most dead things."

I find my heart resting to a quiet stillness, my breathing returning to a shallow, easy pattern. I feel as if I should bow my head and offer thanks to this frozen, damaged creature that flies no more. There is something compelling in its cold, leathery skin, its wicked, sharp claws.

"I've studied everything about you," says William.

"Do you think it lived around here?" I ask, nodding toward the bat. "Was this its hunting ground?"

"Everything," he reiterates.

I turn my attention to him, surprised to see how small and insignificant he looks. "Why would you bother?" I say.

"Your life, your likes," he says. "Every photo, every story."

As much as I try to ward him off with indifference, I can't help feeling violated by this intrusion. How dare he steal my life like that, study it in fine detail without my permission? "What in God's name are you looking for?" I ask. "Because you won't find it in me."

"I sincerely hope I do," he says, and there is a desperation in his look that contradicts his menace. "Every photo," he says. "But the one photo that fascinated me more than anything else was of you being carried from the restaurant."

"At last! You got it right. I was carried . . ."

"By a policeman," says William. "You had something in your hands."

The napkins. So, we have come to this. "What do you *really* know about the napkins?"

He stands, smiling, as if he's tricked me into revealing some secret code. "I know that they hold the key . . ." he says.

"To what?" I demand.

For a brief second William freezes, a rush of bewilderment

crossing his face. It's so fast that I almost miss it, then he adopts a calm, fake-serene expression, smiling again. He isn't in control of the game, after all. He's making it up as he goes along, and I feel a surge of power. Normally, I'd want to break away in blind panic at a moment like this, afraid of any situation where nobody is in charge. But not this time.

"I want you to tell me more stories," he says.

"Stories?" I say.

He nods. "There's so much bullshit surrounding that siege. No one ever tells the real story. That thing you told me about the stairs . . . that was real. I need to hear that stuff . . ."

I feel a curious tingling in my fingertips, and I shake my hands to remove the pins and needles. Why doesn't he scare me? He knows about the napkins, but he hasn't read them. Could he possibly understand the girl that Theo wrote about? Or would she give him goose bumps that would creep and crawl along his skin like ice?

"I don't tell stories anymore," I say. "Not unless I want to."

I take a step closer to him, *my* turn to be menacing.

"And the stories I tell, William, will be the ones I choose to tell."

Closer.

"They'll break your heart. They'll leave it shattered, because that's what I have to share."

His eyes widen.

"And I'll tell you those stories gladly, William, when I'm ready."

I am almost standing on his toes now. He has no comeback, no retort or further bargaining chip to play. He looks up at me, small and terrified.

"You're different," he says.

"That's what makes me so interesting," I whisper, then I turn to leave. William, however, has not played his last card after all. He grabs me by the upper arm and wheels me around.

"Wait!" he yells. "Don't leave . . ."

"Let me go!" I struggle to keep my voice calm. He is strong, and his grip is beginning to crush my arm.

"You've got it wrong," he says. "I'm not here to hurt you . . ."

How can he make that statement? How can he know with such certainty? I look down at his hand gripping my arm painfully. I see the play of his muscles, his grip, the tension in his skin, the force he is exerting.

"You *are* hurting me," I say.

"Just listen, there's lots I want to talk to you about . . ."

"You're hurting me," I repeat.

He doesn't respond, just intensifies his grip, squeezes harder. With one flex of his wrist he could bend my knees. With another, he could force my face into the ground. With another, he could have me begging him to stop. I am no match for his strength. We both recognize that, both read the messages flying back and forth from my arm to his hands, from my eyes to his heart. We stare at each other, caught in a moment, and neither of us know how to move on.

"You were right," I hiss, surprised at how breathless I sound. "I am different now."

Then I swing my free arm as hard as I can and smack him in the side of the face. There is an awful crack that resonates around the alley, and William drops his grip, stunned, his hands going up to the red mark forming on his skin. My hand is aching, but I ignore it, concentrating on a tiny trickle of blood that has formed under his eye. My ring, an eighteenth birthday present from

Nancy, has cut through his skin. He glares at me, and I glare back, gulping in air, failing to get enough. We stand this way for a few seconds, shocked, his hand smudging the trickle of blood into his cheek, breaking the clean red line that has started to flow. I can feel the bruising on my palm, the pain in my ring finger where it was squeezed between gold and bone, the jarring in my arm.

Then he speaks, his voice quiet, hurt, his words devastating. "When are you going to stop believing in him?" he says.

I turn and run.

JOHN WAYNE
O'GRADY

It was dark again, and the hostages prepared for the gloomy inevitability of spending yet another night with this madman. The men in the bathroom were in pitch dark, so they amused themselves by telling stories about their lives outside. The cook had been made as comfortable as possible with a rolled-up windbreaker-pillow. He woke not long after being dragged into the bathroom, his head a screaming mess of pain. Within minutes, he was vomiting and complaining of dizziness. It was clear that he was suffering from a concussion, and the Vietnam veteran had banged on the door, calling out to O'Grady for some medical help. Eventually they heard Constantine outside the door, hissing at them to shut up before O'Grady did something really bad.

"O'Grady said you'll just have to help James as best you can," said Constantine.

Outside the bathroom, the female hostages were doing only

marginally better. The old woman complained of chest pains, and her complexion seemed to have deteriorated to a pale gray. She was made as comfortable as possible, and she quickly fell into a fitful sleep. As it grew late, the need for food began to cloud every decision and action, until the two burger-queens plucked up the courage to ask O'Grady if they could prepare something to eat. He refused, saying they would have to be punished for their rebelliousness. They then begged the gunman to allow some medical help for the cook. This caused O'Grady to descend into another dangerous tantrum, so they withdrew to quieter, darker reaches of the restaurant to stay out of his way.

There seemed to be no purpose to the gunman's actions now, no strutting or lecturing or organizing of the "comrades." He wandered about aimlessly for a while, then slumped into his favorite chair near the landing, turning his head toward the police lights that flooded down the stairway.

The young girl had been given a pair of gym shorts from the smaller of the two burger-queens. A safety pin was found and the shorts were pinned into place under the skirt, which had been rinsed of any urine.

"I was supposed to be at the gym last night," said the burger-queen as she tightened the shorts around Freda's tiny midriff. "What a joke, eh?"

The girl did not laugh. She tugged at the shorts to test their staying power, then went to sit against a wall. She'd only just settled when Constantine tapped her on the shoulder and led her to an out-of-the-way corner of the restaurant.

"I want you to come to the storeroom," he said.

"What for?" asked the girl.

"You know . . . your medicine."

"I don't need medicine," she replied.

"Look," sighed Constantine. "Wouldn't you like to be away from him for a while? There's a flashlight in the storeroom, I haven't told O'Grady about it. We could put that on and see . . ."

"See what? You writing on your napkins?" hissed the child.

"So what if I do write on the napkins?" snapped Constantine, his voice growing louder and angrier. "At least it gets us away from that bastard for a while. God . . . Five minutes is all I'm asking for. Come on . . . be a good kid."

"No," said Freda, backing away from Constantine. "I don't want to."

"*He* wants you to," said Constantine. "He told me. He wants you to have your medicine. Don't go bothering him, just come . . . For a minute or two."

Now the girl hesitated, looking in O'Grady's direction, and the manager took her by the arm and led her gently, but firmly, to the storeroom. They went inside quietly, and were gone for several minutes before returning back to the gloomy restaurant.

Constantine went into the kitchen without a further glance at the girl and searched through the refrigerators. The red-haired woman walked into the kitchen after Constantine. She whispered in the manager's ear that the gunman seemed lost in his own world.

"Whatya want me to do about it?" hissed Constantine. "You saw what happened to James."

"No, no, no . . ." said the woman, her face as red as her hair. "I wasn't meaning that. I thought we could probably cook some food up . . . we need to eat."

"Do what you like," muttered the manager. "Most of it is going bad in the fridges, but there's still meat in the freezer . . . if it hasn't already thawed."

"Do you think . . . ?" she began to ask, but Constantine had walked away.

Several of the women came into the kitchen then to prepare food. As they opened fridges and cooked meat as silently as possible, a reverential soft light illuminating them from the gas burners, they relaxed into whispered conversations.

"I'm Suzy, by the way."

"God. Isn't that stupid that we've never exchanged names? I'm Melissa . . ."

"Kylie."

"Carmel."

"It's so quiet up there," said Suzy, glancing up at the ceiling.

"You don't suppose . . ." began Melissa, then she stopped.

"What?" said Kylie.

"Nothing . . ."

"Go on."

"You don't suppose they've given up on us, do you?"

There was a brief silence as they each struggled with this thought, then Suzy spoke up. "I think they're getting ready to come in again. They haven't turned on the lights since the raid last night. . . . So I think . . . maybe . . ."

"Of course they are," said Melissa. "I didn't think . . ." She looked at Carmel, the boy's mother, and shrugged apologetically.

"I saw a microphone," said Carmel. She'd been quiet throughout this discussion.

"You're joking! Where!"

"Ssh. At the entrance this morning. I think it was a microphone. When I was checking the doors. It was poking under the door. I didn't say anything . . ."

"God. They're listening."

"Yes."

They contemplated the significance of this piece of information. If the police had been listening all day, then they would have heard the threat on Constantine's life. They would have heard the cook's attack, and the way O'Grady beat the men. They would have heard it all, yet they still hadn't moved in.

"Do you think they can hear everything?" asked Melissa.

"I . . . I don't know. It wasn't a big microphone . . . It may not have even been a microphone . . ."

"Maybe they only heard the shouting," said Kylie.

The others agreed that this was probably all the police could hear with a microphone stuck all the way up the stairs.

"Maybe they *won't* come," said Suzy.

"Why?" asked Melissa.

"Because they'll know that he means business. It'll be too risky."

They allowed this depressing thought to sink in, finishing the rest of their preparation in silence. Once the meat was cooked, they sat on the floor to eat.

"We'll find a way out," said Suzy, and the others nodded their heads.

They talked about nothing in particular after that, enjoying some normal company after the tension of the last day or so. The women quietly debated about asking the gunman if they could take some food in for the men. Carmel, the boy's mother, was all for it, but some of the others were more cautious, not wanting to risk another tantrum. In the end, it was decided that they would ask if they could take food for the boy and the cook, then judge O'Grady's mood from there. Suzy, the red-haired woman, volunteered to speak to him, and she went into the restaurant, making sufficient noise for the gunman to emerge from his reverie and shout, "What the hell is going on?"

"Nothing," said Suzy. "We were just wondering about . . . um . . . food for the boy . . ."

"There's no food," said O'Grady wearily. "Can't you see what they're trying to do with us? Can't you see how scared this reeducation program makes them? They'd do anything to stop you knowing the truth. Gather up the others, it's time we had a talk."

Suzy went into the kitchen shaking her head and told the others that they were required by O'Grady. This time they sat in the seats, in the darkness of the restaurant, O'Grady in the long spike of light that spilled out from the landing. He looked like a prophet, bathed in an unnatural glow.

"Well, here we are," said O'Grady. "And what a long way we've come. There's six of us now . . . six comrades to go forth into the fray and do battle. I had thought that we might have taken longer to get here, but it's time to accelerate the program. And I think you're all nearly ready, yes I do."

Several of the women had eager expressions on their faces, hopeful that this new phase in their "education" might actually lead to their freedom.

"Yes," he continued, "just the final test to go."

There was a slight murmur as he said the word *test,* a suspicious reaction to the caprice of the man. O'Grady put the shotgun down against his seat and held his hands out to them, palms forward, playing the prophet role to its fullest. He pointed to Suzy and asked, "How will you spread the word?"

She blushed instantly, and looked around for some kind of support from the others. They gave her encouraging looks, and she cleared her throat.

"I have two sisters," said Suzy. "And I know that they . . . they, too, hate the corporate . . . puppet-masters . . ."

"Why?" asked O'Grady.

"Because . . . they work for a multinational firm and they've seen what terrible things the corporations do to innocent people. They don't like it . . . and they're ready for the truth just like I was."

"Good! Good!" boomed O'Grady. "How ready are *you* for the truth?"

"Pardon?" said Suzy.

"Would you take up arms?"

"Arms? You mean . . . guns?"

"Yes," said O'Grady. "The puppet-masters won't give in easy. Will you fight them down to the wire? Maybe even shoot a few of them?"

"I . . . er . . ." Suzy blushed, obviously caught in a moral dilemma, not wishing to pledge to an action she would never carry out, yet desperate to be freed from this underground hellhole. "Yes," she said, with as definite a note in her voice as she could muster. "I'll join a gun club . . . or something. I'll learn how to shoot . . . anything."

"Excellent!" boomed O'Grady. He pointed to Kylie, one of the burger-queens. "You next."

Kylie took Suzy's lead and waffled on about how she could see the truth now, and how she would hold study nights and get all her friends to listen to the truth of John Wayne O'Grady. And, once again, he challenged her willingness to take up arms for the cause. She answered that she would.

They each in their turn followed this course, seeing it as their only door to the outside world. The old woman, Mary, told how she would enlist her bowling club and make sure that they told all their grandchildren. Carmel, whose boy was still locked away from her, told how she would run classes at her son's primary school and spread the word of John Wayne O'Grady. Each of them was careful to mention the word *truth* several times and O'Grady's name even more. All through this the gunman beamed at them, soaking in the false glory.

When it came to Constantine's turn, the manager stood up

and said that he would personally resign from Family Value and stand outside their restaurants handing out pamphlets. O'Grady laughed, telling Constantine that he had, once again, chosen the fool's way out. That the Left today was wasting its time with pathetic pamphlet drops and court cases when anyone with half a brain could see that direct action was needed.

They fell silent after that, waiting for the next move from O'Grady, when the girl spoke.

"What about me?" she said. "You haven't asked me."

"Asked you?" boomed O'Grady, bursting into a laugh. "Will you listen to that? She is my best comrade. My best soldier. You'd all do well to follow this child. Yes, indeed."

He patted the girl on the back, beaming proudly. "Mine is the plan of inspired genius," said O'Grady, rubbing the child absently on the back. "Mine is the only way to shake people out of their complacency. Look at this child . . . look at all of you. Before you met me you were self-centered slobs who never gave a single thought to the society you lived in. Anything went wrong and you blamed someone else, but you were only blaming your fellow comrades. Now you know the truth. Now you know who to blame. Yes, we are close now. The program hasn't failed. It is nearly there . . . nearly there. Good work, all of you. Even though the puppets have put us in darkness and given us cold, you have all stuck to the program. Is there any food? Surely it's time to eat."

"I'll go prepare some," said Suzy, walking quickly into the kitchen before O'Grady had a chance to see that they'd already helped themselves. The others followed her, but they were too hasty, too fidgety and nervous about their departure, and the gunman grew suspicious.

He walked slowly into the kitchen, his eyes adjusting to the gloom, and saw the already prepared food that was meant for the men.

"What the hell is this?" he asked.

"We . . . ah . . . prepared some earlier," said Suzy, deciding to go for the truth rather than lie.

"When?" asked O'Grady.

"When . . . um . . . when you were resting."

"The hell you did!" shouted O'Grady. "How dare you accuse your commanding officer of sleeping on the job? How dare you?"

The women closed their eyes, the tiny glimmer of hope snuffed out in an instant, crushed under the unpredictable temperament of John Wayne O'Grady.

"You scheming bitches!" he screamed, picking up the trays of uneaten food and smashing them against the wall. "You liars. All of you. Liars! You're not ready. None of you. Get the hell out of my sight."

They shuffled out of the kitchen, thinking they'd got away with no more than a roasting, but O'Grady followed them.

"Oh no, you don't. No way!" he shouted. "Not in here. You can all go into the women's bathroom. All of you. You'll be punished, you hear me?"

"But Mary . . . the old woman . . ." began Suzy.

O'Grady waved his hand at her dismissively, and they knew that there was no point in arguing. The women made their way into the restroom, taking whatever they could grab for warmth and comfort with them. As far as they were concerned, it was going to be a long, cold night. The girl shuffled in behind them, but O'Grady grabbed hold of her arm and pulled her close to him.

"Not you, honey," he said. "You haven't done nothing to upset old John Wayne."

Freda struggled against him, but O'Grady gripped her tighter, putting a deep blue bruise on her arm that her mother would only notice days later.

"Just you and the fool now," whispered O'Grady as the restroom door closed behind the women. He locked the door, then turned to his last two captives. "Look what I'm left with," he said, shaking his head. "You two are my bookends." He pointed to Freda. "I'd hoped that twelve would go into the world, but we'll just have to start the revolution with the one, honey. With you."

"Me?"

"Yes. Will you stick with old John Wayne and make sure he doesn't have to do this alone?"

"Okay," said the child, a look of wonder on her face.

"You can do it, can't you, hon? You're gonna be my revolutionary."

"With a gun?" she asked.

O'Grady laughed, slapping Constantine on the back with a loud *whack* that sent the man stumbling forward. "Did you hear that, Theo? She needs a gun. She is well and truly ready."

"This is not right," said Constantine.

"Not right?" shouted O'Grady. "It's the only right thing there is at the moment."

He leaned his shotgun up against a wall and walked over to the girl, holding her against his stomach in a warm embrace that lasted for well over a minute. There were tears in O'Grady's eyes, rolling down his cheeks and falling onto the child's head. The girl's face was impossible to read. Eventually Constantine broke into the "tender" moment and said, "Can I go into the bathroom now?"

O'Grady ignored him. Still clutching the girl to his stomach, he asked, "You like music?" She nodded. "Well, how about John Wayne O'Grady sings you a song? Eh? A cowboy song?"

She didn't reply.

O'Grady sang. "Hush a bye/ Don't you cry/ Daddy's gone to get the horses/ Blacks and grays/ Dapples and bays/ All the pretty little horses. . . ."

Constantine coughed loudly, but O'Grady kept singing, so he stepped into the man's line of vision and spoke in an even louder voice, shattering the musical interlude. "Look, I think she needs her medicine now."

O'Grady stopped singing. "No medicine," he said irritably.

"But her cough . . ."

"I said no medicine!" shouted O'Grady.

The manager paced around the restaurant, muttering to himself as O'Grady continued to hug the child, oblivious to Constantine. Eventually, Constantine made it back to the storeroom door, and quietly opened it, then slipped inside. O'Grady didn't notice the departure, he was too busy whispering to the child who was squeezed up against his heaving stomach. "You can't do bargains with the truth, honey. You know that now. The truth takes no prisoners, gives no quarter. The truth will always get to you in the end. Remember these things. You're my only hope."

O'Grady looked up for a moment at the gloomy restaurant, but his eyes seemed unfocused and distant.

"We're all alone, hon," he whispered. "Just you and me. I like it like that. Just you and me."

NAPKiN

N

Crazy. The prick is in love with that kid. They
hug each other, and just now he sings to her.
He looks at me. Why does he do that? He hates me.
Do you remember the flowers? The unusual rose . . .
Heard a noise. Remember me. I know you will. I'll
be . . . He's out there. The crazy kid is with him.
They'll come for me soon. When you read this, make
sure everyone knows what happened. Okay? If I
don't get out. I gotta get out of this. I can't
die. I just want to go . . .

FREDA OPPERMAN

Somehow I make it home, walking, running, dodging cars on the road, making sure I don't step on the cracks. Yes, I make it home to my street, but why does my breathing still pitch and roll and grab me around the throat? And why do my eyes see things that simply cannot be there?

My front door is open. The gateway to Fortress Opperman, that unpassable place, sanctuary to the good and the iconic, is available for all the world to enter. How can this be? This is the first time in my living memory that I've ever seen our front door open like this. Is everything in my life to be ripped open? I stand on the footpath, stunned.

A man passes with his dog, a large hound on a leash. The animal pulls and tugs, sniffing into our yard, down our path as the man waits patiently, oblivious to my presence.

"What do you think you're doing?" I shout.

"Pardon?" says the man.

"That's my house in there! My house!"

"Sorry . . . The dog . . . He wanted . . ."

The man shrugs and pulls the dog away from the yard, urging it on down the street. He glances back at me, shaking his head.

I was made promises, Goddamn it! Promises.

I walk toward the door. Nancy is inside. I can hear her bird-like footsteps. She is going from there to here, from here to there. Looking for something. Words, perhaps? I stand on the "welcome" mat and contemplate the open doorway. This breach of Opperman security. My mind clicks through a series of portals, releasing snippets of my encounter with William. Blood. Pain. Anger. Attack. And his parting words.

When are you going to stop believing in him?

I remember the moment I stopped believing in Santa Claus. It wasn't due to some blunder my parents made. There was probably lots of evidence that I ignored, because Santa is a powerful myth to let go of. No, I stopped believing because of questions and answers. I asked my father if Santa was real, and instead of giving me the usual Hugh Opperman vague brush-off, he said, "Freda, even if you don't believe in Santa, you'll still get presents at Christmas. That's the way it works."

That's the way it works. We can let go of our beliefs, our logic, our ethics, our morals, any truth, just as long as what we replace it with still gives us goodies.

In the evidence given at the inquest after the siege, the police showed a torn-up Anti-Corporation Group pamphlet they'd found in O'Grady's trash. I think it was probably the one he took outside his restaurant. The one that resulted in his demotion. This pamphlet was all about the destruction of natural rain forests in

South America, a favorite subject of O'Grady's long-winded lectures. "The national production of rice and grains is crucial to many Latin-American countries, yet the farmers of these nations stopped growing these crops. Production dropped from 80 percent use of the land to 20 percent. And what took over all that land? Cattle . . . beef . . . Family Value hamburger fillings for hungry slobs who live thousands of miles away."

The police also found used packaging from Family Value takeout hamburgers in O'Grady's trash. Somehow I don't think it was ideology that made him give up his shitty life to become a revolutionary.

I heard him talk about the future of his revolution, heard his voice quiver and break at the thought of the glory that would be his one day. I listened to the hurt in his voice when the men went against him. Saw the way he held that shotgun, nestled it in his arms, rested its weight as if it were a natural extension of his body. Saw the look on his face whenever he pointed it at one of the hostages. I even held it myself, that magical, powerful thing that solved all of his problems.

O'Grady stopped believing in Santa for a much bigger prize.

And me?

All is silent inside the house, until I hear shuffling. Ah, nibble, nibble . . . who's that nibbling in my house? Nancy Opperman is in here somewhere. That minimal passing through the air, that wingless beat. She is here, nibbling away at forbidden fruit.

I walk in the door and quietly lock it behind me, then go straight to my room. It is a mess, a jumble of scattered belongings. The box has been removed from the laundry basket, and I go immediately to the curtains. They are untouched. Reaching behind, I slip the napkins from their resting place. Look at them now. Theo's letters, roaming far from acceptable topics such as the weather, breaching good manners by daring to speculate on a nine-year-old girl, his charge, his ward of the restaurant. How dare he write about me? How dare he try to deny it, too.

"What are you writing?"

"Nothing. Ssh."

"Is it about me?"

"No. It's about him."

"What are you saying?"

"That we all hate him. That we don't want to be his soldiers. That we never wanted to be his soldiers. That he's a big joke."

I remember that.

Theo was the joke, making up lies to fool a young girl. Lies that kicked up and spat in his face. He *was* writing about me. Freda, who held the gun. Freda who was crushed into the smell and heave of the sick bastard. Freda who was bad herself.

William thinks he knows the truth, thinks these napkins will reveal all the missing parts of me. He has seen photographs. Perhaps he has even talked with Nancy Opperman. Her duplicity may have gone even that far. They thought I'd be a pushover, but they haven't been looking closely enough. They thought I was passive, meek, troubled, and confused. Watch your back, sweet William.

With the napkins safely locked in my hand, I go in search of N.O. Her office is first, and I stop to listen. The *shuffle-shuffle* is still distant, coming from some other part of the house. I look inside. It is so neat in here, so ordered. Her desk sits before a large window, arranged in an orderly fashion, stark contrast to the scene outside where Mother Nature runs wild, doing mad cartwheels across our backyard. It's almost as if N.O. has deliberately set this juxtaposition up, the sane woman inside, the crazy one out.

It is quiet as I walk in, breathing the faint odor of Nancy's perfume, the traces of her in every corner of the room. Neat photos sit framed on the walls, parts of my mother's history. There's all sorts of images here, such as the newspaper clipping announcing the bankruptcy of the Family Value franchise that owned the underground restaurant—N.O.'s victory dance. And here is a photo of me with Nancy, huddled together on a couch, with television lights looming over us and a camera so menacingly close. We are small, crammed into a brilliant corner, with dark shapes closing in on us. This was one of Nancy's triumphs, an interview on national prime-time TV. Young Freda Opperman, and her mother. How old was I? Ten?

"What will he want to ask me?"

"Oh, I expect he'll ask about what happened. Don't worry, I'll be there. If you feel uncomfortable, just squeeze my arm, okay? I'll speak up for you."

"What does he want to know?"

"Just stories, love. Your stories. This is for all the other boys and girls out there who worried about you. This is to let them know that you're fine. Remember all those pictures and letters they sent?"

"Will I . . . will he . . . what if I can't . . ."

"You'll be fine. I'm there. Just be polite, darling. Just be pleasant and nice and talk about the good things, the people who were kind. Just about that. You don't have to mention anything else . . .

I squeezed so hard and so often, I gave Nancy bruises that lasted for days.

The filing cabinet is ajar, strangely untidy for N.O., and I go to it, opening it wider for a quick peek. There's a mass of files crammed into the top drawer, but one sits up slightly above the others, as if it's waving to me. Obviously, Nancy has been in a bit of a hurry. I pull the file, which bears no name, and sit with it at Nancy's desk. There are bank statements and accounts, reports about something called the Opperman Trust. I've heard of most of Mom's organizations, but I've never come across the Opperman Trust. Judging by the balance on one of the statements, it's doing very nicely. It would take a large injection of cash to build up a balance like this. A lottery win, perhaps, or a successful court case against a giant corporation?

Several letters have been clipped together, and I release them, scanning their contents. Mostly they seem to be from people asking for help, but who are they? Destitute strangers who thought Nancy Opperman would be a soft touch? That doesn't make sense, especially considering that Nancy has coughed up some fair-sized amounts of money from the Opperman Trust for these folk. "*. . . to cover medical expenses . . . professional counseling . . . ongoing educational costs for your son . . .*"

I sit back and let go of the breath I've been holding ever since I found this file. So much seems to have been done under the Opperman banner. So many tireless efforts to change the world, to assist the needy, to fight a good cause. And yet, I am attached to this effort by name only.

I pick up a cigarette lighter from Nancy's desk and twirl it around. My mother's a nerve-end smoker, seeking out the ciggies whenever things are going badly. Obviously, she's been giving them a workout lately. Six months ago, if I'd found this file, I would have shoved it back into the cabinet and forgotten all about it.

There's so much I've forgotten.

The burden of remembering is coming back to me, and not in the guise of an artificial cause created by my mother or a phony crusade that bears my name. Taking the napkins and the cigarette lighter, I go in search of my mother's shuffles. She's in the living room when I find her, making such a mess I almost "tch tch."

"Cleaning up, Mom?" I say.

Nancy wheels around, her face bright red. "Freda! Where have you been?"

"Oh, come on, Mom. You know where I've been . . ."

"Before that," she says, her patience obviously running thin. "When you were supposed to be at work."

"Dad's," I answer nonchalantly.

"What were you there for? I dropped you at Guardian Angel!"

It's fascinating to watch her try to maintain a veneer of normality, even when her world is crumbling around her. Here stands my mother, knee deep in rubble, rooting around in her own living room for missing napkins that she *knows* I've hidden somewhere, and she's chastising me for being late for work.

"Looking for these?" I ask, holding up the offending face wipers.

"No," she answers, blushing a deeper red. Then, "Yes, actually I was."

"What did you think I was going to do with them?" I ask. "Show the world?" I don't give her a chance to answer. "I have a lighter with me," I say, producing her little plastic flamethrower. "We could burn them now if you want."

"Don't be ridiculous," says Nancy. "That wasn't what I was looking for them for . . ."

"Oh, Mom. No lies, okay? You've always wanted to do this."

I shove the napkins under my arm, then hold up the lighter. "Do you reckon we'd need a big flame to start with? Or will a little one do?"

"Freda," says Nancy, that warning tone in her voice. "What's going on?"

"Just a little bonfire, Mom."

I spark the lighter. The pathetic little flame struggles to shoot from the gas jet. Running low. Holding my hand over the flame, I say, "Let's burn those pesky napkins, shall we?"

Nancy stares at me incredulously as I continue to hold my hand over the flame, its heat digging deeper and deeper into my flesh.

"Freda?"

Starting to sear now, to burn away at the skin, the binding that holds me in.

"Stop it!" she shouts, knocking the lighter from my grip.

"See," I say, holding her gaze. "I knew you couldn't do it."

Nancy retrieves the lighter, and I stuff the napkins into the back pockets of my jeans. It makes an unsightly bulge, but that's nothing compared with the stinging pain in my hand. Nancy and I glare at each other for a moment, then she turns away under the pretense of picking up a few scattered cushions.

"This has just been a misunderstanding, Freda. That's all . . ."

She tidies up, cleaning the detritus from her frantic search, putting everything back to "normal" again, that state she craves, that state she lost so decidedly in the past.

"So, tell me, mother," I say, watching her rearrange the cushions. "Exactly how did you dig up William, then?"

"William?" says Mom, her surprise so fake that I laugh. She drops her pretense. "He approached me," she says. "At Guardian Angel. Said he'd get an article into the university magazine. He talked about his own life a bit . . . and I thought if you two met . . . He had a good understanding of what has been done for victims of crime since the siege. Honestly, I had no idea he would write what he did . . ."

"No, you just thought you'd get a bit of publicity out of it."

"Freda," says Nancy. "That's not what I was after at all. I know you won't understand this, but what I did was for you. I thought . . . with William . . . I thought he'd be helpful. I thought he'd help you see how you've made so much good out of what happened."

"Me?" I laugh, but it's a sad sound that emerges. "I haven't done it, *you* have . . ."

"Of course I've done it, but only because of you and what you did. You made it through those horrible long hours in the restaurant and now you've got your adult life ahead of you. Sure I've protected you, but I can't do it forever. You're not nine anymore. I made sure that what the public saw back then was exactly what you were, an innocent child. So don't blame me if I'm also trying to make them see you as an innocent adult."

"So much of my life is bullshit," I say. "Why does it have to be like that? You do everything in my name, but I've got nothing to do with it. I just found out about something called the Opperman Trust . . ."

"How did you find that?"

"By snooping. How else? You've been giving money to strangers . . ."

"No. Not strangers . . ."

". . . in my name. It's all crap. And you wonder why I cling to these napkins? At least they're real."

Nancy shakes her head, that same sad, defeated look she gets whenever I mention the napkins. "I wish to God you could let go of them," she says. Her voice sounds dog tired, as if she doesn't believe I'll ever hear that message. "They're not you . . ."

I take out the napkins, hold them up to Nancy, but they hurt my hand. Each corner digs into my burn, and I shove them back into my pocket. Tears blur my vision, make me lose her for a second. Lose my mother. I wipe away the warm trickle that runs down my cheek and see her anew. "These napkins are all I've got," I whisper.

"What about me, Freda?" says Nancy, her eyes wet now. "You've got me."

"I'm sorry, Mom," I say, looking down at my feet. "You weren't there."

"Oh, Freda . . ."

She wants me to absolve her, to give her release from this awful moment, but she's played one too many games with my story. I can't forgive that, not yet. "I know that William knows about the napkins," I say.

"Are you sure he knows?" she says. Still playing, stalling for time. She's already come to the same conclusion, why else would she ransack her own house?

"And I'm guessing that you told him," I say.

"Oh, God, Freda. No. Never . . ."

For the first time in my life I see real panic in my mother's eyes. There's more to this little game than has so far been revealed. It frightens me that I don't know who's running the show. Nancy or William.

"Freda, believe me. I didn't tell William," she says. "He hasn't been straight with me, either. He made some promises. I'll talk to him. I'll sort it all out." She's still trying to be in control. "Give me a few days. It'll be fine . . ."

"No," I shout. "Not anymore."

She glares at me, her eyes cold. N.O. has never coped well with me shouting. Eventually she says in a voice that is measured with reserve and bitterness, "Then let me at least get something for that burn."

"Don't bother," I say, turning to leave.

"Where are you going?" she asks.

"Underground," I mutter.

I walk out then, her confused expression a lasting image in my brain. She'll work it out soon enough. What else is left to me now but the underground, that place of unfinished business? But not down those stairs. No, I can't go there. Instead I shall go where I am closest to my true self, a ghostly half spirit who doesn't belong in any world.

I head for the bus stop, tired, the napkins uncomfortable in my back pocket. The stinging in my hand has me close to tears, but I ignore it. This is not finished yet.

Each passing car seems to herald a shift in the afternoon, as the day recedes toward night. Lights come on—overhead, on cars— pinpoints in the evanescent gloom. When at last my bus arrives, I pull myself on and sit, too tired to think at all.

My stop comes, and I get off the bus, half running through the darkening suburban streets toward my father's workshop. Dad is trudging up the hill, going home, and I wave to him from a distance. He's confused by my arrival, having deposited me in the city only a few hours ago.

"Hi," I say. "You going home now?"

"Yes. What's up? Did you leave something?"

"No. Um . . . I need a place to sit for a bit."

"Here?" he says. "Why don't you come home with me? Or . . ."

He doesn't finish his sentence, caught short by the need in my eyes or the flush of my cheek. "Hang on a second," he says, tossing a toolbox into the back of the truck and lashing it down with an elastic strap. "You sure you want to park here?" asks Dad, turning to me from the truck. "I mean, it's no trouble having you . . ."

I shake my head with as gentle a rejection as I can muster. "No, I just want to be alone for a while . . . do you mind?"

"Of course not."

"I like it here," I say, peering in through the still opened doorway to his warmly lit workshop. I can see the fellas are huddled around a piece of lumber in the vice, blowing away ghostly sawdust from its edge. This is the company I need to keep right now, these ethereal carpenters with their sure hands and their steady gazes. These guys are slow to conclusions. I like that.

"What are you looking at in there?" asks Dad, following my gaze into his supposedly empty workshop.

"Another world," I say.

He grunts, used now to me uttering odd sentences. I turn to him. "Dad," I say. "Do you remember that time I came up the stairs during the siege?"

He gives me a startled look, then nods his head. "Of course I do. It was . . . well . . . nobody could make much sense of it."

"What did you see?" I ask.

"I saw you, Freda."

"What did I look like?"

"Look like?" Dad is more than startled now, he's disturbed by my question, as if I've stepped over the line of good taste by bringing up the subject.

"I'd like to know," I say.

He sighs. "You looked . . . small," he says. "That's what I remember. Like a tiny doll in this huge, bright place. Fragile . . . At first I was relieved that you were unharmed. Then . . . I thought for just a second, I thought that you'd break or something."

"I did break, didn't I?" I say. "You survive, and everyone thinks you're still in one piece . . . but you're not. That's the thing people forget."

Dad turns away to give the toolbox a few shoves, testing to see if it's set tight. It is. "I remember how upset you were," he says. "I guess it was because you wanted to be with us . . ."

His voice fades away like the daylight around him, unable to finish the thought behind his sentence. I let him rest the matter there, in his assumption that little Freda, underground Freda, was upset because she wanted to be with her parents. He might imagine that I was called back by the harsh command of John Wayne O'Grady. That I ran underground again, quivering, afraid of what the man would do with that terrible gun. Why should I hurt him with the truth?

"Sure you don't want to come with me?" he asks.

"No, I can close up the workshop for you."

"Okay, Freda," Dad says, standing awkwardly in the street. He makes a small, jerky movement toward the cab then stops, returning to me with one last thought in his eyes. It comes to nothing, and he waves quickly, then climbs into the truck and drives away. I watch him vanish, staying on the street for a moment or two, then I walk into the workshop.

The fellas don't pay any attention to me, too busy concentrating on the piece of wood. I wonder for a moment what the fascination is for this hard, scratchy stuff that we cut from the trees. It's always given me splinters. Going over to Dad's scrap box, I push aside all the scraps and scratch around for a few minutes with no particular purpose in mind. A memory comes to me, a happy recollection of my time spent in this workshop as a younger girl, and I get down on my knees to poke around under one of the benches. Eventually my hand rests on a piece of soft timber, thrown under the bench many years ago. I pull it out, feeling its lightness as if it were hollow inside. I remember this wood, Dad used to give me pieces to play around with. He called it balsa wood, and I'd take blunt saw blades or old knives and carve at it for ages.

This piece is long, square on all sides, and I hold it on the crook of my arm, letting it nestle there. Removing Dad's piece of timber from the vice I put the balsa in. I have to be careful about how tightly I close the vice, not wanting to harm its surface. Then I take one of my father's spokeshaves, a two-handled tool with a sharp blade that I've watched him use many times before, and I begin to gently carve.

Carve out a shape.

This feels right. The most natural thing I've done in weeks. I shall make an artifact. I will forget all about my role in society or what constitutes a good person. I shall carve out this thing for me, and for me alone. And it will soothe me. It will take me down to the place below the stairs where I can drink deep again, wash my face and head in the waters of remembering and not come out screaming.

In the background, the fellas watch me, offering no ghostly advice, making no sound at all. Perhaps they have more faith in memories than I have. I hear a faraway child's voice. It comes with each stroke of the instrument, each shaping of the wood. This child is not crying, nor calling out in pain or fright.

Instead she is singing an incredibly sad, lonely song.

JOHN WAYNE

O'GRADY

Something woke him . . . a distant sound . . . muted . . . was it singing?

"What the hell is going on?" bellowed John Wayne O'Grady, sitting up too fast and feeling slightly queasy.

The girl emerged from the staff restroom, flinging water from her hands, and walked through the kitchen to the restaurant. She looked pale, with dark rings under her eyes and a wild, feral demeanor. The place was empty, and O'Grady struggled to remember what had happened. He'd been sleeping, and a noise had woken him.

"Where is everyone?" he asked.

The girl pointed to the bathrooms, and O'Grady nodded. Those bastards in there, let them rot.

"I heard singing," he said. "Was that you?"

The girl shrugged, and O'Grady scratched his head in frustration. Everything was getting out of hand. "What about Theo?" he said. "Where's he?"

The girl shrugged again, and for a brief second O'Grady panicked. Had Constantine somehow escaped? He calmed his mind, forcing it to run through the problem logically. A vague memory came to him. He'd been holding the girl, feeling the frailness of her, stroking her hair—something his parents never did to him—singing to her when the manager came buzzing in his ear with some annoying request. O'Grady shut his eyes, and finally an image came to him. Theo Constantine had gone into the storeroom, despite being told not to.

Theo had defied him.

O'Grady stood and marched over to the storeroom door, but it was locked from the inside. He searched through the set of keys in his pocket, but there was no key for the storeroom. "Get the hell out of here now before I get really angry," shouted O'Grady, banging on the door.

"No," came the sullen reply from the other side.

The girl joined O'Grady, a passive expression on her face. She looked on as the gunman paced outside the storeroom door, trying to think of what to do next.

"What's he doing in there?" muttered O'Grady. "Do you know?" He directed this question at the girl, and she instantly blushed.

"No," she mumbled, looking down at her feet.

"You know, don't you. What's he got in there?"

"Nothing," she said.

"What? Is it girlie magazines or something?"

"Girlie?" asked the girl.

O'Grady laughed and banged on the door again. "Come on, Theo. You got a few seconds to make your way out of your cubby before I blow the door open."

There was a pause on the other side of the door, then Constantine said, "Please don't do anything. I'm coming."

"You'd better be quick about it," said O'Grady.

The storeroom door opened, and Constantine emerged with a sheepish grin on his face. "Sorry," he said.

O'Grady laughed. "You sly old dog, Theo. Whatcha been doing in there?"

"Nothing . . ."

"I know," said O'Grady.

The manager shot a quick look at the girl and hissed, "Little snitching bitch!"

She looked at her shoes, avoiding eye contact with him, her face red, her shoulders slumped.

"Don't believe a word she told you," shouted Constantine. "She's a liar."

O'Grady slapped Constantine on the back and leered at him. "My, my, my," he said. "I just don't get you at all, Theo. After all you been through, you've still got time for a girlie magazine?"

Constantine shot the girl a puzzled glance, then looked back at O'Grady, trying to hide his confusion.

"At any other moment in history," said O'Grady, "I'd admire you. But I'm afraid you're gonna have to be punished."

"No!" shouted Constantine, but he was too late. O'Grady poked the end of the gun into the manager's chest, a violent jab that sat Constantine onto the seat of his pants. He remained on the floor sobbing, rubbing the painful bruise on his chest. "Jesus," he said, crying like a child. "You're gonna kill me. Just stop it."

O'Grady stared at him, a look of sheer disgust on his face. "Grow up, boy," he snarled.

"You nearly killed me!" sobbed Constantine.

O'Grady grinned at the girl. "Poke him. See if he's still alive."

"Poke him?" asked the girl.

"Yeah. Just give him one in the ribs."

The girl jabbed Constantine in the ribs with her fingers and the manager snarled back at her, "Leave me alone, you little freak."

"Yep, you survived your punishment all right," said O'Grady. He bent down to Theo's level and spoke in a quiet voice. "Go on out there and check on the doors for me. It's been a few hours since we had a look. Take too long, or try anything silly, and the next jab you feel will be a cartridge from this shotgun. Okay?"

Constantine stood reluctantly, giving the girl a defiant grunt before making his way to the stairwell and vanishing from sight.

"Well, sly old Theo," said O'Grady, peering into the store-room. He began to search the room, looking for Theo's girlie magazines. Pulling away at the shelves, O'Grady threw toilet rolls and bags of plastic spoons to the ground, but no magazines appeared. The girl stepped into the room after him. She was nervous about something, agitated.

"What are you doing?" she asked.

O'Grady ignored her, and the girl leaned against the door, her breath coming in short, rasping bouts, her face growing redder and redder. She worked hard at controlling herself, placing her grubby hands over her face to cover her mouth and nose. After a minute, she was able to breathe normally again, and she looked into the storeroom to see that O'Grady had virtually ransacked the place. The gunman was about to bend down and peer under the desk, when the girl called out to him.

"Show me the gun again."

"Not now," muttered O'Grady.

"I wanna know how you shoot the puppets," she demanded. "You said you'd teach me."

O'Grady looked at her and sighed. "You're a determined little miss, aren't you."

"Teach me! Scaredy-cat! Too afraid . . ."

"That's enough," barked O'Grady, and the girl stopped. "Nobody calls me afraid, okay? 'Cause I'm not afraid. I'm a soldier, and I'm your commanding officer. If you wanna be a soldier, too, then all right." He stood, wiping the grime from his already grubby trousers.

He walked into the middle of the restaurant. "Okay," said O'Grady as the girl joined him. "You're locked away in your classroom . . . with tables up against the door so the teacher can't get in."

"Where am I standing?" asked the girl.

"On another table addressing the comrades," said O'Grady, a grin on his face. "Tell 'em the truth, hon."

She climbed up onto a table, her legs wobbly. "Okay . . . um . . . There is no value in Family Value . . ."

"Yes, that's the way," laughed O'Grady. "You're up there, giving them the truth, when the puppets come to the door."

"And they try to shoot me . . . ?"

"No, no, hon. This is where you gotta be careful," said O'Grady. He walked over to her table and indicated for her to sit down. She sat with her legs over the edge of the table, swinging back and forth as O'Grady spoke. "When they come for you, hon, they're gonna be nice about it. They're gonna say they love you, that they want you to come and play with them. They're gonna use every trick in the book."

She listened wide-eyed, imagining the kindly teachers, the smiling policeman, all beckoning her to open the door and release the children.

"What do I do?" she asked.

"Do?" said O'Grady, standing abruptly. "You . . . you point your gun at them. You shout, 'Make a move and I'll shoot you dead!' You show them you won't be fooled."

"Okay," said the girl, standing on the table. "Let's pretend I shout that at them, but they won't go away. Now do I shoot at them?"

"Yep. That's when you shoot them."

"Show me," said the girl, hopping down off the table.

"Show you?" He laughed, pointing at the girl. "You just want to hold old John Wayne's gun again? Don't you?"

She nodded, and the gunman stepped in behind her, placing the gun in her hands.

"Now don't go squeezing that trigger, okay? This is just a practice run. First thing you do is aim at where the bad guys are."

He helped her aim the gun toward the imaginary posse of teachers and police officers, steadying the Barrett for her as she swayed with the weight.

"That's good. Of course, this is just pretend. Next you squeeze the trigger real gentle because you don't want to throw your aim off with any sudden movements."

"Can I do that?"

"No, not now, hon." He went to retrieve the gun, but the girl held it tightly.

"Give me the gun, hon."

She refused to let go of the shotgun, her finger slowly squeezing the trigger, her heart racing at a dangerous rate. Every muscle in her body tensed, waiting for the sound the shotgun would make, the explosion, the dramatic destruction. Tighter and tighter she squeezed, amazed at how hard it actually was to pull on the trigger.

"You gotta stop that . . ."

Her finger ached as she held the trigger on the edge of release, a mere millimeter away from the point of contact. Taking one last breath, she pulled with all her strength, and the trigger mechanism was released.

An empty, hollow *click* rang in her ear.

A click. A nothing. No explosion, no release. Just a disappointing anticlimax.

"It didn't go off," said the girl. "What's wrong with it?"

"Nothing's wrong with it," said O'Grady, taking the gun from her. He didn't seem surprised that it hadn't exploded, he didn't examine it, or check the cartridges, instead he placed the shotgun against the wall and sighed. The girl watched him, a suspicious expression on her face.

"Why didn't it go off?" she asked.

"It wasn't loaded," said O'Grady matter-of-factly. "Never has been."

The child stared at him for a full twenty seconds, a look of incredulity on her face. She shook her head a few times, as if she might be able to shake his words out of her brain. Surely he didn't say that?

"What do you mean, it wasn't loaded?" she asked. "I don't get it."

"There were no cartridges in the gun," said O'Grady. "Don't go on about it. It's no big deal. I wanted to avoid any accidents. I would have loaded it if I needed to . . ." He pulled a handful of shotgun cartridges from his pocket to show her. "See, I got these. I coulda blown the bad guys to bits if I needed to. Just didn't want any accidents, that's all . . ."

The child stared at the cartridges. A low growl began in the back of her throat, a rumble that eventually formed itself into a word.

"Liar," she said.

"Now, hon," said O'Grady. "There's no need for that . . ."

"Liar!" yelled the child, staring at the cartridges.

O'Grady put them away in his pocket again, shrugging. "I haven't lied to anyone," he said. "Nobody asked me if the gun was loaded, did they? So technically it's not a lie."

The girl screamed at him then, her voice cracking with a powerful emotion that had boiled inside her these past two days.

"You lied! You lied!" she repeated, her mouth dripping with saliva, her face red and overheated.

"I did not lie!" shouted O'Grady.

"I hate you," shouted the girl.

"Oh, you hate me now?" said O'Grady, mocking the child and her anger. "Well that's too bad because I'm the only person around here that likes you. The manager thinks you're a little freak, those people in the bathrooms don't care for you. And out there? Nobody has come to rescue you, have they? No police, no mommy or daddy. You'd think if you were so important to them they'd be in here by now. But they don't care a damn about you. I'm the only one who cares. I'm your John Wayne, so you'd better think twice about whether you hate me or not."

"You're not my John Wayne," shouted the child. "You said that you told the truth, but you didn't."

O'Grady walked over to her, a conciliatory smile on his face, but when he went to put his arm around her, she pushed him away.

"Okay," he sniffed. "I gave you the truth. Now you decide what's real or not. You go on up there and have a look for yourself. Go on. Go out to those steps and see if they come running to you. They don't love you. They're the puppets, and they know you're a member of John Wayne O'Grady's gang. They'll see it in your eyes, they'll know that you held the gun, that you practiced to be a revolutionary. Remember what I said . . . they're gonna be oh so nice to you, those puppets out there. Go on up to them. Make up your own mind. Then we'll see if you don't come back to me."

"I will go out there," shouted the girl. "I will."

"Go then," said O'Grady. "I want you to. Go and get that fat man for me. You're a part of my gang now. You've got the truth. They'll see it. The puppets can do that."

The girl hesitated for a moment, confused. She didn't feel so fierce now, she felt small, lonely, afraid. O'Grady pushed her gently toward the doorway, repeating his order. Eventually she walked toward the landing and disappeared into the police light.

When she was gone, the gunman let out a bellow of rage. He went to the wires taped to the wall. His face contorted with emotion as he picked up the battery, arm quivering, then paused. After almost a minute, he let out a huge sigh that transformed into quiet sobs. John Wayne O'Grady leaned up against the wall and slid down to the ground crying.

An empty gun beside him.

FREDA OPPERMAN

I wonder what influenced John Wayne O'Grady to settle on the Barrett as his choice of weapon? There would have been a host of brands to choose from—Winchester, Remington, Beretta, SKB—all beautifully crafted, all made from the finest materials. Each worked to precise specifications, smelling of that same combination of steel and gun oil.

My balsa-wood carving is coming along fine now, and I'm amazed at how easy it is to recreate a shape after so many years. The guys have started to take an interest in what I'm doing, arguing among themselves about what I might be making. Some remember when I was younger, quietly carving behind my father's bent back, making no other sound than the *scrape, scrape* of my blade. They shake their heads now, worried that I might be creating something bad. What can I say to them? These strokes that I make with the spokeshave come from a deep, secret code that's been locked away in my muscles, held prisoner inside me all these years. This is not the sort of thing a good girl does.

Pausing for a moment, I look at the straightness of my carving, and it gives me secret thrills that cause me to sit down to catch my breath. It is a beautiful thing, so simple and rigid, possessing no doubts about its purpose, no hesitation about what action to take. Retrieving a piece of rough-grade sandpaper from Dad's bench top, I begin to rub my carving, smoothing out any trace of squareness, creating the over-under shape that will give it the authenticity I want.

Now the guys are dead-worried, which is a funny joke given that they are also dead. They mutter loudly in ghostly voices, which thankfully I cannot hear. I'd hoped that they would understand what I am trying to do here, but it seems that they can only see the crude surface of my actions, and not the heart and soul that lies beneath. Come on, fellas, look at me. I'm bringing to fruition a long-held desire. This is the end of my journey of discovery.

I release my carving and place another piece of crude balsa in the vice. This will have to be a two-part carving, glued together to get the right length. I stop for a minute, glancing at my father's clock. Nearly midnight. And cold. I stoke the wood burner, coaxing the small gathering of dull coals with paper and twigs until I have a blaze, then adding more and more to the flame. Pieces of scraps, balsa from my carving, anything that burns, until a pleasant heat emerges.

A car stops outside, I switch off the overhead light and sit quietly in the darkness. Footsteps approach. Someone walks to the garage door and listens. There are no windows facing the street, so whoever it is out there has no way of knowing I'm in here. Perhaps it is my mother. Perhaps it is William, sent by Nancy to seek me out. Eventually, the owner of the footsteps gives up and goes back to the car. I hear it drive off, but I sit still in the dark awhile longer. After a pause a car sweeps past. Maybe it was the same car. I don't know.

Suddenly, I feel exhausted, and I close my eyes. The warmth of the heater allows me to drift off into a quiet sleep. I wake in a gentle mood and switch on the light. The balsa is still in the vice, waiting for me. I stand. Rub my fingers over it. Remember things I haven't thought of in a long time. I don't know if I'm up to this, but I also don't know if I can stop.

I work away at the second part of the carving. This shape is more difficult. It is more angular, blockier, and requires concentration. The clock tells me it is 1:00 A.M., not a good hour for concentrating. It is nearly 2:30 by the time I finish this shape, and I sit wearily, looking at it for a long time.

Then I sleep and wake again. I take my two pieces and drill holes in them, inserting a couple of dowel plugs for strength. Watching my father all these years has paid off. I glue them together. I sleep again. It is 4:30 when I wake, and still no light shines in the windows. I take my balsa construction from the vice and hold it out in front of me, looking down its length to check the trueness of its twin-barrel structure. This gun is straight and fine, but it will never fire a shot. And in that way it perfectly resembles O'Grady's shotgun. A piece for show, for bravado and intimidation, not intended to be fired in anger.

Therein lies its truth.

The guys have been woken by me, and are all looking crestfallen, upset that "their" workshop has been used to create such a thing. I take a pot of stain from my father's shelf and rub it into the stock of my gun, my second carving, bringing out a deep, rich brown texture that really should not be there. The stain gives the wood the appearance of toughness, of durability and depth. I am rubbing tradition into my fake gun, a thousand million memories of shots that have killed and maimed and terrified people all over the world.

The guys are openly alarmed now, trying their hardest to stop me, but their hands go through my body. Surely they understand that you cannot halt tradition? That it is a powerful weight, an invincible force that sends the proudest man to his knees, the frailest old woman into hysteria, the weakest child into spasms of fear that cause her to lose touch with the real world.

I was only nine years old. Lost in an evil, cold place, repeatedly told that I was alone. I was spinning around, desperately search- ing for a rock-solid place to hold on to. Your mind does strange things to you when you're in such a state. It offers you light that isn't there, fantasies that will never come true, magic in ordinary objects.

Such as guns.

The stock is finished, but the barrel is whitish, and looks like softwood, not metal. Sighing with disappointment, I know that my imitation is poor. Once the assembled ghosts realize this as well, they laugh, pointing at my milky gun barrel. The girl is a failure.

Oh, you are possessed with mirth, are you? Well, maybe I haven't finished, yet. There must be something here to give this barrel a dull sheen or luster. I search around the workshop, but being a cabinetmaker, my father does not have paints, only stains and shellacs and waxes. The guys are smirking now.

They have no idea. Theirs is the domain of drawers and doors and fine dovetail joints. I've come from a different world, a place where the thin veneer of society barely holds back the evil I see beneath. A place where a nine-year-old girl has to play danger- ous games to survive.

Fearsome games.

Standing with a sudden sense of urgency, I take an empty jar and fill it with some stain. Then I bend down to my father's workshop floor and pick up some old, grimy sawdust and mix it with the stain. But when I rub it into the barrel, it only produces another brown, wooden color that makes the whole thing look pathetic. I throw the gun onto the ground and burst into tears, overwhelmed and exhausted. I see the stairs again, the bright, harsh light of them. I see *her* making the long, lonely walk toward the top. Little frail Freda, little fearful Freda, a far cry from that fighter who wanted to be a cowboy. Just a pigtailed little girl who thought there might be a glimmer of hope beyond the doors. But all she saw were puppets.

Picking the carving up from the floor, I search once more through my father's shelves and find a bottle of machine oil. It will have to do. Rubbing with an old rag, I color my gun barrel, making it resemble steel, something that could crack a man's jaw open with one hit. That can bruise a fragile chest. My metal must be cold, unswerving, obeying my commands. A gun has no interest in ideologies. It will serve any master for any purpose, no matter how corrupt or vague that might be.

It will serve me.

I finish my coloring and hold the gun out, satisfied that it is as close as I'll ever get to O'Grady's Barrett. The fellas have turned their backs on me now, as their final protest. I swing the gun in their direction, but they pay no attention to me.

"Oi!!" I shout. "Oi!"

Slowly they turn toward me, sad expressions on their semi-transparent faces.

"You tell me what I was supposed to do, huh!" I say. "Ever been in my situation? No, I didn't think so. Let me tell you, there's precious little option when you think you're gonna die. So don't judge me!"

They shrug their milky shoulders, perhaps deciding that I am lost to them now. Locked away in a place where they will not talk to me again. I pull my face into as much of a rebellious expression as I can muster, and flounce away.

Someone will come. Someone will find me here with this thing and try to take it away from me.

I switch off all the lights in my father's workshop except for the tiny lamp that sits on his desk. It struggles to illuminate the space, creating a gloomy, shadowy world around me.

I'm ready now . . . in the dark.

Taking a seat on a tall stool, I face the door and wait. Minutes pass, ten, fifteen, I'm not counting. Eventually I hear a noise outside. A tiny creak precedes the opening of the workshop door, and the unmistakable shape of a teddy bear stands in the entrance. He pauses for a moment or two, adjusting his eyes to the gloom. He sees shadowy benches, silhouettes of timber, tools . . . then he sees me with my Barrett. I stand and point the gun at his chest. "Open your mouth," I say. "And I'll shoot you dead."

The effect is electrifying.

William bounces backward, as if hit by an unseen force, only to crash into the doorway and bang his head. Staggering for a moment, he looks once more at my Barrett and drops to his knees, sobbing wildly and uncontrollably. Through his hysteria, I hear him say, "Please . . . no . . . I'll be good . . . don't hurt me . . ."

And I know that my nightmare has only just begun.

LITTLE **FREDA O,**

ON THE STAIRS

When she was completely exhausted, emptied of rage and fear and horror of the puppets, she felt a sense of calm come over her. There were so many men out there. So many guns. Soon there'd be a fight. The bad man would win. He told her that. He knew everything.

He told her that, too.

She couldn't believe how simple it all was. Just listen to the bad man. That little girl who wanted, who prayed, who ached for those people out there, receded into the hard white glow of the lights, until she was nothing more than a halo.

Now the struggle was over.

Little Freda O. turned, back to the dark place, back to the way out. She saw the manager leaning against the wall. He hated her. She knew that.

"He wants you," she snapped, poking him in the ribs the way the bad man had showed her to.

The bad man.

As she walked back down the stairs, the manager rising up beside her, a faint noise scratched behind her. Fingernails on glass, perhaps? Or Sunday shoes scuffing at the top of the stairs? She let it fade behind her, until there was nothing but the cold, stale air from below to fill her senses.

Then she went back down into the darkest of places.

JOHN WAYNE

O'GRADY

The manager and the girl stared at the gunman. Each had come down the stairs with different thoughts on their minds, individual reactions to their experiences in the harsh police light. As they entered the gloom of the restaurant they were confronted by O'Grady, poised in a shooting position, the gun aimed at their heads.

"If I fire this gun," said John Wayne O'Grady, a crazy look in his eyes, "you die. Simple as that. You fall down and you're dead. Do you want me to shoot you, manager?"

Constantine looked up at the gunman slowly, his reactions dulled, deep in a state of shock and denial. He'd collapsed on the stairs, become lost in his mind, going back to one moment where he was happy, driving his car to his girlfriend's house, enjoying the tingle of nervousness in his stomach, the pleasant agitation in his whole body as he negotiated the winding roads. She was nice. He was on his way to see her, with the morning sun slowly burning away the cold, the radio playing his favorite song, and the flowers crackling in their cellophane wrapping on the front seat beside him. He was happy . . . enjoying that tingle . . . listening to that voice . . . on the radio?

Constantine looked around at the restaurant. What was happening?

"Well?" demanded O'Grady. "Do you want me to shoot you?"

There was a broken chair lying sideways on the restaurant floor. How did that happen? There was a smell in the air, dank and stale. What the hell was going on? He met the gunman's eyes, saw the situation, then registered the terrible question.

"No," said Constantine, his voice raspy and broken. "I don't want to die."

"I didn't think so. And what about you, child?" asked O'Grady, swinging the gun in Freda's direction. "Do you want to die?"

The girl shook her head emphatically, eyes wide open, her breath short and shallow.

"Of course not," said O'Grady. "And am I gonna shoot you with this gun?"

Now the girl smiled, her tension easing, as if she'd just figured out the answer to a trick question. She shook her head at O'Grady and said, "You can't shoot me with that gun."

"That's right, hon," he said. "I can't." He lowered the gun and smiled at them. "So now we understand one another. I'm the commanding officer. I'm in charge. I will have no insubordination. I will have no dissent. I *will* be taken seriously."

Constantine nodded enthusiastically. He wiped his face, wondering why it was covered in saliva, then shook himself, as if waking from a nightmare.

The girl walked over to O'Grady and looked up into his eyes. She was so small. The gunman put a hand on her shoulder, a kindly gesture of goodwill or care, and a tear came to his eyes.

"I saw them," said the girl. "Out there."

"You saw the puppets? And did they want you to play with them?"

"Yes," she answered.

"And still you came back here."

The girl nodded.

"Then you're as ready as you'll ever be. And I have done some good. I'm glad about that. But now my time has come. I'm getting out."

Constantine's eyes lit up at the thought of the gunman's departure, but the girl recoiled, reacting as if she'd been slapped in the face.

"You're leaving?" she said. "But . . . what happens, then?"

"Don't worry, hon. Everything's gonna be fine . . ." said O'Grady.

"No," she shouted. "You have to take me, too . . ."

The manager grabbed the girl roughly by the upper arm and dragged her away from O'Grady, as if removing her from the man's presence might break the hold he had over her. "You've got no idea what you're doing," said Constantine.

The girl swung around, slapping the manager in the stomach. "He can't go!" she yelled. "What about me?"

"You'll stay here with me . . ."

"I hate you!"

The gunman looked at the child, at her sad, lonely expression, at the abandonment in her stance, the way she began to sob.

"You don't want old John Wayne to go, hon?" he said.

She shook her head, saying, "I don't want to be left here."

"I suppose you could come with me . . ."

"No," hissed Constantine. "You don't understand what he means. Just stay here, everything will be all right. Your parents will come . . ."

"They're dead!" shouted the girl.

"They're not dead . . ." began Constantine, but he got no further. The sensation of cold, hard steel in his ear brought about an immediate end to his reasoning with the child. He didn't have to turn around to know that O'Grady had shoved the barrel of the gun against his head.

"Leave her be," said O'Grady.

Constantine backed away. "Hey, sorry. No problem. She wants to go with you, then it's fine by me. Just lower that gun, eh?"

The girl stared at him, then burst into laughter. "You're such a scaredy-cat," she sneered. "Afraid of John Wayne's gun. Scaredy, scaredy . . ."

"Shut your filthy little mouth," hissed Constantine.

"Now, now, Theo." O'Grady smiled. "Keep it polite."

Constantine stared at them, and a look of revulsion distorted his face. "What the hell have you done to her?" he whispered.

"Don't you get it, Theo?" said O'Grady. "You're the odd one out, here. You're the kid in the school yard that nobody wants to play with. You're the manager in the restaurant who drives the staff crazy. You're not wanted."

"Hey, look. It's okay," said Constantine, holding his hands up. "She wants to go with you, then that's fine. Leave me out of this . . ."

"And how would you propose I leave you out, Theo?" asked O'Grady, a terrible smile on his face.

Constantine's eyes flickered from the man to his gun, from the threatener to the threat. "What's going on?" he said.

"Why waste a good comrade, eh?" sneered O'Grady. "Who knows? Those men and women in the bathroom might come to their senses one day and join the revolution. You, on the other hand, are just plain useless."

"Listen," said Constantine, thinking on his feet. "I'm sorry if I've offended you. I'm not going to get in your way when you leave . . ."

O'Grady laughed, as if the manager had cracked a hugely funny joke. "That's where you're wrong. You *will* be in my way. I'll tell you what you're good for, Theo. You're a natural-born human shield. Let's just hope that the cops aren't in the mood for target practice."

O'Grady leaned forward to take hold of Constantine, and the full realization of his plan hit the manager.

"No!" yelled Constantine, running for the storeroom door.

O'Grady shouted "Stop!" but the manager was not obeying any further orders. The gunman lunged after him, his long legs making up the space between the two men in a few strides. They reached the door at the same time, and Theo managed to open it a crack before O'Grady grabbed it.

"Just behave yourself," hissed the gunman.

"No," panted Constantine, using his heavier weight to force the door open against O'Grady's resistance, squeezing himself through the crack.

The door slammed behind Constantine, pushed closed now by O'Grady's force, and the distinct sound of a key being turned in the lock could be heard from the other side.

"Shit!" yelled O'Grady. "Shit! Shit!"

He banged his fist on the door. "You'd better believe me," shouted O'Grady at the closeted manager. "I'm mad enough to shoot."

There was no reply. He paced back and forth, stopping every now and then to scream at the manager through the door, but there was no answer from inside.

"I'll do it! I'll do it!" he shouted.

No answer.

"I will!"

Silence.

Then a tiny voice spoke beside him, a determined voice that was heard clearly by both men.

"Do it," said the girl. "It won't matter."

FREDA OPPERMAN

I never really knew what it felt like to point a gun at another human being until now. Sure, I'd held O'Grady's gun, and I'd fantasized about it, but that is nothing compared to the real thing. Up until now, a gun wasn't much more than a pointed finger, a stick, a coat hanger that went off on cue and never missed.

BANG! You're dead.

You're dead, William, a dead man, a dead man sitting there. Did you see that? A dead man . . .

This is so different from my childish fantasies. This glorified stick has caught both me and William in its deadly web. We are bound together, joined by an invisible thread that ties us as frail humans, as weak-minded receptacles of anger and shame and violent intention. We are the pause between my trigger finger and his recoil, between my voice and his panic. I am everything to him, now. His life, his death . . . his imagination.

I have his attention.

William tells me a myriad of things through his deep, brown, teddy-bear eyes. He pleads with me one moment, then is angry the next. He is sad, then outraged, lonely then vulnerable.

I feel torn, repulsed by my actions, disgusted with the power this gun wields, yet exhilarated at the same time. William is up against the roller-door now, breathing in jagged gulps that threaten to send him into hyperventilation. You poor little bastard, you poor little boy. Stay calm, William. It's okay.

"Everything's fine," I say.

"What the hell do you mean by that?" he yells, never once taking his eyes from the fake Barrett's barrel, so realistic in the gloom.

"Really, you're going to be all right." I'm trying to sound soothing, but each time I open my mouth he seems to panic more.

So I put the gun down. I place it carefully against the stool and go to him. "It's okay, William," I say, placing my hand on his shoulder.

He stares at me, his fear still evident. He searches my eyes for a moment, then a snarl forms on his face. I have one second, perhaps even less, to react. To run back to my gun before he takes it himself. Such is the timing of these moments, when animal instinct takes over and rational thought is put behind us.

We both move at the same time, me twisting around and reaching out for the gun, he grabbing hold of my top to drag me back.

"Stop it!" I cry, kicking at him with my feet.

"Bitch! Bitch!" he yells, tearing my top with a gaping rip that gives me a quick shudder. This rip loosens his hold for a second, and I'm able to take the gun in my hand and swing around, pointing the barrel so close to his face that he cannot get a proper focus on it, cannot see that it is fake.

"Let go of me, you slime, before I blow your head off."

The effect is instant. William releases his grip and I quickly stand, taking in the look of sheer hatred in his eyes. Oh yes, we're back to square one again.

"Get up," I command. "Now!"

William slowly stands, his eyes locked on my balsa-wood enforcer, his legs as wobbly as jelly.

"Move over to that desk."

I push him with my will toward Dad's desk, force him like a puppet on a string to sit in my father's chair and behave himself. Then I go to the workshop door and close it, locking the dead bolt with the key, which I put in my pocket. We're alone now, teddy bear and Freda, alone with the gun and the terrified ghosts in the corner.

"It's time you and I cleared the air a bit," I say, panting heavily after my desperate fight for the gun.

"Yes," he says. "I know."

"Why have you sought me out, William? I assume that's behind you asking my mother if you could interview me. And no doubt you snooped in my past and found out about Shelley and God knows what else for the same reason. So, why?"

"To get you to face up to the truth," he says.

"Oh, the truth." I'm trying to sound mocking, but it doesn't come out right. Besides, he hasn't listened to that word in the same way that I have. He probably still believes in it. "And what is the truth, William? That I'm somehow not as innocent as I seem?"

"You can only guess at the truth," he hisses. "Because you're so stuck in your rigid justifications, your phony fairy tales about the poor innocent child who survived the siege."

"I was innocent!" I yell.

There is a ripple behind me, and I know that the fellas have grouped to support me, even if they do disapprove of my methods. There's no way they're gonna float around and allow someone to accuse me of not being innocent. They've been in this workshop for too long, smelled my father's resignation, his shame.

William smiles. This is all wrong, me demanding things from him. I'm the one holding a gun, even if it is fake. He has come to me because *I* am what he seeks. I allow that fact to calm me, give me clear sight. He'll reveal what he wants, either slowly or clumsily, he'll tell me what I need to know eventually.

I don't speak. I become the opposite of that ranting, raving madman who held me for so long. I am silent, withdrawn, and already I can see it unsettling my captive. William fidgets for a while, trying to match my silence with his own, trying to face me down. It's a game of chicken. Who will break the impasse? Who will claim victory? After many long minutes, William sits a little straighter, trying to look satisfied.

Change is coming.

"Mary O'Conner," he says smugly, counting off a finger on his left hand.

It's a good tactic, because he has broken the impasse with something intriguing. I must either ask who this person is, which puts William in control, or continue my silence, which will only make me look churlish. I sigh, just to let him know I understand the tactic, and say, "She is . . . ?"

"She is dead," says William. "A sixty-year-old woman when John O'Grady held her captive in that restaurant and locked her in a bathroom, she never fully recovered from the siege and died several months later. Her family did not sue anyone."

"Oh," I say, hanging my head. I remember that poor old lady. She spent most of the siege confused or sleeping. And then she died.

"Ken Farraday," says William.

Oh, please. I know where this is heading. William is trying to make me feel guilty for not following up on the lives of my fellow comrades.

"Listen," I say. "Cut the testimonials, okay? I don't want to know about them. They got out alive, too. Let them deal with their own shit. I've got two dead men to cope with."

"Ken Farraday," repeats William.

"I don't want to know . . ."

"Ken Farraday . . ."

"He better not be dead, too!" I shout.

"Tall," says William, enjoying the fact that I have no idea which of my hostage companions was this Ken person. "An ex-basketball player. Amateur only. His life seemed to go back to normal fairly quickly after the siege. He formed a relationship with one of the other hostages, Suzy Matic, who O'Grady had once suggested was his girlfriend. They were only acquaintances, caught in that restaurant because they were meeting to discuss a surprise birthday party they intended to throw for a mutual friend. Suzy and Ken married two years after the siege and had a son six years ago. He is tall like his father, and spends every Saturday afternoon at the cemetery putting flowers on Ken's grave."

"Oh, God," I say, my head spinning with all this information. "Why? What happened to him?"

"Suicide," says William matter-of-factly.

"You little bastard. You're enjoying this. You're getting a kick out of making me suffer through the fate of these poor people. God. I suffered, too. Do you think I wouldn't want to go back in there and change how things turned out? I can't even remember what happened, you prick. But I'd do anything to make it different . . ."

"James Barrowclough," says William.

"Stop it. I don't remember."

"James Barrowclough."

Suddenly the name is familiar. I'd heard it so many times at the inquest. He was the cook, the one who'd tried to attack O'Grady. Alone. Why did no one else join in? Why were we so scared?

"I know who he is," I say. "I suppose he's dead, too?" It's a terrible joke, and I regret it the instant it spins from my mouth. Thankfully, William shakes his head, and I rest easy in the knowledge that James has survived. He always was a fighter.

"On a disability pension," says William. "From the injury he sustained from O'Grady. Guardian Angel fought a court battle for him and won him some extra compensation. I'm amazed you don't even know that."

Little prick. He's turned one of the positive stories into a criticism of me. I wouldn't know anything about James's court case unless Nancy decided to tell me. Perhaps that's the point of all this? William is stating the obvious, that my life has been orchestrated for so long by N.O., but I already know that. Or perhaps it's that Miss Freda Opperman, *Hope of the Nation!* has been callous and uncaring in her disregard for those who shared her ordeal?

Then I remember the file in Nancy's office, and the strangers who received so much kindness. N.O. said they were not strangers, and now I see exactly who they were.

"The Opperman Trust," I say. "Those people received money from the Opperman Trust."

"Do you think money made any real difference to their lives?" asks William. "They all had to watch as the newspapers photographed you and wrote about you and defined your role in the siege. The media gave you your 'out' clause, you were the innocent bystander who was caught up in the madness. Do you think Ken Farraday couldn't have used an 'out' when he slumped into his dark depressions? Suzy used to hold him, used to soothe him and tell him he was okay, but he'd suffered some deep shame in that restaurant, and nothing anybody said to him would help. Do you think if he could have walked from there as a hero, he would have been able to get through his shame? He was one of the many men there. They outnumbered O'Grady, yet they all ended up in the men's room. He wasn't absolved of his sins the way you were. Why the hell didn't they just overthrow O'Grady? If one more man had joined James, they just might have done it."

"They couldn't do it," I say. "Nobody could. O'Grady was too strong. Look at James . . ."

"They could have tried," he shouts. "Why didn't they try?"

William starts sobbing, and I look away. There's a truth circling here, but I don't want to meet it. I'm afraid of what it might unleash. Turning back to my captive, I see in him once again the quality that breaks my heart, that softness in him, where dreams might grow. William meets my eye, staring at me, his tear-streaked face blank and hard.

"John Blake," he says eventually.

"Who?" I say, irritated with his game.

"A Vietnam War veteran. One of the hostages."

I groan. "No more," I say.

William ignores my protest.

"John seems to have been the least affected by the siege," he says. "He was a member of a veterans' society, and went back to his friends who'd been through worse stuff during the war. He probably thought it was all a picnic. But you know what I reckon? He had a 'family' that knew how to support him because they'd been through the same sort of shit. A real family. Ben McAllister and Paul Reisingham had a similar thing. They were the two guys who worked on weekends in the underground Family Value kitchen. Paul took time off from college to travel overseas and ran into Ben in London, who was about to go work as a volunteer in western Somalia. On a total whim, Paul joined up, too, and they have both spent the last seven years working for aid organizations around the world, giving support to the needy from Bosnia to East Timor."

William is giving me a pointed look, as aware as I am of the false promise in the famous last gasps of Theo Constantine.

"Okay," I say. "So they've led a good life. You tell me exactly what that is, because I've been searching for it now for nearly ten years and haven't even come close. My mother's take is to do as much for others as you possibly can, pour money into their problems from her secret trusts. And if anyone gets in her way she runs them down. Did she ever give a moment's thought to the corporate executives and their families when the newspapers were trumpeting what bastards they were? Is that a good life? Perhaps I should have just done nothing."

"But you didn't do nothing that night!" shouts William, starting to stand up until I wave the fake gun at him. He sits back down again heavily. "You didn't just stand by and watch. The others were in the restroom. They heard things . . . I've talked to them. They heard stuff that didn't make sense . . ."

"That's not true!" I shout. I'm losing my breath again, and have to gasp for a few seconds, clutch my chest, before I can trust my lungs to do the right thing. Then I speak. "It would have come out in the inquest . . . they would have said . . . you made that up, you little bastard."

"I'm telling the truth," says William, oh so smug.

"How could you even begin to understand what happened that night?" I ask. "You're just a pathetic jerk who talks to survivors, who carries around a list of names that belong to dead or not-dead people. What is your problem? Are you some kind of sick ambulance chaser? Do you get off on people who've been through traumas? What the hell do you want?"

"I want to *know*," says William, gripping a screwdriver that has been left carelessly on my father's work desk. He holds the handle in his pudgy fist, the star-pointed end waving in my direction. "I understand what those people went through after the siege. Every little thing is their secret knowledge. I understand them completely."

"You're wasting your time with me, William. If you think I'm gonna offer you some sort of revelation, you'll only be disappointed. I don't remember. I don't even want to try . . ."

"You remembered about the stairs . . ."

"Only because . . . because . . ." My voice trails off, the horror of the stairway coming back to me.

William toys with the screwdriver, his actions growing more and more confident with each moment. I shift the fake gun in my hand, just to remind him that it's still there, and he stabs the point of the screwdriver into the bench top.

"Wood is so soft," he mutters. Then he picks the screwdriver out of the bench top and throws it like a circus knife at the floor, but it simply skids away under my stool and vanishes into the darkness.

"Look at you," he says. "You're frozen. O'Grady froze you. He froze everyone. Cordoned off. Contained. Isolated. That's what he did to you. That's your big excuse."

This is personal. I can hear the voice of that madman whispering in my ear, telling me again and again that you can't make bargains with the truth. It's so insistent, almost as if he's trying to tell me something, a message for later . . . for now. A wave of deep sadness washes over me, and to my surprise I can also see it in William's face.

Frozen.

He's stuck, too. That's what I've seen in him all along. That's the quality I could love. He needs my story to ease a deep, wrenching pain from something that happened to him.

"You said you once did something wrong," I say. "When was that?"

"A few years ago . . ."

"Not ten?"

He looks down at the ground and shakes his head. No, not ten years ago, but it's related to then. It has to be. Isn't that the point he was trying to make with all those survivor stories? We were all left with a terrible legacy. O'Grady wanted to release a virus of truth into society, but instead he released the shattered and the brokenhearted. Some tried to do good, some gave in, and some did bad things . . .

"You were there," I whisper.

He nods. "Haven't you known all along?"

Before I get a chance to answer there's a banging at the garage door, and the voice of Nancy Opperman breaks through. "Freda! I know you're in there. Open up."

NAPKiN

N

Very late. He's banging on the door. I ran in here and locked it when I had a chance. This might be the last one I'll write. He's gonna shoot me through the door. I know it. That crazy little bitch is telling him to shoot. I have to stay here under the desk. I don't want to die. I love you. What a mess. How the hell did we get to this?

Theo

FREDA OPPERMAN

Death was always just around the corner in the underground. We were thrown into the far reaches of our fear. You make all sorts of bargains down there. Theo Constantine criticized me in one of the napkins for smiling at O'Grady. I would have hugged and kissed the man if I thought it would make me safe. I looked at him, and to him, again and again, waiting for a sign that he liked me, that he wouldn't hurt me, that I was *okay*.

I felt so much love for the man when he smiled at me. I know that ordinary people would be disgusted by such a revelation, so I never mention it in polite society. Even so, it's true. When he smiled, or showed warmth to me, I felt like my whole heart would burst. Not in the early stages, but later, when I was left with so little. Each time he smiled at me I would think, "So it's okay now?" Then he would shout or bully or push that gun at someone. He became an unpredictable father to us all, our "commanding officer," but no matter how much we prayed to him, he wouldn't listen. The only certainty about John Wayne O'Grady was his gun. Each of us had to steer our own course through his crazy religion.

To survive.

And now I find that William is also a young survivor, a fellow traveler within a society that cannot fathom what it means to make bargains for your safety. We should, perhaps, form a club. Meet near the bathrooms and talk about real topics, such as fear, hatred, pressure, and violence . . . and mothers perhaps?

The first thing Nancy sees when I let her into the workshop is the gun under my arm. She is alarmed, but hides it behind a quizzical look, as if to ask where I found this thing. Then she notices William in the gloom, sees the fear in his eyes, and in the mere ticking of a second my mother works it all out.

"Freda," she says, her voice urgent.

I ignore it, locking the door again and pocketing the key.

"Take a seat, Mom," I say. "William and I were just chatting."

"There's something I need to tell you about William . . ."

"That he was in the siege?" I say, resisting a sneer.

Mom looks a little taken aback, then she nods. "So, you know already. I wanted it to come from him . . . He promised me he'd tell you."

"Save it," I snap, waving the gun around.

Nancy stares at me, as if I have somehow transformed into an alien, and I laugh at her.

"Oh, really," I say. "Don't be so amazed by this gun. Isn't this situation what you've feared all along? This is your nightmare come true, Mom. The furtive scribblings of a long-dead man have finally proven to be correct."

William looks alarmed now, and I turn to him.

"Okay, William. Boy who had a mother, boy who was protected, just how the hell did you know about these napkins? And don't give me that photo story, because I've seen that shot, too, and I could have been holding anything."

William shuffles uncomfortably in his chair. "I heard you," he says. "You and Constantine . . . arguing . . . outside the bathroom door. He wanted you to come with him to write something . . . and you said napkins. I never even thought about it again . . . until recently. I've been thinking a lot about the siege, and I remembered that. It seemed important, because it was the only chink in your perfect armor."

"So you tracked me down, then?"

"No," says William, shocked that I could accuse him of such a thing. "I went to Guardian Angel to sue Family Value . . ."

"That's right, Freda," says N.O. "I can verify that . . ."

"Mom," I say, sighing. "Just try to listen for a minute or two."

I turn again to William, devious plotter with my deceptive mother. "So, you thought there might be more to Freda Opperman than met the eye, eh? And you organized an interview with me to find out?"

"Sort of," mumbles William. "You weren't the first. I talked to all of the others . . . I guess I was too afraid to approach you. Then when I went to Guardian Angel and saw your mother there, I realized that it was you I needed to talk to. We were both kids . . . but you came out an angel, and I was a nobody."

So, I am the end of William's line. What then does he really seek of me? Confirmation that I am no angel? There's a deep, horrid truth William harbors, as insidious as my napkins. It plagues him, makes him seek out frightened girls in the hopes that they will . . . what? Tell him he is a good boy, perhaps? That he isn't? Doesn't it all boil down to that in the end? Pulling the napkins from my back pocket, I hand them over. "Here," I say. "You might as well read these now. The truth about me is in there."

He takes the napkins and starts scanning them randomly, his eyes flickering in the gloom, his body tensing with each sentence he reads.

Nancy, who had been standing throughout all this, sits awkwardly on the edge of Dad's bench, having scanned the room for the least filthy spot. Her short legs swing slightly as she tries to balance herself. It's hard to tell what's making her the most uncomfortable. The fact that she's in Dad's space, the fact that her daughter is holding a gun, or the fact that the ghostly gentlemen behind her are giving her the once over.

The fellas crowd around her, perving, nodding to each other with approval. You can almost hear them saying, "Not bad," and I roll my eyes at them. Really, this is a serious moment, not to be debased by ghosts in leather aprons.

Eventually Nancy speaks, revealing her primary concern, a topic that comes as no great shock. "Where did you get the gun from, Freda?" she asks, sounding calm, but I know better.

"From my memory," I answer. "That thing you've always been afraid of . . ."

"I've never been afraid of your memory," says Nancy, a softness in her face that I've rarely seen before. "It's what others will do with your memory that frightens me."

"And so you invented a good girl," I say.

"And so I protected you," counters Nancy.

We meet there, mother and I, with our eyes, our souls. We meet for a brief moment and forget to clash, forget to bang the shields of our past against each other. Then Nancy speaks, and once again it's dark all around me.

"How can you point a gun at him, Freda? You of all people. How can you do that?"

I turn to William, this young man who has concealed the truth from me, looking up from the napkins. He was that boy who I envied with all my heart. Curled up against his mother when all I had was a plastic table. Wrapped in her care, when all I had was the tangible disdain of Theo Constantine.

"I have unfinished business," I say. "And William is helping me get it done. I can't go on until I carry this through." I nod at the napkins still in William's grasp. "You read them yet?"

"Mostly," he answers.

"And?"

William sighs. "Do you think it's possible to ever live a life that doesn't do damage to another person?"

Before I have a chance to answer, Nancy Opperman, in her newfound role as counselor to young survivors, speaks up. "Who have you hurt, William?" she asks.

I sniff, annoyed at her intrusion, and annoyed that she can't see the whole picture. "He's hurt me, for a start," I say. "Both of you have."

"I'm sorry, Freda," says Nancy. Her apology might be late, but at least she's trying. "I thought . . . when I got to know William and learned that he was that other child in the siege . . . I thought that somehow it would be healing for you and he to get together." She shrugs.

"Oh, Mom," I say, shaking my head. "Look at this." I hold the gun up. "Look at it. Does this look like a healing to you?"

Tears form in Nancy's eyes, and even though each one burns me like that flame from her lighter, I can't let her go, can't turn my anger away.

Now the fellas take a step forward, indicating to me that I've simply gone too far. They place their glowing hands on Mom's shoulders, soothe her pain. It's a bizarre sight, not because of the ghosts, but because I have never seen my mother look so vulnerable before.

William hands back the napkins. "It was my mother," he says. "That's who I hurt. Who I punished . . . I guess." He looks me in the eye. "You think those napkins are right, don't you? You think you helped kill Theo Constantine. Well . . . you don't have a monopoly on those sorts of feelings, okay? My mother was thirty-eight at the time of the siege. I was her baby, the last of four boys, and she'd taken me to Family Value as a treat." He pauses, looking down at his hands for a while, then he raises that teddy-bear head and meets my eye again. "There are very few people I know who can even begin to understand what it felt like when I was locked in the bathroom with the men."

I nod. Perhaps I do know, William. Perhaps I've known all along that you harbored such a thing in your memory.

"You couldn't leave it at that, though. Could you?" I ask. "You couldn't leave all that anger behind. Someone had to pay . . ."

He nods like a little schoolboy, caught with his hand in the cookie jar. Oh yes, he made her pay, that mother who cried for him, who had to put an abrupt halt to her pleas at the brutal hand of John Wayne O'Grady and his gun. Someone always has to pay, in the end. And I wonder now, who have I hurt in the process? My father, who sent me down those stairs? I have no anger toward him for that. Nancy? It would be simplistic to think that she was my sacrifice. Yet someone always pays, and I suspect I have offered up a life elsewhere. In some other place.

"The crazy thing is," says William, "I was jealous of you after the siege. Why was your photo in all the papers and not mine? Why did they write about you? Why not me? I was terrified in that dark place. They didn't even care about that."

"It protected you," I say, placing the gun crossways over my lap. "Being anonymous."

He gives it a quick glance, then nods his head. "Yes," he replies. "But it wasn't enough. I grew older, and started to make a bit more sense of the world . . . or maybe I realized that none of it made sense. I started to remember, too. Lots of stuff, things I thought I'd never feel again. You know, my mom was almost manic about making home life normal after the siege happened . . . which worked out fine for a ten-year-old kid. I guess by the time I was well into being an obnoxious teenager, I hated all the normality because it was such bullshit. Nothing was normal. Everything pissed me off. I mean, everything! My memory, my life, my family . . . and especially my mother. It didn't matter what she did, I was critical, angry, vicious. I was a total shit . . . but I couldn't stop it. I punished her again and again for abandoning me. At least, that's what the shrink told me I did . . . later. Mom saw it differently. She just kept loving me, even when I hurt her. And believe me, I deliberately hurt her."

William stops for a brief moment, and I stand up, holding my balsa-wood gun like a toy, and stretch. I catch Nancy exchanging a glance with my captive out of the corner of my eye and sit again, pointing the gun deliberately at William's stomach. Oh no. We're not cozy yet.

"Well, that's fine," I say. "You treated your mother like a bastard, and I was a murderous little bitch, according to Theo Constantine. Shall we all meet again, same time next week for survivors anonymous?"

"Freda!" says Nancy, shocked at my appalling lack of manners.

"Oh, Mother," I shout. "Will you stop that? I have a gun here, for crying out loud. This is not a nice situation. So stop pretending. Little Willy here has given us his true confessions. He hates his mommy." I turn to William and shout, "Get over it, okay? She didn't lock you in there. The poor woman was scared shitless by O'Grady and his shot . . ."

"My mother is dead," says William.

Horrible.

Oh, shit. Shit! Shit! Shit! I hate this crap. I hate it. I stand up and knock some wood and tools from my father's bench just for the hell of it, my heart racing so fast I feel faint.

"It wasn't suicide," says William in the background, but I choose to ignore him. I *choose* to ignore everything. Damn them. Damn any moving, living, breathing thing.

"Freda," says Mom.

I wave her away with my hand.

"Freda." She stands, takes a step toward me, and I swing the gun on her, fix her with all the rage that burns in me.

"Stop right there!" I yell.

Look at them both, their worried looks, their fears. Damn them. Why do they have to be weak? Why are we all so weak? It was just one man, Goddamn it. One man and three days and one gun and two dead and so many survivors split apart forever and ever and ever.

"You wanna know what I think, William? I think we hurt people all the time . . . I think we can't help but hurt people. It doesn't matter what we're trying to do."

"It's okay, darling," says Mom. "It's all okay . . ."

"No, it is not!" I shout. "You wanted stories, William? Well, I think it is time for some fucking stories. Okay, Mother?"

Nancy Opperman gets that look again, that terrified expression.

Rage works. Anger. It shines a light on otherwise dark places. It brings the horror to the surface. I can see O'Grady. I'm crying, and he's confused. He's just said something to me.

"God," I whisper. "He was going to get out of there alone. He was going to leave us and end the siege . . ."

"O'Grady?" says Nancy. "But why . . . ?"

"It was me. I stopped him. I *begged* him to take me with him."

"Oh, Freda . . ."

"I begged that bastard to take me with him. And when he wouldn't take me I . . ."

Stop it! Don't look at me like that. Don't move, Theo. Don't say what you're about to say. How can I remember this? It will kill me. They don't understand. Even William, who somehow drove his mother to the darkest of places.

"No! I won't remember!"

Nancy moves toward me, touches me. "That's okay, darling . . ."

I push her away and she falls to the floor. I stare at her. How did she get down there? How does anything happen?

"I remember," I say, barely able to speak.

"Freda . . ."

"I betrayed Theo Constantine. To prove to O'Grady that I was a good soldier."

I sit back on my stool and sob. The gun almost slips from my lap, but I still have the presence of mind to grab it at the last moment. To hold it to me. This symbol, this replica of the real thing, has helped me to remember. It is fitting, because the remembering brings me so much pain, just like a gun. It cuts me and tears holes in my fragile fabric. It rips me apart with the bullets of certainty.

Nancy gets off the floor and William asks her if she's okay.

"Shut up, both of you," I shout. I lift the gun, raise it to the vertical, and wipe the tears from my eyes with the back of my free hand. "Just shut the hell up and listen. Because I'll only say this once. I see things. You understand me? I see things . . . and this is the one and only time I'll tell."

IN THE COMPANY
OF GHOSTS

John Wayne O'Grady wondered if he'd heard right. Had the girl really told him to shoot at Constantine through the door? He looked at the door, then back at the child again, shaking his head as if to clear away the debris of words and phrases that had gathered in there.

"You mean that?" he eventually asked.

"Yes," said the girl. "Shoot it. Shoot it at the door."

John Wayne O'Grady, molder of minds, smiled at the direct

solution from the mouth of this child. Of course, she didn't think the gun was loaded. She was just a kid, she had no idea. He wondered if next time it wouldn't be better to only use children for his plan. They were so uncomplicated.

"I've done a good job on you," said O'Grady, patting her on the head.

The girl nodded, just as a loud crash sounded from inside the storeroom.

"You okay in there, Theo?" called O'Grady.

"Yes," came his timid reply. "I dropped something."

"The girl here says I should shoot the door open," said O'Grady, leaning down so that his mouth was close to the vent.

"Bitch . . ." hissed Constantine.

O'Grady shrugged his shoulders and sat with his back to the door, gesturing for the girl to sit beside him.

"Can we go after you get him?" asked the girl, nodding toward the storeroom door, an anxious look on her face.

"Yes," sighed O'Grady. "The next phase of the plan is about to begin. Right now armies of revolutionaries are waiting for me to come out. Men, women . . . children, too . . . They've been hiding in the hills, waiting for this moment when I emerge triumphant, John Wayne O'Grady."

The girl seemed agitated throughout this speech, impatient. O'Grady continued to dwell on his thoughts, until he noticed the girl's demeanor.

"You listening to me?" he snapped.

"Yes," answered the child, shivering now.

"I don't know," said O'Grady. "You might not be ready to be a soldier . . ."

"I am ready!" insisted the girl, her eyes wild with fury.

"No, no," said O'Grady patronizingly. "Here's how we'll do it. I'll leave first, and you stay here . . ."

The girl screwed her face up into a ball of rage and screamed, "No!"

"Now listen," said O'Grady, taking her hands in his. "Listen to your commanding officer."

The girl fought against his strength, spitting angry words at him. "You said you'd take me. You said we were going!"

"You don't understand!" shouted O'Grady. "Listen! I didn't say you'd have to be locked away in here. You'll just have to wait a few minutes extra, that's all. They'll let you out . . . the police will come to free you. It's better this way. I can go organize the army and you play at being a normal kid. They'll never know that you're a soldier in old John Wayne's army. They'll think you're just a girl . . ."

"But you said they could tell by looking in my eyes," she said, her face creased with confusion.

O'Grady stopped short. "That's exactly right," he bluffed, trying to make his eyes as sincere as possible. "Normally the puppets can tell by looking in your eyes if you're with old John W. But there is a way to trick them. You just keep yourself to yourself, don't look at them too much, and don't say much at all, then they won't ever know. Trust me."

The girl stared at him suspiciously, and the gunman grew agitated himself. He started to move, gathering his gun, looking around for his bag. There was no time now for reassuring the child. Once the cops outside had seen her on the landing, they would be thinking the same thing. Time to move, to put an end to the siege.

"You have to take me," said the girl, pulling at his clothes, pleading with him. "I'm a good soldier. I am. And I can prove it."

"How would you do that?" muttered O'Grady, checking his gun.

"I know things that you don't know," shouted the girl.

O'Grady stared at her for a brief second, then he smiled. "Like what?"

"I know things about him," said the girl, nodding toward the storeroom door.

"Theo?" said O'Grady, standing. "What about him?"

The girl started to shiver, and she pulled her arms tight around her.

"You're not going to do that coughing thing again, are you?" asked O'Grady.

"He's writing," whispered the girl.

"Writing?" asked O'Grady. "Writing what?"

"He's writing down what happened," said the girl. "He's been doing it all along. He's been writing down what you say and what I say and what the truth is. On paper napkins. In there."

O'Grady scratched his head. "What would he wanna go and do that for?"

"He's writing down on a napkin that I'm in John Wayne's army," said the girl, her voice slowly rising in intensity. "That I held the gun. He's writing down that everyone here laughed at you. That they never wanted to be in your army. That they thought you were funny . . . No. That they thought you were a joke."

John Wayne O'Grady pushed past the girl, knocking her off balance. He was determined, moving back toward the storeroom door where a flashlight flickered through the grill, and the faint sound of scratching came under the door. A shadow crossed his face, a dark menace.

"You've got one minute to come out of there, Theo," he said, his voice low, horrible. "One minute, or I'll kill you."

———

"Once it started," I say, eyes locked with William's, "I couldn't stop it. No . . . I didn't want to stop it." I pause, watching his expression. "Are you sure you're ready for this?"

"I don't know," he says.

And neither do I.

"John Wayne O'Grady was bashing on the door of the storeroom where Theo had locked himself away. He was shouting that he would shoot him in one minute . . ."

"I heard that," whispers William. "I had my ear up against the bathroom door and I heard him."

"Did you hear me?" I ask.

William shakes his head.

"I spoke, too . . ."

———

"He doesn't like you," said the girl, arms folded, face set with determination.

O'Grady looked at the child. How did she know all this? Why hadn't he spotted Theo's deception? Then he realized, the medicine, it had all been a ruse by Constantine to get into the storeroom and write his stories. What about the girl? Was she part of it? O'Grady regarded the child anew, her cold expression, her steely determination, and he shivered. What the hell had he created here?

O'Grady scratched his head furiously, pacing back and forth, his eyes darting around the gloomy emptiness of the restaurant. "Damn that fat arsehole," he muttered. "Damn him to hell!"

"See, I *am* a good soldier," said the girl.

"Oh, hell, yes. You are one bloody fine soldier. Better than them men. Better than any of them. Shit, I'd fight in the trenches alongside you for sure, kid."

"So, will you take me now?"

———

"You'd understand about proof, wouldn't you, Mom?" I ask.

She nods her head, the weary lawyer, weighed down by family anecdotes.

"Then you understand that I had to prove to him that I was an invaluable ally."

"What I understand," says Nancy, "is that in the eyes of the law, and in the eyes of any right-minded person, you would be innocent. No matter what you said or did. You'd be innocent."

Having started these images rolling, they won't stop. I see O'Grady bashing at the door, yelling at Constantine. The deadline passes again and again, and still the manager wouldn't come out. I see it in the gloom of that shabby place. The tall shape of O'Grady hammering his fist against the storeroom door. It must have been made of some hard material, because with all of his strength, O'Grady could hardly shift it.

And then . . .

Oh, God. And then he said . . .

———

"I'll take one of them burger-queens in the bathroom as hostage instead," said O'Grady. "Why didn't I think of that before? The small one . . . she'll be lightweight . . ."

"What about me?" asked the child.

O'Grady looked at her, distracted, then went to the wall where the bomb wires were taped and started connecting one to the battery. The girl watched him from the storeroom door. She could hear Constantine rustling about inside. Her whole body twitched, nerve endings that would snap at the slightest provocation. Why was he fiddling with those wires? Why didn't he answer her?

Then she heard the voice of Constantine wafting like a thin whistle through the vents.

"Ow, shit!"

"What are you doing?" whispered the girl through the door.

Theo did not answer at first, and the girl told him that O'Grady was busy.

"I'm putting things against the door," came Constantine's reply.

"Why?"

"Because I'm not coming out."

"I think he doesn't want you now," whispered the girl.

"That's just a trick," said Constantine.

"It's not," hissed the girl. "He doesn't want you . . . and he doesn't want me, either. He's a horrible, mean, bad man!"

———

"I knew that if he got one of the girls, he wouldn't need me," I say. "That's how it was. She'd be his soldier. O'Grady even said that the hostages in the bathroom could become revolutionaries one day. If he got one of them, I was certain he'd leave me behind."

"If he'd taken one of the girls," says William, "he might have got her killed . . ."

"Instead it was Theo who died," I say.

"But not by you," says Nancy, a worrying hint of doubt in her voice.

"No, not by me," I say. "What you have to remember is that I was convinced the gun wasn't loaded."

"Of course you thought it wasn't loaded . . ."

"No, Mom," I shout. "Don't do that. Don't leap to my defense. There was stuff I did that *was* bad. I made him take Constantine, for instance. We were his bookends. He called us that. If he took Theo, then I came along as part of the bargain. So just let me simply have the truth without any reinforcement, okay?"

Nancy nods, and I see in the shadows a shape, lying in the darkness. So long, strong, steely, powerful. It could break anything. Hadn't I watched it smash grown men to the ground? Hadn't I seen the way everyone was scared of it? Hadn't I held it myself, felt how heavy it was?

It could do anything, including break down a door.

————

The girl went to the shotgun and picked it up, almost overbalancing with its weight. She tried to arrange it into the same shooting position O'Grady had helped her into before. Eventually, she had it right, her hand on the pistol grip, her finger barely reaching the trigger, her other hand on the fore end. The weight of the gun was causing her to shake and wobble.

Aiming the shotgun at the door, the girl started squeezing the trigger, until she remembered the disappointing *click* from her earlier attempt at firing. Instead, she grabbed the stock in both hands and banged the gun against the door. The effort of holding its weight meant that her battering was mostly weak and ineffectual, a feather's touch.

John Wayne O'Grady ran back to her from near the stairway. "Shit! Stop that now!"

The girl froze, glaring at the man. "You have to get him out," she said.

"Now, hon," said O'Grady, his voice even, calm. "Put the gun down, okay? Old John Wayne has loaded it now. When you were on those stairs. So put it down."

She didn't move, clutching the gun, her body swaying with the effort, her legs turning to jelly. O'Grady took a small step toward her.

———

"He ripped the gun out of my hand. God, it hurt so much. I was crying, but he didn't care one bit. After a while I looked up at him, and all he was worried about was his precious gun. I thought he was patting it or something . . . but that doesn't make sense. Maybe he was checking the safety and stuff like that. Still . . . how could it . . . God. That's it. He was so wired up on pills and lack of sleep . . . he must have accidentally released the safety on the trigger. That has to be it. He wouldn't have deliberately taken it off. Would he?"

———

"Jesus!" yelled O'Grady. "What the hell did you think you were doing? You wanna blow yourself apart? This is my gun, right? And only I use it."

"I want to get out of here," shouted the girl, picking herself up off the floor. "I want to get out! They hate me! The puppets hate me . . . and I want to go . . ."

"All right, we'll go. Shit, you nag worse than a wife, you know that? We'll just go." He glanced at his watch and swore again. "Shit! This is taking too long. The cops will be in here soon."

As if in answer to his suspicion, there was a faint noise from the stairwell. A tinkle, as if a tool had been dropped, but it was difficult to tell if the noise came from inside or outside the restaurant.

"Shit! The cops are coming!" yelled O'Grady.

He carefully lay the gun against the wall, then turned to the storeroom door and started banging it with his fist again.

"Theo! Open this door! Open it, you turd! You're coming with me. I need protection."

They heard a loud crash from inside the storeroom, then the frightened voice of Constantine. "I won't open."

O'Grady flew into a rage, banging and kicking the door, flying with fists and feet until he almost fell backward like a doll. The door was untouched. O'Grady retrieved the gun, kicked the door once, then yelled, "Step back, Theo!"

"What are you going to do?" came the frightened voice of the manager.

"Just step the hell back now!" shouted O'Grady.

Another loud crash came from inside the storeroom, and Constantine moaned through the vent. "I've hurt myself now. I fell over, you bastards. Leave me alone. You'll kill me."

"Step back, Theo. I'm not joking."

"No! You'll kill me."

The girl started sobbing, her voice rising in volume and pitch as O'Grady pleaded and Constantine begged for his life. Then the high-pitched alarm sounded from the dumbwaiter in the kitchen, screaming in the gunman's ear.

"The cops are coming . . ."

"Please don't shoot. Please!"

The girl's cry broke into a hysterical string of words that shattered O'Grady's head and drove him to the point of exploding.

"I wanna go home!" she screamed. "I wanna go home!"

"Move away!"

"Iwannagohome . . ."

Another noise from the stairwell. Louder. The alarm piercing.

"They'll be here any second!"

"Iwannagohome!"

"Leave me alone!"

"Fuck it! Just fuck it all!"

O'Grady started beating against the door with the barrel end of the gun, lost in his rage. The gunmetal was having some effect, splintering the wood, which only served to increase O'Grady's frenzy. He continued the battering, the girl's screams, the manager's pleas, the crack of the metal against the door, the noises up the stairs, all driving him on. He continued to chip away at the wood, with the two opposite ends tearing him apart.

Then the inevitable happened.

The gun exploded.

———

"The noise was deafening. I remember the flash of light . . . and I think that came after the noise . . . or before it. That's all. The next thing I remember is standing up . . . and I couldn't hear a thing."

———

O'Grady lay on the ground, his face covered in flecks of blood, his eyes momentarily blinded by a flying splinter of wood. He shook his head and found that he could see out of one eye, but the other was red and closed. The girl was screaming from somewhere behind him, and he twisted around to look at her. She had a wild, animal-like snarl on her face, her face dotted with minute cuts, her hair covered in tiny splinters of wood. Her hands were clenched into tight balls, which she held beside her head, as if to ward off any more flying debris from the door. There were no words now to her scream, no pleas or demands, just a cry from her terrified heart.

O'Grady rose gingerly to his feet and inspected the door. A gaping hole had been blown open by the blast, knocking the doorknob and lock completely out. The whole thing hung on one hinge, a flimsy resistance now, and O'Grady peered into the storeroom for any sign of the manager.

"Theo?" he called. "You okay?"

There was no reply.

"Shit," said O'Grady, suddenly overwhelmed by dizziness. He leaned against the doorjamb and tried to regain his balance, breathing hard as his heart raced. Eventually, he was able to lift his head properly, and he noticed something out of the corner of his eye. On the ground. Feet.

"Theo?" said O'Grady. He cautiously pushed at the store-room door, meeting resistance. Constantine's barricade. O'Grady ripped the door from its remaining hinge and lay it on the restaurant floor. Working furiously, he dragged the boxes out of the way, revealing Constantine lying on his back, slightly twisted, as if he'd tried to get away from the blast. There was no gunshot wound on him, just a myriad of tiny cuts from flying splinters, and a large, ugly bruise on his cheek. The blast must have propelled the doorknob into his face. O'Grady bent down to the manager and shook his shoulder.

"You okay there, Theo?"

No response. He noticed for the first time the gray, pallid tone of the manager's skin. Looking for obvious signs of breathing he saw none, and O'Grady panicked. In a fit of blind terror, he thrashed around like a man caught in a cage, only stopping when a disused pot fell from a shelf above, giving him a glancing blow to the head. He stood motionless, slightly stunned, the body of Constantine at his feet, and tears trickled down his face. After a pause, the girl spoke beside him, her face covered in grimy tears, her head shaking involuntarily.

"Is he all right?"

"No," said O'Grady. "He's dead. I killed him. How did this happen? I only wanted to change something . . . Shit. What a mess. What a mess."

The girl bent down and picked up one of the napkins, Constantine's scribble at an angle across its surface. She tried to focus on the writing, but the words danced around the napkin. Sitting down with a thump, she closed her eyes, but no more tears would come. When she opened them again she could read Theo's last words.

Dear N
I'll never forget your kindness to me.
You let me see that life can be good. Thanks.

What *is* innocence in the end? Is it the state of grace that all babies are born with? That unfathomable wisdom they seem to hold in their eyes? Is that innocence?

We grow. We live, we breathe, we knock our bodies up against other bodies. We do damage. To others . . . to ourselves.

What is innocence?

O'Grady was afraid to use that gun, right up to the very end. He never deliberately fired it at another human being. Is that innocence?

Is it a little girl who just wanted Wild West stickers? Who had no ideas about how to get out of hell? Who was afraid of silhouettes because she thought they were puppets out to get her? Innocence was my enemy. Innocence was weak.

I look at William and my mother, my heart still racing from the telling, my head thick and sore.

"It was just as the inquest found," I say. "Constantine was killed by the doorknob."

"The inquest found that he was killed by O'Grady," says Nancy.

I shrug, a memory coming back to me. Sights . . . sounds . . . *she* was there. "Theo looked so strange to me . . . so gray . . . and there's something else. God . . . It's incredible. She sang . . ."

"Who sang?" asks Nancy, a look of bafflement on her face.

"God . . ."

———

The girl stood, clutching the napkin in her fist. She looked down at Theo and shook her head. No, he couldn't be dead. She wouldn't let him be dead. She stared at him as hard as she could, willing him to breathe, to come back to life and worry about O'Grady or the napkins or the gun . . .

He would not move.

Then she saw something else. A shadow, perhaps? A flicker near the manager. An outline of a girl. Gray. Hollow. Needing to be filled in. She knelt down beside the manager, just as she'd seen the shadow do. She filled that position. Next to Constantine's body. She lifted his head gently, aware of the stillness of his chest.

"Can you hear me, Theo?" she asked.

There was no response.

"It's all right now. Everything's okay."

Then she bent closer to him and whispered a promise in his ear. "I'll look after the napkins for you, Theo."

She wasn't sure, but she thought she could see a faint flicker of comprehension on his face. Stroking his hair, she began to sing to him, a soothing song that she'd heard somewhere.

"Moon, moon/ Shining and silver/ Moon, moon/ Silver and bright/ Moon, moon/ Whisper to children/ Sleep through the silvery night."

———

"I think I heard you singing," says William. "I'm not sure . . . it's something that I think I heard."

I nod, but my thoughts are with Theo, lying in my arms, most likely dead, as I sang his soul to heaven. "Do you think *he* heard me?" I ask.

William shrugs. I don't look to Nancy. I know she'll say yes, just to support me.

"What was the song?" asks William.

"Hm?" I say, distracted by the memory of Theo's face.

"The song?"

"I dunno." I shrug. "Does it matter?"

———

"Police! Don't move! Police! Don't move!"

The voices shouted from everywhere. Officers in flak jackets and gas masks, armed with assault rifles, stormed down the stairs and took up positions of cover at the entrance. Tear-gas canisters bounced into the middle of the restaurant and burst into smoke. A man moved through the gloomy haze and vanished around a corner to where the bathrooms were.

The police waited, cautious, not knowing if he was taking up a firing position or not. If they'd followed him they would have seen a lone figure in the near darkness. Crouching. His hands shaking as he held the shotgun the wrong way. This was a dangerous thing to do. The smoke started sweeping around the corner, stinging his eyes. The man reached down to the trigger and touched it. He let out a small shiver.

There was a loud bang and a bright flash of color. The man was dead.

––––––

"I heard the gun," says William. "And I started to cry. I think some of the other men were crying, too."

"I heard the gun, too," I say. "But it didn't sound real."

––––––

The officer who found the girl was a young man with two daughters of his own. At first he'd seen Theo Constantine's body and had called control, then he'd noticed a slight movement in the gloom, as if a shadow had evaporated. Scanning the tiny space, he saw her, wedged under the desk, clutching something in her hand.

"It's okay, sweetie," he said. "It's all over."

He knew she'd be frightened of him in his gas mask, so he moved slowly. She didn't budge, didn't even acknowledge he was there. He kept talking to her, letting her know he was friendly, human even. Reaching down, he gently placed his arm around her middle and lifted her into the air. She coughed going through the restaurant. Then, as he carried her up the stairs to her waiting parents, she said, "Don't look at me."

He was happy to oblige.

––––––

Anyone who tells you that remembering is a good thing is a liar. It is neither good nor bad. It is not a weight, not a lifting of burden. It is an understanding. A knowledge that goes beyond events and numbers and narratives. It is accepting that when you seek out the past, you know *exactly* what you are.

So I have remembered, I have sung my song again, and still John Wayne O'Grady is with me.

"Keep yourself to yourself, that's what O'Grady told me," I say.

William nods. He understands that only too well.

I have a fake gun in my hands.

"Freda," says Nancy softly. "I think we should go now."

"I can't," I say.

She raises her eyebrows at me, but it's not her I'm interested in. I look to William. "Can you possibly leave?" I ask.

"I don't know," he says. "It's like I've been back there . . . for real."

"Me, too," I say, looking down at my gun. "What do we do now?"

"I can't say . . ."

"Oh, please," says Nancy, leaping off the bench and pacing around the room. It is light outside now, dull gray at the window. "This is ridiculous," she says. "Give me that gun or put it down or whatever. Let's go home now. Hm? This is not the restaurant, it's your father's workshop. You're not back there . . . you're nineteen years old. So cut this maudlin nonsense and let's be a bit positive. Can we?"

I stare at Nancy, amazed at her outburst. Even though I've seen it aimed at so many foes, I've never been the recipient up until now. William is staring, too, perhaps agreeing with her, or perhaps wondering how she blew into all this mess. Before I get a chance to answer her, I hear the sound of a key in a lock, and my father enters his workshop.

"Freda?" he says, looking around the gloom. Then he sees Mom. "Nancy? What are *you* doing here?"

"Hugh," says N.O. stiffly.

Dad steps into the workshop, shocked, I think, by the intrusion of real-life bodies.

"This is William, Dad," I say, remembering my manners.

"Hm," says Dad, but his eyes are locked on my gun. "When did you do the carving, Freda?" he asks.

"Carving?" shrieks Nancy.

"What carving?" asks William.

"Can I see?" says Dad, and I hand the gun to him. "It's good," he says, looking it over. "You've got a real talent."

"What's going on?" says Nancy.

Dad stares at her, then passes over the gun. As she takes it I see the look of amazement on her face. It's so lightweight. So unreal.

"You made this?" asks Nancy.

"Balsa wood," I reply.

"What?" says William. He marches over and takes the gun, testing its weight, swinging it around. "I don't believe it. I don't believe it." Then he glares at me, and I wait for it, because he has every right to attack me. I have menaced him with this most hated replica for my own needs. I have put him back into hell. After a long pause he smiles, and says, "Shit." Then he shakes his head and sits with the gun, repeating the word a few times for anyone who'll listen.

Dad looks embarrassed, as if he's just ruined the surprise party, so I help him out by asking, "How come you started so early today?"

"Oh," he says diffidently. "I actually rang you last night. No one was there. So I swung by your house early and it was deserted. I thought that maybe you'd be here. I suppose I was worried about you. When I left you yesterday you were so . . . you looked so sad. I guess . . . Well, I guess I wanted to ask if you were all right."

"I don't know," I say. "I've just remembered things from the restaurant . . ."

"Oh," says Dad, even more embarrassed and uncomfortable. "You mentioned . . . before . . . that time on the stairs."

"Yes," I say.

"Do you know that I often think of that time . . . and of when they carried you out."

"Really?" I ask. "What do you think?"

"I guess I remember things, too," he says. "I saw something . . ." He glances at Nancy. "It's not important."

Nancy rolls her eyes and says, "Oh, for heaven's sake. Stop doing that. Just say what you have to say. I'll block my ears if necessary."

"That won't be necessary, actually," says Dad. "I saw a girl . . . in the doorway. But it wasn't you, because you were in the car with your mother. I know it doesn't make sense, but I did. It's always bothered me . . ."

I stare at my father, so full of surprises. "I think it does make sense," I say. "I think I dream about the same girl."

Dad nods, and an understanding passes between us.

"What shall we do with this?" asks William, holding up the gun.

"Burn it," I say. "Horrible, disgusting thing. Burn it to hell." I remove the napkins from my back pocket. "And burn these, too."

"Are you serious, Freda?" asks Nancy.

William leaps up immediately, eager, alert to the symbolism of the action. "Where can we make a fire?" he asks.

Dad goes to his little combustion stove in the corner and opens its door. "Um . . . there's still some coals in here," he says, giving me a knowing look.

I toss the gun to William, and he doesn't have to be asked twice about what to do. He breaks it into pieces, a look of satisfaction all over his face. For a moment I'm envious, wishing I could do this—destroy the memory of our oppression, but strangely, I think I managed to expunge this weapon of destruction from my system when I carved the thing. It is fitting that the gun is destroyed, and I try to think of some words to go with the ritual, but my mind is tired. Too many words have come out. All I can think to say, as William shoves the balsa wood into the stove, is, "Terror breeds more terror. It needs to be burned quickly."

William nods. Then I pass the napkins to him. "These are next."

He takes them and picks the first one off the pile. For a moment he looks at it, then says, "Who's 'N'?"

"Pardon?" I say.

"'N,'" says William, showing me the napkin. It is addressed to "N." William shows me other napkins, the later ones, each addressed to or mentioning an "N."

"I don't know," I say. "I've never really paid it that much attention. I guess I was too obsessed with what he wrote about me . . ."

"Hm," says William, and he begins to toss the napkins into the stove.

"Wait," says Nancy Opperman.

"You're joking, aren't you?" I say.

"No. I've just had a thought. William searched for you and the other survivors all this time because he . . . I guess he needed you in a time of crisis."

"What's your point, Mom?"

"Theo Constantine wrote these in crisis. He addressed some to an 'N.' Whoever that was . . . that's who *he* was looking for."

William withdraws the threat of a fiery grave from the napkins and we look at them afresh.

"His girlfriend?" I say, hazarding a guess.

"I'll find out for you," says William. "Tracking people down has become one of my specialities."

"What exactly do you do?" I ask. "You're not a student, are you?"

"Unemployed," says William. Then he gives me a grin and adds, "Until now."

I place the napkins in my bag. It's not the outcome I'd envisaged, but I suppose they now have a purpose . . . again.

We leave soon after that, Nancy and I, taking William home on the way. As we drive he tells us a story about when he was in high school. Some friends of his were talking about an antiglobalization protest. William wanted to go because he supported the movement, but when they started making arrangements he made up some excuse to get out of it.

"The thing is," says William from the backseat, "when the day came I actually *did* go to the protest."

"So, you marched with your friends after all?" says Mom.

William is silent for a long time. Then he says, "No."

"Oh," says Mom, a little confused.

"I stood on the footpath and shouted at the protesters," he says. Then he adds, "Abuse. Angry abuse . . ."

I turn around to him. "Did it feel better?" I ask.

He nods his head. "Yes," he says. "For a while. It wasn't them, you understand . . . ?"

I nod. Of course it wasn't them.

"It was him," says Nancy, her voice almost lost in the background hum of the car.

We arrive at William's place, and he steps out with a promise to call. Then we head for home. The morning light seems overly bright to my tired eyes now, so I close them, a myriad of images running through my brain like highlights from a bad movie. Guns. Shouting men. O'Grady's ranting. I'd rather take the glare, so I open my eyes to the world again and look over at my mother, driving, still in control.

"Why was it so necessary to prove that I was good, Mom?" I ask.

She glances at me, then asks what I mean. I sigh, then say, "I think you know."

"I wasn't proving anything," she says, bristling at the perceived attack in my question. She's got it wrong. I'm not on the offensive. There's still a few more "bodies" from my past I need to bury, that's all.

"What about 'Lead a good life'?" I say. "What about the press conference? What was all that trying to prove?"

Nancy Opperman maintains her concentration on the road. There is little traffic around. I wait. Eventually she speaks to me in her civil-lawyer's voice. "Have you ever read a newspaper report about a mother who's been accused of murdering or neglecting her children?" she asks.

"Yes. Sure, but what's that got . . ."

Nancy holds up her hand. "I'm talking about what the media does. Those mothers are ripped apart. Forget about the subtleties of their situations, or their mental state . . . they are slaughtered so we can all feel better about ourselves. I'm no fool, Freda."

"But I was just a kid. You even said I couldn't be prosecuted . . ."

"Not by the courts, no," says Nancy. "But there are a hundred ways for you to be tried by the media. Of course I protected you against that."

"And Theo's last words?"

"It wasn't planned," says Nancy. "They just came out. You'd been saying something about 'good life' in the back of the police car. Don't you remember?"

I shake my head. All I can remember is the feel of another body against mine, the warmth of the car, the pain in my hand as I held the napkins, and the absolute determination I had not to open my eyes.

"Well, you were saying that," says Nancy. "Can you imagine how I felt reading what I did read in those napkins? I thought I'd be sick . . . and all you wanted was for me to hold you tight and not let anyone see you. You kept saying, 'Don't let them look at me.' O'Grady taught you that, but at the time I thought that you were scared they'd see what Constantine had written."

"I was," I say.

"So, when that question kept coming up at the press conference . . . it seemed like a fair enough reply. I gave him some last words."

"And everyone was ready to believe that he could have said that."

Nancy shrugs. "Why not? This *is* a good life. Even Constantine was thinking that at the end when he wrote his last napkin."

I shake my head, turning away from her, staring into the morning light so that it hurts my eyes.

"What?" she says.

"Nothing."

"What?"

"I can't . . . I don't know. I just can't . . . How can you be so certain of that?"

"I don't know," she says, pulling into our driveway. "Maybe it's the one thing we *can* be certain about."

I climb out of the car exhausted, only too aware of the unfinished business of the napkins. Nancy would come with me if I asked her. She'd hand them over for me gladly.

"Mom," I say, and she turns.

"Yes?"

"I think I'd like to take driving lessons."

Mom looks at me for a second or two, a little nonplussed by my prosaic statement. Satisfied that there's no hidden meaning behind it, she nods and says, "Fine."

We go inside. There's some cleaning up to do.

A LETTER

Sunday, July 22

Dear Naomi,
Just a little card to go with the flowers because
I'm not sure if you'll be home or not. These
flowers are a thank you, I guess. Thanks for
being such a nice friend. Thanks for going out
with me to the movies. And thanks for being my
"girlfriend." Is that OK if I call you that? I
hope it is. I'm looking forward to your reply. If
you're not home, I'll call you after work. About
five o'clock. Sundays are always slow days.
All the best + best wishes.
                              Love, Theo
P.S. I hope you like the color of these roses.
They're so dark and unusual, but beautiful, too.

FREDA **OPPERMAN**

She opens the door to me and I'm immediately struck by how ordinary she is. No makeup, a practical dress with a plain cardigan to cover it. I don't know what I'm doing here, now that I've come. What right do I have to bring these napkins to this woman who smiles at me? She is no taller than me, but rounder and fuller, the result of being older or of having children. I should speak to her, explain myself, but I can't. She raises her eyebrows and offers a friendly smile. "Yes?" she says.

Do I say I am here because she is Naomi, a girl whose name starts with "N'? Is that enough reason for me to open my bag and pull out the napkins?

"I . . . um . . . Are you Naomi?" I eventually stammer.

"Yes," she says. An upward inflection. One slightly raised eyebrow now, friendly, inviting, and waiting.

Yes, she is Naomi, part of a long ago record. A woman who went on a few dates with Theo. As far as William could tell, she was the *only* girl to go on a few dates with him. And for this she receives the booby prize, the poisoned chalice of the napkins with their bile and their hatred scratched into the paper.

"I don't think . . ." I begin to say. "I mean . . ."

"Do you want an appointment?" she asks, cutting short my incoherence.

The question is so unexpected that all I can do is reply, "An appointment?"

"That's okay," she says, opening the door wider to let me in. "I've got an opening. Come in, sit down."

And I follow. I enter her life with the unmistakable feeling that I should not be here. She leads me to a small living room which has a cozy gas heater for warmth. There are photos on the wall of children, and a man who I suspect is her husband. He isn't rugged or handsome with his balding head and his ordinary features, but his eyes are warm and kind. I like him immediately. Like him in a way I could never like Theo. This man is dependable and solid. Lucky Naomi. She turns to me and says, "Take a seat. I'll just finish with Mrs. Ashbourne, then I'll get to you. Help yourself to some fresh coffee in the kitchen."

"Thanks," I say, trying hard to hide my bewilderment. What sort of "appointment" have I let myself in for?

She passes through some sliding doors, which are left open, perhaps to allow some of the heat from the living room to seep through to the next room. I venture a little snoop through the doors and see an elderly woman sitting in front of a large mirror with her hair in rollers. She has a black cloak draped over her, and is reading a magazine. I almost burst out laughing with relief. Naomi is a backyard hairdresser.

"That didn't take long," says the old woman, dropping her magazine.

"Do you remember where you left off?" asks Naomi, taking the woman's hair in her hands and gently stroking it. Mrs. Whatsit continues a long, detailed story about someone named "Arthur," one of those memories that seem to come to elderly people, but it is only peripheral to what is going on in that sunroom.

It's the hands. Naomi's long fingers, her pale skin, those light blue veins showing as she strokes the old woman's hair with smooth, even caresses. Her hands speak back to the woman, offer all the response of a listener. They nod, they murmur, they agree, they *connect*. Would those hands touch me if I sat in that chair? Would they listen to me? I'm terrified.

Calloused hands held me tight upstairs, speaking to me in a calm, direct way. Birdlike hands have clutched me in the cold morning atmosphere of the police car, testing to see if I was hurt. Meaty hands patted me so many times, offering me no solace at all. And *his* hands, rough, uncaring, treated me like a doll.

How can I let those hands stroke me? She would see right through me in an instant. I am an imposter who doesn't belong. I would scream at her touch. Or I would cry a thousand tears that would soak her in my shame.

This was foolish to ever think I could come here. I stand abruptly, sending my bag to the floor. It tips over on its side, open, revealing. I pick it up. Mrs. Whats-it is being shown her cut by Naomi, who holds a hand mirror at the correct angle, shifting it this way and that for approval.

I steal out of the living room and open the front door, feeling a most dreadful sense of defeat. I should run. I want to run, but I can't. I go to a rosebush with a dark crimson bloom, feeling the silky touch of its petals. This bush is much older than the others around it. Thick, twisting wood grows from its center, giving it a stature and a presence that sets it apart. It is such an unusual color, like an ancient sentinel.

I pluck a petal from the bush and go to place it in my bag, but I stop. Not in there. Instead I place it in my jeans' pocket. Then the front door opens and Naomi emerges with Mrs. Whats-it, who is fumbling through her purse.

"I've got some money in here," she is saying, but Naomi places her long-fingered hand on Mrs. Whats-it's wrinkled skin and the fumbling ceases.

"Don't you remember, hon," says Naomi. "You've already paid me."

"No, no," says Mrs. Whats-it. "I know I haven't given you anything yet. Now don't be so naughty, Naomi . . ."

"You gave me that lovely story about Arthur," says Naomi. Then she sees me among the roses and says, "There you are. I wondered where you went off to."

I'm left to ponder exactly where it is I "went off to" as Mrs. Whats-it is dispatched with a bunch of flowers, freshly cut and bundled from the garden. Naomi returns to me, rubbing her cold hands, nodding toward the crimson rose that I seem unable to leave.

"I love that one," she says. "Planted it for a friend years ago."

I nod. "You didn't take that woman's money," I say.

She smiles and says, "Never do. It's just a little fancy of mine. A haircut's gotta at least be worth some of her memories. Now, your hair. It looks in need of lots of love and attention."

"I've only got a bit of money," I mumble, half hoping to put her off.

"Oh, I'll take whatever's in your bag," she jokes.

Then she turns and goes into the house, leaving me to struggle with the horror of her suggestion.

I stare at her front door, a place I was running from a minute ago. If I go back it will be deliberate. Do I have the courage?

"Come on," she calls.

I take a step toward her. It is an ordinary thing to do, yet for the young survivor it is a huge risk.

I follow Naomi inside the house to the sunroom where I sit in the chair. She takes up my hair in her hands and I flinch ever so slightly. Nothing happens. Naomi chats to me about my hair, and doesn't even seem to mind that I have no opinion.

I surrender then, feeling her touch on my face and scalp, closing my eyes so that there's no distractions. Then I think of William, screaming at the protestors. I think of the young girl who stayed behind, and my heart starts racing. But Naomi doesn't seem to notice, or maybe she does. Maybe her touch is gentler. I breathe, slowly, until all thoughts leave me and there's nothing but the here and now.

Naomi proceeds to cut my hair in a style I'm vaguely aware of having given approval to. When she's finished, she shows me my cut in her hand mirror, then places her now warm hands on my cheeks and says, "Still cold but warming up a little."

"I haven't paid you," I say, reaching for my bag. As soon as I open it I see the napkins. With perhaps the merest hint of a pause, I push them aside and pull out my purse, handing Naomi a small note.

"Are you sure this won't leave you short?" she asks.

"Don't be silly," I say. "It's nowhere near enough for the haircut."

She brushes me down and we leave the sunroom, walking to the front door and out into her beautiful garden again.

"Oh, some flowers. I'll cut you some," says Naomi, and she goes back inside to retrieve the garden shears. She returns quickly, and I watch her cut the roses, choosing the best blooms. She takes a few stems from the crimson rose and says, "I don't normally give people this one. But you seemed to like it."

"I do," I say. "It's kind of ancient . . ."

"It is, isn't it," she says, tying the stems with some string.

As I watch her wrap the flowers tightly, I realize that I have made a choice. It's weird, because for so much of my life I have run away from doing anything, and here I am deciding *not* to give the napkins to Naomi yet feeling relieved. And certain. They don't belong here.

Theo would approve of this choice. He led me to this garden, that frightened, angry man who had something to teach me after all. This was the world Theo held on to as he recorded the spiraling horror of that restaurant. A place where it is possible to cut someone's hair for the stories they tell. He could see what was beyond the police lights, when I was so eager to forget.

Naomi hands me the tied bunch, saying, "Careful of the prickles." We walk to the gate, and I look at my flowers, touching the small, almost white buds she's included.

"They'll open up and change color over the days," she says. "Nothing ever stays the same, eh?"

She opens her gate and I nod, the smell of the rose blooms so rich and powerful. "Thanks," I say, making my way out the gate, but she touches me lightly on the arm.

"Come by any time for a haircut," she says. "Or some more roses."

"Okay."

And I don't look back.

THE **GARDEN**

SEAT

I have one of the crimson rose petals in my hand. It is drying out, wrinkling, but it still looks striking against my pale skin. Theo's rose. That is what I have come to call it. I scattered some of the crimson blooms on my windowsill and let the sun shine on them. I owed him that at least. Mom looks down at the petal in my hand with only a slight interest. We are sitting in our backyard on a garden seat that almost wept with gratitude at being used after all these years. I look around at this wild garden, such a stark contrast to Naomi's. This place is a madwoman doing cartwheels and making rude noises.

Nancy sees this as an odd place to sit, but to me it's perfect. This garden represents all the neglected parts of the Opperman Empire, and I love the way it's decided to grow wild, and not wither away in a sulk. There's something that I'm beginning to understand here, that living can be messy and complicated, and yet we still go on.

"Where did that come from?" asks Nancy, indicating the petal. "Not from our garden, surely?"

"No," I say, smiling. "I . . . I guess I found it."

"Oh."

Or I sought it out, perhaps? I am, after all, a seeker. I look for grace in places unexpected. I look in places that others would call chaos—in leaf-strewn doorways, in colored and neglected gardens, in madness—and hope that I see it shining there. I take prisoners at the point of a gun. I hold them until they weep with the same bitterness that I have felt. I bury the past and take a rose petal with me for remembrance. I do these things in the knowledge that all life is a risk, no matter how you live it.

Theo's petal threatens to blow away with the wind. "Go on," I want to whisper to it. I never went to his funeral service, yet before me in this garden is a new patch of soil, a burial plot. It is where I dropped Theo's fear and his shame. I stood alone and watched each napkin flutter to the ground like a panicked bird, clinging briefly to the side of the hole before vanishing to the bottom. And I realized that I was also burying my own shame.

It was a relief. In that end, words came to me. Shelley's words, and they seemed to fit the occasion:

Teach me half the gladness
That thy brain must know,
Such harmonious madness,
From my lips would flow,
The world should listen then, as I am listening now.

I look now at my mother, sitting quietly on this bench with me. She would have snorted if she'd heard me quoting from Shelley.

"William hasn't called me since he called with Naomi's address," I say. Not that he promised he would, but somehow I did expect to hear from him again.

"He called me," says Nancy. "He's gone away for a while. I'm sure he'll contact you again when he gets back . . ."

"Just like you were sure he'd do me some good?"

"Oh, Freda . . ."

A gust of wind blows up through the trees, hissing at us in our broken seat. The grass swishes back at the branches, then settles again to bask in the winter sun. "When I lie awake at night, Mom," I say, "with that man's voice in my head and the dark shadows flashing across my face, the one thing that calms me is the memory of how it felt to be held by you that night in the police car. Maybe that's all it takes, something as simple as that."

"Holding you isn't always going to help," says Nancy. "You can't honestly believe that. And neither will remembering what happened."

"Maybe . . ."

"You may not have even done all those things, Freda. Repressed memories can be unreliable. There's research . . ."

I take her arm and squeeze it tightly. "You don't have to put me back together from the stars, Mom. Okay?"

"I know that. I just don't want you to punish yourself . . ."

"I'm not. I don't know what to think about what I remembered. I know I'm not that little bitch Constantine wrote about. And I'm not O'Grady's soldier, either. I guess I have to work it out for myself, so just be here, okay? I can do it."

"I know," she says.

I squeeze harder.

She nods. "I know."

The grass is slightly flattened at my feet, and I see a small patch of blue wildflowers. They are defiant, holding their own against the tide. A bee lands on one of the flowers, gathering pollen, and the wind blows up again. Blades of grass whip about the bee, hitting it from all directions. The bee hovers for a moment, then flies off on the breeze.

"Harmonious madness," I say, looking out at our garden. Nancy places her hand on mine. I feel her warmth. Her skin. Her touching me, letting me know where I finish and she begins. We breathe together, skin to skin, and I nod my head.